Thai Kiss

by

Matt Carrell

Author's note

This book is a work of fiction. All characters portrayed herein are fictitious and any resemblance to real persons, living or dead, is purely coincidental.

Thai Kiss is available as an e-book on Amazon

Please find Matt Carrell on Twitter and Facebook, and visit his web site at www.mattcarrellbooks@gmail.com.

CHAPTER ONE

The flight

When your best mate gets washed up on the beach with a hole in the back of his head, it's time to reflect. I turned it over and over in my mind but there was only one conclusion. If I stuck around, I'd be next. They said it was an accident, that he'd been drinking and hit his head as he went over the railings of Brighton Pier. Sure… and Hollywood is itching to film my life story.

Tommy hadn't touched a drop of alcohol for months and he hated that pier with a passion. There was something about the way you could look down between the wooden slats and see the water sloshing about underneath. He nearly drowned in a swimming pool when he was a lad, his brother held him under for a joke that went too far and he'd been terrified of water ever since. Tommy wouldn't go near the pier of his own accord.

He used to like to drink, but then the doctor told him to take a year off the booze or his liver wouldn't make it to his fortieth birthday. It was tonic water only from then on. I had to cover for him… pretend he was knocking back the gin and he had to make out he was getting drunk like the rest of us. It was bad enough drinking "cocktails" instead of beer, but if the lads knew he was teetotal they'd have given him hell. All feels a bit trivial now. Someone did make his life hell… the last bit of it anyway.

I booked the flight at the last minute and spent the whole taxi ride to the airport convinced that the car behind was following us. Then it would overtake and the driver would turn out to be some middle-aged bloke looking glum while his wife gave him an impromptu driving lesson from the passenger seat, or a tosser in a Subaru trying to impress his girlfriend. No sign of any heavies coming to offer me an unwanted change to my itinerary. The M25 is England's most infamous motorway; it's intended to speed drivers round the outskirts of London instead of forcing them through the city's gridlocked streets. Most days it's a parking lot for a couple of million angry motorists. I chose such a day to make my escape. Occasionally the traffic flowed, but most of the time we just edged bumper to bumper towards the airport. There was plenty of time to stare at the electronic signs warning stationary drivers not to exceed fifty mph because of congestion. The guy in the control centre must have been chuckling as he put that one up. I spent the journey nervously checking out neighbouring vehicles and thumbing my nearly new passport. It was six months old and had been used only twice - once when I took Clare to Marbella and once when I went to Thailand with Tommy. The man in the photograph looked like a complete stranger, but it wasn't... it was me, Paul Murphy, hospital porter and part-time drug dealer.

No one ever called me handsome. "He's nice looking," they'd say. Nice? Could be worse.The guy in the picture wasn't smiling, Passport Office rules, but he looked happy enough. Dark, curly hair that was maybe a bit too long. Clear brown eyes, Clare always said they were mischievous. A strong chin... or two. Too much beer and home cooked food were starting to take their toll, but at six feet three inches I reckoned I could carry it off. Oddly enough I kept catching a glimpse of another guy in the driver's rear view mirror, it couldn't be the same person. This one looked drawn and pale, the eyes were bloodshot and two days without a shave made him look dirty. Maybe that was a good thing, nobody would recognise me as the nice looking bloke in the passport photo, but then a lot had happened since that was taken.

I didn't really relax until I'd fastened my seatbelt on the plane. I scanned the cabin for any suspicious looking faces but it just made me laugh. I spotted several shifty looking characters on the flight, which should have spooked a man in my advanced state of paranoia, but I figured I'd nothing to fear. There were plenty of families, the parents already looked exhausted and the kids looked bored. An ideal start to an eleven hour flight. And there were dozens of student types, off to find themselves by backpacking through Asia and all set to immerse themselves in a foreign culture. I gave it about three days before they'd be gagging for a KFC or asking the locals if there was a Nando's nearby. They were off to get drunk and get laid and give their CV a much needed boost in the process. The shifty characters were older and they weren't going East to find themselves; they were in search of someone else entirely. They were probably not sure exactly who the person was, only that they'd be young, beautiful, brown and willing to do whatever the man wanted in exchange for a few pounds.

I was pretty sure I'd made my escape. The plane left the stand and by the time they served breakfast the next morning, Thai Airways flight TG 911 would have about 90 minutes to go before landing in Bangkok. It gave me time to think about how a humble hospital porter could be on the run from Brighton's most feared gangster. Sure, it's only a little tinpot seaside resort and Terry Connor wasn't exactly the head of the Russian mafia but he arranged for my mate to be killed and I was certainly next in line.

If I told you I grew up less than half a mile from Brighton's fancy Marina you'd probably think I had it pretty easy. The issue for the town planners was that the roughest council estate in Brighton was there long before they identified the one place where the south coast's rich and famous could moor their gin palaces. They simply made sure there was a nice fast east to west road. The millionaires could make a quick getaway without even looking at the sprawling expanse of run-down housing on the hill immediately to the north.

I once played in a charity tournament at a local golf club and found myself sitting at a table with a bunch of policemen. They were all northerners who'd been posted to Sussex by the Force. I mentioned I was a local boy and couldn't resist admitting I grew up in Whitehawk. There was a physical reaction, they all lurched back in their seats and I swear they reached to check if their wallets were still there. It's what happens when you tell people you come from that estate. Tommy would have been furious; it's the sort of thing that draws attention. What would a Whitehawk boy be doing at a fancy golf club? Any decent copper would wonder whether he had a little sideline they should look into. Fortunately these guys were more interested in the free wine and once they got over the initial shock, they ignored me and carried on bragging about all the villains they'd nicked over the years.

If I really craned my neck from my bedroom window on the estate, I could just about catch a glimpse of the odd mast. Even then I thought that someday I'd have one of those boats. I'd be piling along the coast road in a Porsche or a Ferrari, with some gorgeous little thing who couldn't wait to take her top off on the deck of my yacht. What happened to Tommy put it on hold for a while but I'd be back, that was for sure.

There are quite a few ways of surviving a Brighton council estate. You can be "hard", or at least give a convincing impression that the smallest slight will be met with extreme force. Having girls fall at your feet is another, considerably more appealing, option. Sport is a third alternative, but it has to be a man's sport. Bend it like Beckham and you're cool whatever you look like, but captain the school table tennis team and you're a nerd by definition. Or you can make them laugh… being the funny guy in the group will generally save you from being at the bottom of the food chain. If you can make the girls laugh, then you're into option two as well, and things are really looking up. I never really cracked any of the four but I was a big lad so nobody came looking for a fight. I played in goal for the school soccer team mainly because no-one else wanted to and was amusing enough company to score a few points with both sexes. It didn't take me long to work out that I didn't have to say much to the girls, I just had to look like I was listening. So I never rose to the top of the pack, definitely not Alpha male material. I did what was required so no-one wanted to kick my head in and was big enough to sow a seed of doubt as to whether they could if they tried.

Did I mention I'm a Roman Catholic? Well that helped too. I got to go to school away from the estate because my mum was a proper churchgoer. It was called a Comprehensive. It sounds fancy but means they stick everyone together regardless of how smart they are and just hope for the best. So it barely counted as a proper education, but it meant I could occasionally put my hand up in class without risking a stone through my window at home. There was etiquette to follow of course. It was a ten-minute walk from the bus stop to my front door every evening. My school blazer and tie were stuffed into my sports bag well before I got near the estate. If I hadn't done that, the chances are I'd have made it home eventually but the uniform would have become a trophy for a local hard man.

I bought myself a golf club membership on my twenty-third birthday. On the fourteenth tee there was a sign that said; "the object of the game is to stay just behind the group in front, not just ahead of the group behind". The exact opposite was the recipe for success in my school. Try hard enough to keep the teachers off your back, but not so hard that the tough kids think you're a clever dick. I pulled it off perfectly. Leaving school at sixteen, I passed four GCSEs I couldn't admit to back on the estate, but I'd never got into a fight and the other kids liked me enough never to burgle our house. My mum worked at the local hospital so I was a shoe-in for a job as a porter. As jobs went, it was no great shakes but I met Tommy and after a while he showed me that there was a way for young kids to make their way in the world. You didn't have to be born with a silver spoon in your mouth; you just had to be smart and patient.

Tommy, my brother the dealer

Tommy was like the big brother I never had. He'd worked at the hospital for a few years, really knew his way around and everybody loved him. There was a regular Friday night trip to the pub, but if Tommy wasn't going, people lost interest and drifted away when the shift ended. At lunchtime, everyone gravitated towards his table and I could bathe in the reflected glory, as they all knew I was his best mate. He went through girlfriends at an astonishing rate but it never put the ladies off. As he tired of one girl, the next would be standing in line certain they could rise to the challenge and be "The One". It never happened of course.

He was definitely a good-looking bloke with grey-blue eyes the colour of a mountain lake in springtime... or so the girls told me. Tommy had short blond hair and that unshaven look that takes so much longer to maintain than if you get the razor out every day. I could never be bothered with that sort of thing, but Tommy had a big female fan club and was eager not to let them down.

He and I hit it off straight away. Tommy was the master at appearing to work his tail off, whilst actually doing the bare minimum. I became a devoted apprentice. I guess I should have been pissed off when I realised what he was doing but he had a way about him, you just couldn't get angry. Like the time we literally bumped into each other as he came out of the dispensary at the back of the Accident & Emergency department. I'd delivered a corpse to the mortuary minutes earlier and he'd stolen some class A drugs from a locked cupboard. I might not have realised anything was amiss, but our collision made him drop the box in his hand and there was no sign of the paperwork he'd have if he'd come by it legitimately.

"What the fuck?" he said. "Oh it's you."

"What you got there then, Tommy?"

"Leave it, I'll tell you over a coffee… OK?"

I'd already worked out what was going on before taking even three sips of the slurry that passed for coffee in the staff canteen. Tommy was stealing drugs and then getting me to deliver them to his contact in the hospital reception area in a box marked as samples. I genuinely thought the guy was from a laboratory and it was legitimate.

"You were never at risk mate. I wouldn't have done that to you. The top brass keep an eye on me because they know I have access to all parts of the hospital. They don't notice you. If you were caught I'd have taken the blame anyway."

Tommy had a way about him; he could look you straight in the eye and tell you a barefaced lie. Not only did you believe him, you'd be eternally grateful he was willing to talk to you at all. It was the sort of skill that gave the likes of Tony Blair a decade or so running the country; it just made Tommy a very successful drug dealer. Anyway, if I did have any doubts, he banished them with the magic words.

"I wasn't sure I could trust you, it was part of a test and you passed with flying colours mate. You can be a full partner now. Welcome to the Firm… if that's what you want."

At that moment I couldn't think of anything I wanted more in the whole world. I gave him one of those playful, blokey punches on the shoulder.

"Yeah, I'm in."

And that's how it all started.

Clare and the lobster that never was

Clare looked amazing in that nurse's uniform and she knew it. Not exactly beautiful but she had no shortage of admirers. I didn't really think I'd much of a chance but strange things happen when it's a staff party and someone else is picking up the bill. Clare had long natural blonde hair and every time I saw her she'd have it styled in a different way. It was like she was trying on new personalities but hadn't quite found one she liked. At work it was all tied up in a bun under her cap but, whenever I saw her socially, it would be a slightly different but equally sexy Clare. Sporty ponytails, fluffy curls and even schoolgirl plaits all put in an appearance. On the fateful night, Clare clearly spent a few hours with the straighteners and went for that look they use on shampoo commercials to show that split ends are for poor people. The scarlet dress was a little too tight but none of the men in the room could see a problem with that. Clare was a tad overweight but it was all in perfect proportion, she looked fabulous.

I thought I was all set for the evening. At the start I'd propped up the bar with Tommy, but he disappeared after taking a call on his mobile. I wandered round for a while and got chatting to a group of student nurses. They were happy to talk to anyone who knew more about the hospital than they did. It would be a while before they realised porters were close to the bottom of the food chain. The girls started to drift away until I was left with Gemma. She was giving plenty of signals that my luck was in and I was happy to let her talk about… well I have no idea actually, I wasn't really listening. I was watching Clare work the room. It was a moment of impulse when I saw her standing alone. I told Gemma I was going to get more drinks and strolled over to where Clare was draining her glass. She was drunk.

It took another couple of vodka tonics to get her to admit some guy treated her badly, and she was "trying to forget". I made her laugh and then listened while she told me all her problems. At least I looked her in the eyes and nodded at all the right times. I was actually thinking how the Albion were going to line up against

Crystal Palace on Saturday and what she might be wearing under that dress. To my complete amazement, I got the answer to the second question about an hour and a half later. As we left the party I got plenty of envious glances from the other men and a look of sheer malice from Gemma.

I was certain Clare would give me the boot the following day but it didn't happen. She told me how lucky she thought it was that our paths had crossed. It would have been nice if she said how I drove her wild with desire, that she didn't know the meaning of passion until she met me, that I was handsome or charming. Clare set her sights a bit lower I guess.

"I'm so lucky, you are so reliable."

"I know you'd never let me down."

"I love it that I can really trust you. Carol's boyfriend just went off with her best mate."

"I feel so comfortable with you, you don't make me feel like I have to be looking my best all the time."

You get the picture. But she seemed happy enough, so why complain? I moved into her flat and life was pretty good. The sex tailed off a bit after the first few months but it was still amazing when it happened and she was up front about it.

"Blow jobs and lobster thermidor," she announced one evening.

"Sounds like the menu of a restaurant I'd like to visit," was my witty retort.

"Do that and you are dead lover boy," she said.

"OK, what about blow-jobs and lobster whatsitsname?" I asked.

"Just two of the things you'll never get at home," she smiled.

Her flat, her rules.

I wasn't getting out so much since I moved in with Clare. She was happy for me to go to the football on a Saturday when Albion were playing at home and I played for a local team on Sunday, but she wasn't remotely interested in coming to watch. I was banned from the flat once a week when she had her night in with the girls. Otherwise, it wasn't a smart move to come home late, especially with beer on my breath. If I was doing a late shift at the hospital she'd phone the porter's office to speak to me instead of calling my mobile. So many of her mates were messed about by blokes, I guess it was understandable. The last one she was seeing before we hooked up was a prize dick as well. He promised her the earth, then one day he packed his bags and fucked off to Marbella. Clare said he took her out on her birthday, spent the night at her flat, then the next morning she got a text as she was on her way to work.

"Off to Spain to make my fortune, will be back for you when I'm rich," or words to that effect. She barely mentioned him since that night at the staff party so I reckon she was handling it pretty well.

Tommy was constantly trying to get me to join him on one of his boy's tours. He said that was where he first got a taste for drugs but more importantly, where he got the idea that selling them was a great way of paying for his own supply. He'd come back from Ibiza, Falariki or Kos with more money than he had when he went away. Tommy always had the knack of finding a local dealer and the balls to then go and sell the stuff he didn't want for himself. Occasionally he'd find a girl who'd unwittingly carry some surplus supply back into the UK. It was always a girl. One night with Tommy and they'd do virtually anything for him. Then he discovered Thailand.

His first trip was courtesy of a nurse he started dating at the hospital. Selena was from a wealthy family and Tommy was certain their relationship was her way of getting back at a domineering father. Apparently he hoped for great things from his daughter, he wanted her to be a surgeon like daddy. Selena probably had the brains but none of the drive. She wanted to do a worthwhile job and have a good time until she found a wealthy bloke to marry. In the meantime she intended to have some fun and take as many opportunities as she could to raise her father's blood pressure. The poor man had barely got over his daughter's choice of employment when she turned up at home with a messenger boy who pushed the sick, the dying and the dead round a hospital for a living. Selena's mother never denied her anything and was happy to hand over her own credit card to pay for the holiday with Tommy. Whether it was motherly love or her own attempt to provoke Selena's father was uncertain but they didn't care, it was a free holiday.

Unusually, I didn't get so much as a text message from Tommy while he was away but on his first day back he was full of it. He'd fallen in love with Thailand and found a way to take our little sideline and turn it into something very special indeed. The beaches were the best he'd ever seen, the food was incredible, the women were extraordinary and, if he could, he'd have moved there the next day. The most exciting part for him was that he met a guy named Clay who was going to be the key to making us our fortune. Then Tommy would retire and open a bar somewhere I never heard of before - a place called Pattaya.

Tommy met Clay in a bar near the beach.

"I knew he was a dealer the minute I set eyes on him," Tommy claimed.

I laughed. "So did he have one of those signs round his neck then? Ecstasy tablets, buy one get one free."

"No mate, don't be an arse. I can always tell by the body language. I watched him for a while, the way he used his phone, turning away whenever he got a call. Looking around to see who was watching him. Always looked a bit jumpy and nervous."

"So what did you do?"

"I just asked him for some stuff. I asked what the locals take and if he could get me some."

"Jesus mate, he could have been a copper," I said.

"Wrong colour matey. Anyway, I've seen blokes like that loads of times, I was sure he was dealing and he said he could get me as much as I liked. It isn't buy one get one free, this guy deals in thousands at a time."

"So did you get Selena to bring you some back then you evil bastard."

A shadow passed over Tommy's face for a second, then he laughed.

"No mate, it didn't work out. She dumped me on the third day. I spent eleven days on my own. As far as I know she's living with some Thai bloke who rents jet skis on the beach in Pattaya. I guess she finally found someone who pisses her Dad off even more than I could."

I tried to look like I was feeling sorry for him, but I did get a little boost from the thought that not absolutely everything drops into his lap.

"I'm sorry mate, that must have been a real kick in the balls. So you spent all that time on your own then?"

That's when Tommy's trademark smile returned, he put his arm round me and told me about the women of Pattaya. I started to think I was wrong. Everything did drop into his lap and if a little trial was ever sent to irritate him it was God's way of making what happened next even sweeter.

Four pints of lager gave Tommy time to set the scene in Pattaya.

"Fifty quid maximum mate, plus your drinks and a couple for her." Tommy was explaining how much it might cost to take a girl home from a Pattaya bar.

"I can't believe you're paying for it. They drop at your feet over here."

"It's not like that, really. I thought it was a bit grim to start with too. First couple of nights with Selena we'd watch the blokes in the bars. Really old some of them. There are blokes in their forties and fifties going home with fucking teenagers. We thought it was disgusting."

I wrinkled my nose to show I shared his distaste.

"Then Selena goes off with this Thai bloke and I end up in a bar on my own. I guess I'm looking pretty miserable and this cute little Thai girl comes up and starts to chat with me. We play a few daft bar games and have a couple of drinks then she asks if I want to take her home. She never mentions money at all. I only realised the next day that I must have paid this bar-fine thing. It was about ten quid so I wouldn't have even noticed when it went on my bill. It's what the bar charges to let the girl go for the night. So we went for something to eat, had a couple of drinks in a club on Walking Street and back to the hotel."

I was still struggling to believe my mate paid for a hooker, but he seemed to think it was completely normal.

"She was awesome between the sheets. Fabulous body and up for anything. We were at it all night. Then in the morning she just said, 'You can give me some money?' It never felt like she was charging me for it, I was giving her a present."

"No way," I said, "that's disgusting. You don't need to pay for it and God knows how many people she's had before. It's got to be hundreds."

"Could be thousands mate, but who cares. I was careful and she was great. I spent a couple of days with her and then we said goodbye. None of the crap you get over here where they want a ring on their finger after a couple of shags."

I was far from convinced but Tommy was more enthusiastic about Thailand than anything he ever talked about before. He joined a forum called Pattaya-Dream and was chatting happily to men of all ages who were every bit as hooked as he was. My mate was a sex tourist. I couldn't even admit to Clare that he went to Thailand or she'd have gone crazy. She wouldn't want me spending time with a bloke who went to a place like that. I tested the water with her once, saying someone I knew was thinking of going there for a holiday.

"Well he must be a paedophile then, that's the only reason men go to Thailand. Or he's a drug dealer, I'm sure that's where all the heroin and stuff comes from," she said.

I couldn't really argue with her, I guess that wasn't far off my own perception of the place. Now Tommy was painting me a picture of a beautiful country with great beaches, fantastic food and women who were sweet, fun and sexy as hell. Sure they got you to pay for it but it's not like dating a western woman is a cost-free option. Well, that was Tommy's logic anyway.

Once he got through talking about the women, Tommy started to explain how we wouldn't be stealing drugs from the hospital any more. His encounter with Clay in Pattaya opened the door to a much more lucrative opportunity.

It was Saturday morning, my team was playing away and I told Clare I was going to watch. In actual fact, Tommy and I were on the train to London to meet William in a bar near Borough Market on the south bank of the Thames.

William, the middleman

Borough Market is close to the south end of London Bridge, that's the ugly concrete one, not the ornate pretty one that opens up to let the ships through. The Brokerage was one of those trendy wine bars that seemed to appear whenever a bank branch got closed down and the lease was going cheap. It was exactly like a scene from a spy movie. I went in first and got myself a seat at the bar. Tommy wanted me to watch out for trouble. I ordered a drink and casually looked around, trying to spot anyone who might be a drug dealer. I narrowed it down to the people on a couple of tables closest to the doors. Five minutes later Tommy walked in, studiously avoiding eye contact. He'd been instructed to wear a blue T-shirt and a Nike baseball cap and when he asked how he'd recognise William he was told he wouldn't have to. A slim white guy in a suit stood up and shook Tommy's hand as he tried to cross to the other corner of the bar. Contact was made but by a guy I ruled out as having anything to do with drugs. The man leant towards Tommy and said something quietly; that was when my mate beckoned for me to join them. It was obviously going really well, so I was smiling my friendliest smile as I got to the table.

Tommy looked glum.

"This is Mark. He said it'd be better if you joined us, because if you were still at the bar, looking that suspicious when William arrived, he'd probably drag you outside and kick the shit out of you."

I lost the smile and slid into the seat opposite our new friend. Mark didn't even look at me as he said, "Get some beers for fuck's sake, we haven't got all day."

I got back to the table just as a man I assumed must be William joined the group. He was West Indian and may have been the tallest and widest human being I ever set eyes on. Mark took his cue and made to leave, giving William what looked like a small salute and me and Tommy a look of complete disdain.

William raised his hand in a way that made it clear he was about to speak and we'd be unwise to interrupt.

"Each month you will get a text, it will have three numbers separated by hyphens. These are the different quantities you are being offered. After that will be three more numbers also separated by hyphens, they correspond to the quantities, and are the prices you pay for each amount. We give discounts for volume. You will text back how many you want to buy and then on the twenty-eighth of each month you come here at two p.m. Mark brings the goods and you bring the cash. If you fail to buy in two successive months you will not be offered merchandise again."

He paused to drain two thirds of the beer in front of him.

"The cash should be rolled up and pushed inside those cylindrical containers they put potato chips in. The tubes should be in a TESCO carrier bag. Mark will have a similar bag with the goods. You simply have to exchange the bags."

"How do we know there are drugs… sorry, goods, in the tubes?" Tommy asked.

"You don't," came the reply.

Tommy laughed. "So how will you know if there's any money in our bag?"

William reached inside his pocket and pulled out some photos. The first was a picture of my mum coming out of the LIDL supermarket in Whitehawk; the next was Clare standing by the hospital entrance. Tommy was still smiling at this stage. The next photo was a girl called Tina he dumped the week before, then the smile disappeared. The final picture was of the only girl Tommy really cared about. Sally was sweet, pretty and sixteen years old. She was Tommy's little sister.

William spoke again. "There will be money in the bag. You'll get your first text by the twentieth of next month. Understood?"

We both nodded a little too meekly given that we were trying to make an impression on a hardened drug dealer. Then William was gone. That feeling running down my spine was certainly fear but as I looked Tommy in the eye and he smiled, there was another feeling - pure exhilaration.

Tommy explained it was better if I did the collections, because during the week he could cover for me at the hospital. At weekends I could say I was watching the Albion or playing football for the Sunday team and Clare would be none the wiser. I stored the tablets in my spare sports bag under some old football shirts and waited for Tommy to confirm we had a customer. Then, having liberated a variety of containers from the hospital, I counted out the pills to make the onward delivery. In our first month we bought five hundred pills, the minimum, and had a hundred left over when the following month's text arrived. In the month before Tommy died, we shifted thousands of pills and ran out of stock before we completed all the orders.

Tommy reckoned it took him months to build his client list. He took the orders and I just made the deliveries and collected the cash, which I had to return to Tommy without even counting it.

"Not that I don't trust you mate. It's just that if the cash is short, I need to be able to look the bloke in the eyes and say I opened the envelope myself. If I couldn't do that, they'd be blaming any shortfall on you."

I had no idea how much we were taking but it was plenty. Every week, Tommy gave me my cut of the profit and it was far more than I got from that poxy job at the hospital in a month.

I couldn't flash it about too much because Clare would want to know where I got it. She hated drugs, her little brother was a basket case, in and out of rehab all the time and dragging her family into it every time he got into trouble. He was doing six months in Lewes prison for possession and her family was relieved. He couldn't get them into any more trouble while he was locked up.

It took a few months before my share amounted to more than a bit of extra beer money and enough to slip my Mum some cash towards the household bills. Then it all took off; our customers couldn't get enough of the stuff. Tommy handed me a brown envelope as we pulled up in the car park at McDonalds. Sitting in a corner booth a few minutes later, I was still getting my head round how much money he'd given me. That's when he told me about Anwar. William strongly urged Tommy to meet the guy... under threat of cutting us off if he didn't.

There was a problem keeping all the cash we were taking in and anything foolish could easily draw attention to the whole arrangement. No way could it go in the bank and money laundering was tricky business. Apparently Anwar would take care of that for us.

"It's easy mate," Tommy explained. "A bloke in say; Bangalore, deposits cash with one of Anwar's network. Then as long as you know the password, you can go and pick it up in, say Paris."

Tommy looked at me as though he just answered all my prayers. I couldn't see for the life of me why that was of any use at all. Tommy started on his burger, waiting for it all to click.

"No... don't get it mate. What's Bangalore got to do with anything?"

"It's just an example. He can stash our money and, when we want it, we can pick it up anywhere in the world."

"So it's like a deposit account then?"

"Got it in one." Tommy was delighted the message had finally sunk in.

"What's the interest like?" I asked, my confidence growing.

"Have you seen what the banks pay these days? It's peanuts. Anwar doesn't pay interest, but he doesn't charge us a fee either, unless we move the money abroad."

I knew there'd be a catch.

"Sounds risky. Couldn't we just invest it?" I asked.

Tommy looked scornful.

"Same problem as with the banks. Besides, my Dad invested money and lost his shirt. Paid into a pension all his life then the company went bust. The bosses had cleaned out the pension scheme just before the firm went under. And he paid into one of those big insurance companies and they screwed him too. If he'd got any sort of pay out, the government would have had most of it back in tax anyway. It's why he never made his fiftieth birthday, the stress of it all killed him."

I'd heard it was cheap blended whisky that did it, but I doubted Tommy wanted to hear that.

"This is dirty money; we need to keep it out of the system," he said.

Tommy had just given me more cash than I'd ever seen in my life. Now he was suggesting I hand it over to some bloke I'd never met, who'd take care of it for me, without the hassle of any unwanted paperwork. What could possibly go wrong? It sounded like a terrible idea, but I didn't have a better one. The decision was taken like all the others in our partnership.

"Well, I'm in," Tommy said, scooping up the last of his ketchup with a handful of fries.

"Yeah, I guess… me too," I replied, without the conviction that I had much of an idea what I'd just agreed to.

I had a plan. I would wait until I had enough money salted away, then I was going to tell Clare my lottery ticket came up. If I could pay my share, we could sell the flat and get a nice house somewhere. I hadn't quite worked out how I was going to maintain the deceit though. She was never going to accept me dealing drugs, not with all the problems she had with her brother. I never really thought past getting the house. Maybe I could claim it was a really big lottery win, then she wouldn't be surprised when the money kept flowing. Better still, Tommy and I'd make enough to start a proper business, maybe a pub or a restaurant, and we could ditch the dealing. Well that was the plan, but now I was on a plane to Thailand, Tommy was dead and Clare had dumped me for some rich bastard who lived in Spain; and guess how he made his money… by dealing drugs, that's how.

I'd seen how Clare's ex only needed to click his fingers to make her come running and I'd seen how a Brighton gangster could execute my mate and get away with it. That takes money and the easiest way to get money is by selling drugs. Thanks to Tommy I knew how to do that and then I'd see Clare and make sure she knew what she was missing, then I'd reintroduce myself to Mr Connor, the man who killed my best friend.

The plane was on its approach to Suvarnabhumi, Bangkok's main airport. In an hour or so I'd be in a taxi to the city centre and the Nana Rose hotel. It was where Tommy and I started on my one and only previous trip. I phoned to make sure that they had plenty of rooms but decided making a booking beforehand was too risky. I'd stayed one step ahead of Connor's men so far and had no intention of letting my guard down.

Thai Kiss

CHAPTER TWO

Making my own way in the world

My village is near Buriram in Isaan, the eastern part of Thailand, not far from Cambodia. Most families are poor but I was very lucky. My papa had a job and took good care of my mama, me and my sister. He was my mother's second husband; my real papa left when I was just seven years old. My new papa made sure I went to school, studied hard and got my leaving certificate. I thought I had it made when seven years ago, just after my seventeenth birthday, my papa's friend got me a job in a fancy hotel in Khao Lak. It was short lived, in six months I would be back in my village. My first job there was in the kitchens, but I think they liked me and after only a few weeks they said I could be a trainee in the restaurant. I learned English at school and could speak a little bit. My new job let me practice too. My name is Tasanee Charanthea, but everyone calls me by my nickname, Yim. It is the Thai word for smile. My mama told me that was what everyone noticed about me when I was a baby, my smile.

At first I did not pay much attention to the tall, handsome young man who was waiting tables on the other side of the restaurant. Ghai had jet-black hair that was cut very short, he did not try to copy the pop stars on TV. And he had such a nice smile. I was first drawn to his perfect white teeth, then his eyes which were so big and round they almost made him look like a *farang*, that's what we call westerners in Thailand. Ghai's eyelashes were so long I would look in the mirror and wish they were mine. His skin was light too, not dark like mine. Thai people all want light skin, it is the colour of the "*HiSo*"… High Society people from Bangkok, so much better than the deep brown skin of the people who work the fields of Isaan… my people.

I caught Ghai watching me a few times and he would smile nervously. That always made me put my hand over my mouth and giggle. I did not know what to say to him. Then he came to work on my side of the restaurant. Ghai had been at the hotel for two years already when I arrived. I was told I should do whatever he said, he was so kind and sweet it was not hard for me to do that. He had *jai dee*, that is Thai for "good heart". He was shy the same as me and we liked to speak English together. My papa had always frightened away any boys back in my village. Now I was on my own and could choose who I wanted to be with, and I wanted to be with Ghai, for sure. We saw each other every day and I was not looking forward to the Christmas holidays when I would have to go home to see my family. It would be the longest time we spent apart since our first meeting, and we wanted our last evening together to be very special. I had never been with a boy before. He asked me if I was sure. I said "one million per cent."

New Year is more important to Thai people than Christmas. We are Buddhists not Christians, but it is an excuse for gifts and time to be with family, to eat together and relax. *Sabai sabai.* Everyone wanted to know about my new job and who my new friends were since I moved to Khao Lak. I told them about the girls I met and then mentioned there was a nice boy called Ghai who was teaching me what to do in the restaurant. It would be just three more days until I could see him again.

The Wave

"Come look at the TV," shouted Pim, my little sister.
"Where is that?"
"It looks like Thailand, maybe Phuket," my papa said.
I rushed to the TV. It looked like Khao Lak to me, except not as I had ever seen it before. The wide sandy beaches were covered with debris, palm trees were ripped from the ground and the buildings close to the water's edge were completely destroyed. There was a running banner at the bottom of the screen saying there had been a tsunami in the Indian Ocean and thousands of people were dead. I had never heard of the word tsunami. Whatever it was, it was not something that happened in Isaan, for sure. I did not know where the Indian Ocean was but maybe that meant it could not be Khao Lak after all. There are beaches like that all over the world, it would be too much of a coincidence if this had happened to the town where I worked. I was desperate to talk to Ghai, just in case ... to be sure he was safe. He would be

able to explain about tsunamis and point out the Indian Ocean on a map for me. If I could only hear Ghai's voice, then this gnawing feeling in the pit of my stomach would go away. For sure.

"Where's Sri Lanka?" Pim asked.

"Why?"

"They said on TV, the pictures are from Sri Lanka, that's where it all happened."

I was not sure where Sri Lanka might be, it sounded Thai like Sri Racha. They were interviewing survivors. A wave of relief burst through me, the people did not look Thai and they were speaking another language. This tsunami had happened somewhere else and my new home, the hotel and Ghai would all be safe. I was sure of that, one million per cent. I needed to calm down and relax, then this feeling of dread would go away.

"That's definitely Phuket," Papa exclaimed.

The banner changed at the bottom of the screen and the pictures were different. The faces looked more familiar; more Thai and when they interviewed a man who saw it all happen, I could understand every word. He was speaking my language, he was speaking Thai. The banner said they suspected thousands of people had been killed in Phuket. I tried to think where Phuket was in relation to Khao Lak but my brain would not work. Even if I knew the answer, I would not have been able to remember. Ghai did not have a telephone. I had no way of contacting him, no way of knowing if he was safe. I just had to hope that Khao Lak and Ghai had been spared. Then the banner changed again. The pictures looked much the same but this time there could be no doubt and I had the answer to my question, for sure. If I was in any doubt, the presenter put it into words for me.

"One of the worst hit towns on the Andaman coast is Khao Lak, where thousands of people are presumed dead and access for the rescue effort is being hampered by fallen trees and severely damaged roads, many of which have been washed away completely. Resources are reportedly stretched to the limit as search teams and medical workers are trying to handle the situation there as well as in Phuket, little more than one hundred kilometres down the coast. These pictures are just in."

A helicopter film crew flew low over the palm trees, it could easily have been the beachfront at the hotel, or any one of a hundred other beaches anywhere in Thailand. The knot in my stomach grew tighter still and I could feel the tears slide down my cheeks. My mama put her arms around me.

"Everything will be alright, you will see your friends again, for sure. We all have to give thanks you came to see your family. We are all so happy you are here and not at work. I think they would have big problems today."

But Khao Lak was exactly where I wanted to be, with Ghai, wherever he might be. I could barely concentrate on the news reports now. Something happened under the sea and it caused a huge wave to hit the beach. It was still impossible to imagine water could have done all the damage we were seeing on TV. They explained that children and old people were most vulnerable as the water came in, they could not run or swim to safety. I felt ashamed but my heart soared. Ghai was very strong and a really good swimmer. We spent a few days on the beach and he loved to show off. He would hold his breath under water for ages, until I thought he must have drowned, then he would appear from nowhere, laughing at me. If anyone could survive the wave, it was Ghai. He just had to be safe.

I wanted to go straight back to the hotel but my papa would not let me. He said it would be too dangerous and there was nothing a young girl could do, they did not need anyone to clear plates and top up *farang* coffee cups at breakfast time. We tried to call the hotel but it would not connect. My papa told me it was probably because all the telephone lines were down around the town.

It was a whole week before Papa let me go back to Khao Lak. He only agreed because I told him I feared I might lose my job and not be able to get another because they would tell people I was not reliable. One of our neighbours was going to Phuket to help with the clean-up operation and he agreed to take me as far as Khao Lak.

I found the hotel easily enough. At least, I found the place where it used to be. The shell that occupied the plot was barely recognisable from the beautiful building I had left only ten days before. There were workmen from the American company that owned the hotel, they had already started the job of clearing the debris to build again. The men were Thai and should have had more respect for the spirits of the people who lost their lives but they had families to support too, I suppose. They told me that a lot of people died and the bodies had been taken to a temple five kilometres up the road. One of the men agreed to take me there. As we walked to his motorbike, I spotted a bright yellow sunhat with white flowers around the brim. It was tiny, maybe right for a child of no more than three or four. It was covered in blood.

On my last day before I set out for home I brought some cold drinks to a *farang* family lying by the pool. The woman was very beautiful, with very white skin and long blonde hair. Her husband was tall, handsome and looked very strong, they were definitely really happy to be together. I hoped maybe when we were a little older, Ghai and I would be like that. They had a young son who was playing a game on his phone and a little daughter who never stopped smiling. Her mother was covering her in sun block, then she picked up the little girl's sun hat and put it on her head. It was bright yellow, with white flowers around the brim.

In three days I visited four temples and three hospitals. They told me that many of the bodies had been burned, there were simply too many to bury. Injuries from when the wave came, the effect of the seawater and more than a week in the heat made it impossible to identify anyone from looking at a body. They said they had taken samples and might be able to identify people later by comparing them with something taken from relatives, but that would be months away. When they could, they took photos of tattoos or other marks that might help identify a person. For the moment, the best chance of identifying someone was from what they were wearing when they died. Ghai wore a ring with a black stone and a leather necklace with the letter Y for Yim on a small wooden ball. At the end of each day, I went to the temple and prayed for him, then I would go to my room to sleep. The building where I lived was about two kilometres inland, so everything there was as it should be, except for one thing. I shared the room with Lim, who worked in the kitchens at the hotel. Her bed was empty each night, she had not been seen since the day of the wave. So, each night, I lay down in the room and cried.

I went back to the hotel every day for a week and tried to find the places where Ghai and I used to catch a few moments together when we were supposed to be working. If he was looking for me, he would surely try one of those places too. I saw the notice on the fourth day that any Thai workers from the hotel should assemble for a meeting at four p.m. - the company had an announcement to make. It was the first time I had seen some of my old friends for weeks and I could scarcely believe how few of them there were. As new people arrived, I hoped desperately that one of them might be Ghai. It was not to be. Very few of the staff who were at the hotel when the wave hit had survived, those that did were the drivers ferrying tourists to the National Parks in the hills, the cleaners and maintenance staff working on the upper floors of the hotels and a tiny number of others who were in the open when the first wave came and then managed to cling to a tree when the second struck the beach. Ghai might have been serving breakfast in the restaurant.

The American was late, the meeting started at four twenty and finished at four twenty-two.

"We're desperately sorry for what has happened here. It's an appalling tragedy for the people of Thailand and the poor holidaymakers who were caught up in all of this. It will take us time to rebuild the hotel but once we do, we hope you will all come back and work for us again. In the meantime we're happy to offer you a very generous payment, which will help you take care of your families until you find alternative work. We are grateful for what you have done for our company and we hope you will work for us again in the future."

I stood in line with my friends, exactly as the American asked us to do. When I got to the desk, they asked for my name and once they found it on their list, they wanted to see my ID card. Then the man carefully counted out four thousand nine hundred baht and thrust a piece of paper into my hand to sign. It was two week's salary, less than it cost the tourists to stay for one night at the hotel.

As we quietly filed away from the ruined buildings I heard Tam, the head of housekeeping, in deep conversation with a lady called Nung. The two women were talking about how they were called to deal with an irate guest on the third floor of the hotel, minutes before the wave struck the beach. The woman was their least favourite guest, she phoned to complain at the slightest thing. If the daily cleaning was not exactly to the woman's liking, then Tam was summoned to look at a smear on the bathroom mirror, a poorly folded towel or a used shampoo bottle that had not been replaced. Tam and Nung would smile and bow and openly say bad things about the woman in Thai, knowing she did not understand a word. That morning, she saved their lives. Had they not been called to the third floor, they would have been in the laundry room organising the return of the cleaning from the day before. One of the few bodies identified immediately after the tsunami was Tuk, who ran the laundry. The room was in the basement and she was unable to escape as it filled with water.

What Tam said next made me buckle at the knees and I had to grab her arm to stop myself falling to the floor. It was what I was already thinking but sometimes an idea only becomes real when it is said out loud.

"If they haven't turned up alive yet, they never will. Either the body has been burned, they are in one of the piles of corpses at the temple or they have been washed far out to sea. There's no point in hoping to see them again, it's time to pray for their spirit and for their next life."

The man on the motorbike outside the hotel gate had been driving tourists back to the airport when the wave came. He was friends with Ghai and knew about us.

"Where are you going?" he asked.

"To the temple to pray for Ghai's spirit."

"I will take you there."

Ghai's return

I had been back in my village for over a month before Ghai spoke to me for the first time since our final day together. A westerner would say that it was only a dream, just my imagination, but I know it was Ghai. He told me he felt no pain when his body died. He was serving breakfast to a *farang* family, he remembered a lady with long blonde hair and a tiny laughing child who was wearing a bright yellow sunhat with white flowers around the brim. Then everything went very quiet. He heard someone say, "Look, the sea has gone," because first the tide went out a very long way, then there was a loud rumbling noise and a huge crash as the water hit the trees in front of the terrace. Ghai said it felt like the lights had gone out. He watched me search for him but did not know how to talk to me then. Now his spirit was settled, maybe soon he would be given his next life. Until then he would watch over me and our baby daughter, and make sure we came to no harm.

As I heard him say the words, I realised I was already stroking my stomach, I sensed I was not completely alone, Ghai was with me somehow. Hearing him speak sent a little rush of relief through my body, but the thought that I would have his baby was a different matter. There was the joy that part of Ghai would soon be with me, and the cold fear of knowing I had to take care of a small child. It was something I knew nothing about. I had already missed one period but thought it was because of everything that happened since Christmas. I visited a doctor in Buriram, someone who had never met my family. The examination was brief and I knew the answer before he opened his mouth.

Many *farang* think Thai people are promiscuous and very open about sex. That might be true in the big cities and in the bars of Pattaya and Phuket. In the villages of Isaan it is another matter. It is taken for granted that women will bear children from a young age, but only if they have a husband to take care of them. A new mother who has no husband, will be talked about by the people of her village for sure. They will say she is easy, she has no morals and that she is the kind of woman who will sleep with *farang* for money. That is the sort of girl who has a baby when she has no husband. I could not possibly have known it at the time, but of course they were right. I was the sort of girl who would sleep with foreigners for money, it was the only way I could take care of my daughter.

The doctor looked at me as though he was delivering very grave news. Ghai was standing next to me as he spoke, but the doctor could not see him. Only I could see Ghai's spirit. Had his body been there too then I am sure the doctor would have been very happy for us. Instead he was talking to a girl with no husband. That meant I was easy, I had no morals and that I was probably the kind of girl who would sleep with *farang* for money. He confirmed I was having a baby but it was another seven months before I was sure it was a little girl, exactly as Ghai said. He talked to me many times before Dao was born and again when my mother cried and said I brought shame on the family, when my papa shouted at me that I was supposed to find a good husband to take care of me, not bring him another mouth to feed, and when Dao was sick and nearly died in the few first days of her life. If she had gone to be with her father I might have been able to start again, my life would have been much simpler for sure. But then I would not have all that was left in this world of Ghai. He told me she would be fine and he was right, one million per cent. She got stronger every day until they said I could take her home again. I was happy and so was Ghai, and my family told me everything would be OK. Papa smiled and said his grand daughter was even more beautiful than her mother, and I knew he had forgiven me.

Thai Kiss

CHAPTER THREE

Return to Thailand

It only takes a few seconds, it's the time between stepping off the plane and crossing the air-bridge to get to the terminal building. Thailand hits you straight in the face right there. A wall of heat that makes you catch your breath, the ground staff babbling away in a totally baffling and frankly pretty ugly language, and the air-crew wishing you farewell with an elegant little bow while holding their hands up as though they are praying. Presumably they're giving thanks to Buddha that the shift is over and that they're seeing the last of another Jumbo Jet load of sweaty foreigners.

The walk to Immigration seems endless and with throngs of arriving and departing tourists, the risk of getting swept along and suddenly finding yourself on the flight to Frankfurt is quite high. This was only my second trip to Thailand and, both times, I'd obviously arrived at the tail end of a fleet of incoming charter planes. The lines at Immigration were horrendous and, as with every other queue, I chose the wrong one. It was definitely the shortest when I joined it but it's inevitable that at least three of the people in front of me will spark the interest of the border official. Either their appearance and body language screams drug dealer or they're young and female with a low cut t-shirt. In any event it's enough to prompt the immigration officer to a lengthy scrutiny of their documents while the queue next to me gets processed with a yawn, a nod and a chop with the official stamp that says you can enter the Kingdom of Thailand for a maximum of thirty days.

To make matters worse, I'd not moved an inch for at least five minutes and from my place in the line, I could see the Fast Track queue. This was a special line for VIPs who could sail through while everyone else waited their turn. I didn't exactly resent them, because I wanted to be one too, going straight to the front where some flunky waves me through while the common folk look on with envy. I guess in the meantime, I did resent them, just a little.

Thai Kiss

At least the baggage handlers appeared to be more on the ball than their UK counterparts. The queue at immigration doesn't seem so bad when your bag is waiting on the carousel on the other side.

Maybe it's what I did for a living but the toughest part of the process is walking through the Nothing to Declare channel. The Suvarnabhumi Airport version is actually far less intimidating than London. The staff look heroically disinterested and appear to choose their victims for X-Ray screening based on who might have the most interesting luggage, rather than who looks like a dealer in illicit drugs or weapons. I just have a massive, natural guilt reflex. When my school teachers asked the class who had broken the window in the boy's toilet, or stolen writing pads from the stationery cupboard, my throat would tighten, my face would go red and I'd be unable to utter a word without choking. All this, in spite of being totally innocent of the crime. I was certain a customs officer was about to tap me on the shoulder at any moment and, had he done so, I'd have jumped out of my skin. The fact that my luggage contained nothing illegal was no comfort at all. I guess that's what a Roman Catholic upbringing does for you.

Most of the people arriving at Suvarnabhumi look utterly confused, as though they have no real idea where they're going. It was time for me to get a little smug. Tommy showed me the ropes on arrival. Avoid the touts, however pretty, trying to sell the AOT limousine service, and head straight for the ground floor where you'll see what Tommy called the world's best organised taxi rank. The heat smacks you in the face as you go through the revolving doors but you'll then be greeted by a row of booths staffed by passably attractive young women. They ask for your destination and scribble some gobbledygook on a form, half of which goes to the driver and half to the passenger. It's surprisingly reassuring, as though they have logged you in and the file won't be closed until you arrive happily at your destination. And off you go. Twenty miles and less than a half hour later, you're in the centre of town for less than six pounds. In traffic, a London cabbie will struggle to travel a single mile for the same price.

In exactly twenty-nine minutes, I was standing outside the Nana Rose hotel in Soi 4, off Sukhumvit Road in the heart of the capital. It's handily placed for Nana Plaza, a three-storey horseshoe of bars that overlooks an internal courtyard of sorts containing... more bars. This was where Tommy introduced me to Bangkok nightlife three weeks after Clare dumped me.

Thai virgin

The Nana Rose was a ramshackle, five-storey hotel less than a hundred yards from the Plaza. My room offered a perfect view of the street below and the side of the very swish JW Marriott hotel where all those bastards who sailed past me in the Immigration Fast Track line were probably staying. I half expected the connecting door to the next room to swing open, just like when I came with Tommy.

"Come on you cocksucker, let's get you laid," was his opening line.

"No Tommy, no way mate. I'll come for the beers and this Pattaya place sounds alright, with the beach and everything, but no way am I shagging a hooker."

"We'll see. Let's go then."

We took a later flight on that trip and there was just enough time for a shower before Tommy marched me into the street for our first beer. It was barely eight p.m. but the streets were already heaving with Thais on their way to work and westerners on the prowl. Tommy headed for an open-air bar that overlooked the street so we could watch the action.

My only knowledge of Thailand at that point was based on what Tommy told me, and a book called The Beach by some bloke called Garland. We watched the movie too, that made it all feel pretty glamorous, at the start at least. Young, beautiful people in search of paradise, getting stoned along the way. The Nana Rose even looked a bit like the hostel they stayed in at the start of the movie. There the similarity ended. A few of the guests were around our age and in good shape, but most were old, fat and must have got dressed with the bedroom light off. They wore cargo shorts, flip-flops and button-up shirts that would possibly have fitted them twenty years ago but which were now straining to contain their gut. These were the sort of men we were pushing round the hospital in wheelchairs back in England. In Thailand, they were on the town, chasing some of the most beautiful women I'd ever seen. It was inconceivable that Thai girls could go for blokes like that.

"Look at this guy." Tommy pointed to a huge grey-haired man coming out of our hotel. He was sixty if he was a day and each of us could have slipped comfortably into one leg of his vast pair of shorts. He was wearing a pink shirt, at least he was when he stepped out of the hotel. Forty yards down the street, the shirt was plastered firmly to his skin with sweat and had turned deep red down his back and in two large semi-circles under his armpits. The man was closing on the entrance to the Plaza but walking on the opposite side of the road. We already noticed the gaggle of Thai girls standing there and I fully expected them to give the man a wide berth as he passed. Instead they giggled and grabbed at his arm, as though they knew him. Our waitress arrived to deliver a round of beers and I was momentarily distracted from what was going on in the street. By the time I looked back, Tommy was laughing loudly and pointing to a gorgeous Thai girl walking back towards the hotel. She had a fabulous oval shaped face with eyes to match. In truth, if her body had been in perfect proportion to her legs, she'd have been about seven feet tall. She was born to model lingerie and she knew it. As she walked, there was a gentle swaying of her hips that screamed, "You want me, don't you? Look at this, you'd be crazy not to."

And she was right, I did want her, right there and then. There was only one thing that soured the moment. Holding her hand was the huge grey-haired guy and by the time I got over the shock, he was patting her backside as she walked up the steps of the hotel.

"What the fuck? It can't be. Why would a girl like that go with a lumpy bastard like him?"

Tommy was still laughing. "TIT," he said. "This is Thailand."

Nearly twenty minutes and another large Singha beer later, Tommy had been through all the arguments with me all over again.

"It's market forces mate. They could work in a factory for six quid a day, or come here and shag foreigners for the same salary plus a fifty quid bonus for every trick they turn. The blokes take them shopping, treat them well and they get to party every night. Most of them love it, look at the girls in here, do they look like they're having a bad time?"

It was certainly true that the girls around us were laughing and looked like they were having fun. I was pretty sure it was a bit more complicated than it appeared. It was probably just their way of getting through the day. Tommy had said he was going to ease me in gently, so as girls approached us in the bar, he smiled and said, "Maybe later." This time, however, as two almost identical Asian sex fantasies walked towards us, he made room for them to sit down and ordered up some more drinks. As our waitress returned, we spied the lady with the oval eyes emerge from the hotel. It was twenty-one minutes since she went in with Mister Grey.

"Fuck me," I said, "...she's killed him. The old bastard has probably died of a heart attack."

"Well that could easily be the case if he wasn't expecting what she had in store for him," Tommy replied with a smile.

"What a way to go though. If your time is up, you might as well go out with a woman like that. It would do it for me."

"Since when did you like cock?"

I sprayed a mouthful a beer onto the floor, mostly through my nose. It stung like hell.

"You're kidding me, it can't be." He'd told me about ladyboys but this was unbelievable, she was so beautiful, it was impossible. Wasn't it?

Tommy was still laughing at my expense, but he was adamant - Miss Oval Eyes was a Mister. Height, face shape and the size of "her" tits and arse were apparently a giveaway that she'd been born male but years of taking hormones and possibly even the surgeon's knife changed all that. We discussed briefly whether we should check on the old man. Tommy heard stories of ladyboys robbing unsuspecting *farang*, hoping the victim would be too embarrassed to report the offence. We concocted all sorts of scenarios where the poor fat man was trussed up in his room, traumatised from his experience, hoping to be found before morning, but wondering how he could explain what happened. We were still arguing about whether to intervene when Mr Grey appeared at the hotel entrance and then quickly disappeared into the pharmacy next door, only to reappear minutes later marching back in the direction of Nana Plaza.

"What's he doing?" I asked.

"Viagra," Tommy said. "In half an hour, he'll be ready for more."

Tigers and the taste of human blood

I had little recollection of the rest of the evening. There were go-go bars with shiny poles, ping-pong balls being thrown for the dancers to catch and semi-naked Thai girls bumping and grinding in our laps. We played pool and dice games and drank beer and tequila as though global stocks were about to run out. Tommy and I spent ages discussing chat-up lines that we used to get women in England, those witty little one-liners that catch their attention. One I used a few times was, "How do you like your eggs in the morning?" until one girl replied, "Unfertilised thank you." I couldn't use it again and keep a straight face. In truth that wasn't me anyway. I'm not sure I ever actually succeeded with a girl when I made an approach like that. Only time I made a connection was when we just fell into conversation and she picked me. That's pretty much how it works in Thailand, I discovered, so I was in the perfect place. But I was still adamant I wouldn't pay to take a girl back to my room.

I caught on pretty quick that the ritual is almost set in stone. The girls have a set of stock phrases - "Where you from? What your name? How long you stay? First time come Thailand? You buy me drink?" Even I could get through that inquisition without screwing it up. By the time question six comes along in England, it was usually "What sort of job do you do? Do you have a nice car? Do you own your own house? How do you feel about commitment?" Tommy reckoned you could simplify everything in the UK by having a copy of your monthly pay slip printed on the front of a T-shirt. Except we'd have to add, "And I'm a drug dealer too, so I make a lot more than that!" otherwise we'd never have got laid.

I was getting the impression that, compared with England, Thai women were happy-go-lucky party girls who weren't really interested in how much money I had, as long as I bought them a few drinks. Well it was my first day!

Tommy nudged me and cocked his head towards the cute young girl who had gone to get us another couple of beers. "How about that one?" He wet the tip of his finger and pointed at the girl, then made a sizzling noise. Subtle.

"Absolutely no chance, it's definitely not going to happen," I proclaimed.

I had to admit the girls were very special. It was all so easy, so innocent and the one who went to fetch the beer was extremely hot.

"But what if I catch something?" I asked Tommy a little later.

"Thinking about it then?" he asked smugly.

"No... not at all, it's just... well, you know. Theoretically," I muttered, without a lot of conviction.

"Yeah... of course."

We spotted Miss Oval Eyes, hand in hand with another customer as we swapped bars and that stiffened my resolve to go home alone. Then Tommy announced he was taking me to his favourite Nana Plaza bar. It was a go-go with a pool table and sport on TV.

"This," Tommy said, "is what Heaven will be like."

"You'll never find out, it's the other place you're going to have to worry about." It was funny at the time but thinking about it now made me feel guilty. Death, we both thought, was decades away.

I lost count of the beers, the free shots, the tequilas that were downed willingly as chasers or reluctantly as a forfeit for losing at Scissors, Rock, Paper. I was still maintaining that I'd be returning to the hotel alone. Tommy had already made a choice. The girl was called Awe, which is pretty much the feeling she inspired the first time you looked at her. Tommy knew the code of course. He smiled at her and mimed taking his shirt off over his head. She just nodded and went to get changed.

Thai Kiss

"How do I know they aren't ladyboys?" I asked, sending Tommy into fits of hysterics as he pointed out that every girl in the bar was naked. "If she's a bloke, she's not very well equipped," he replied.

I was intrigued, but determined I wasn't taking a girl to the hotel. As I awoke the following morning, I could remember how determined I'd been, but all the pieces from the night before hadn't quite slotted into place. As I reached out to find the light switch there was something, someone, in the way. She was lithe and brown and had long tousled black hair. As my hand touched her back she stirred and turned to face me with huge deep brown eyes, and then she smiled.

"*Boom-boom* one more time, mister?"

Tommy was in his element when we finally met for breakfast.

"It's like tigers, mate. They don't normally eat people but once they taste human blood, they can't get enough of it. Blokes are the same with Thai women, there'll be no stopping you now."

"Where do you get this crap, Tommy? Is there a web site called TotalBollocks.com or something?"

I was irritated at how gleeful he was at the fact that I fell at the first hurdle. The hurdle was named Noy, she told me she came from a town in the north-east of Thailand, in a place called Isaan. She was twenty-two and had worked in the bars for less than four weeks. Apparently I didn't exactly put in a sterling performance the night before, but she explained that I agreed she should stay "long time". That meant I should give her a little extra money but I was entitled to a second "*boom-boom*." She told me I was a handsome man, I was very good at *boom-boom* and I made her happy. She hoped I'd come to see her again. Noy told me I had a very good heart, *jai dee* in Thai, and she'd be sad if she didn't see me again. She told me lots of things Clare never told me in all the time we were together.

The trip with Tommy was still so fresh in my mind, he was so full of life and mischief. It was days before he stopped teasing me about my hopeless lack of willpower with Noy. But he was right about the tigers. After that first night, any inhibitions I had about Thai women went straight out the window. The following afternoon we headed to Pattaya, about two hours south of Bangkok by car. It was everything he promised and more. There were beaches and rifle ranges and go-karts and all sorts of distractions for a couple of young healthy males, but most of all there were women, thousands of them and Clare was suddenly a million miles away.

I'm not sure why I went back to the Nana Rose on my second trip, I guess I was feeling lonely without Tommy and doing something we'd done together made me feel a bit less isolated. I even went back to the same bar for my first beer. I saw Miss Oval Eyes practically frog-marching a young blond guy past the bar, presumably on the way to his hotel. He had that look about him that suggested he was new to all of this. I wondered if he had any idea what was in store for him once he was alone with his new heartthrob.

I even managed to find the bar where I met Noy in Nana Plaza. Everything was the same on the surface, the dancing girls, the strange ritual where blokes throw ping-pong balls instead of giving tips and the stupid bar games you wouldn't be seen dead playing in a pub in England. When I had done it with Tommy it had all been hilarious but on my own it felt a bit empty. Still I was on a mission, scheduled to go to Pattaya the next morning, same plan as when I came with Tommy. I'd relax, take my time and work out how I was going to get even with the man who killed my best friend. In the meantime I was hoping I might bump into Noy again. I was sure it was the right bar.

"I look for Noy, she here tonight?" I was becoming a dab hand at the pigeon English they all speak in Thai bars.

"We have many Noy, which one you like?"

I started to describe her but couldn't get much past "really pretty, dark hair, big eyes." The waitress I was talking to looked at me like I was an idiot. Then I remembered the number. Every girl has a little plastic disc with a staff number on it. She was number 28, same as my football shirt, that was how we got talking in the first place.

Thai Kiss

"Noy, number 28," I said, with an obvious air of anticipation.

"Oh, she have day off, not work today."

Tommy said that was code for, "You're too late mate, she's already out shagging someone else." Thais are always keen to spare your feelings if they can.

The beauty of a Thai bar is there's always someone to comfort you if you're feeling down. The waitress introduced me to two other girls called Noy on the basis it was the closest they could offer to my original selection. I bought drinks and we played a few games, then we had some tequila and about twenty minutes before I decided it was time to head back to the hotel, I remembered the pills I'd tucked into the pocket of my trousers. I had important decisions to make. One more beer, Noy number one, Noy number two or, as the waitress suggested, both Noys? Decisions, decisions, decisions.

It was probably the sound of footsteps in the hotel corridor that woke me up, then male voices whispering. Or maybe it was the TV, showing one of the endless, interminable Thai soap operas. I was certain I turned that off before I went to sleep, but somehow it turned itself back on. The girl I brought to my room the night before might have done it, I suppose, but she must have gone. I couldn't remember her name… or her face. I hadn't even paid her. It was a shame, I like to have some company with me when I wake up.

Another noise in the corridor was followed by the sound of splintering wood. My hotel door lay shattered on the floor and there were three men framed by light from the hallway. Two were dressed identically in roll neck tops and leather jackets, the guy in the middle was wearing an immaculate suit and a matching coat, Gucci I guessed. It was Terry Connor, the man who ordered Tommy's death. I reached for the pocket knife I kept by the side of the bed, but it was too late. The taller guy was on me first, grabbing my arm and bending it back until I was certain it was going to pop out of its socket. Then the other one joined in, slamming his fist into my abdomen. I felt like I was going to be

40

sick on the spot. Connor's face was inches from my own and he spat into my left eye.

"There's no hiding from me you little shit. You think I can have jerks like you making me look a fool? I'm going to have to make an example of you. We dealt with Tommy... now it's your turn."

I was gasping for breath, desperately trying to find the words that would make him stop, make him give me another chance.

"You're such a disappointment young Paul. I had such high hopes but you keep letting me down. I don't know why I bothered with you."

I thought I was going to die, but I couldn't stop wondering why they were dressed in coats and leather jackets. This was Thailand, where it hits thirty-four degrees in the middle of the night. What the fuck was that all about?

The face was there again, so close I could feel his breath. But maybe the pills I took the night before were kicking in because now the face looked like my Dad, not Connor at all. He looked the way he did just before he walked out on my mum... it made no sense at all. The tall guy's grip loosened and I struggled to pull myself upright. I could see the door, back in place again. I was in my room on the estate with football posters on the wall and that window where you could see the boats if you craned your neck.

"Such a disappointment Paul, I just don't know why I bother sticking around."

The words were echoing in my ears as I started to feel like I was drifting. It's the feeling you get when you're surfacing from very deep water, or if you're slowly coming out of a very, very deep sleep. The feeling you get when you're emerging from your worst possible nightmare.

Sweating profusely, I made it to the bathroom with seconds to spare, then emptied my stomach of everything I consumed the day before.

The taxi arrived at 11 a.m. just as I finished paying my bill. Like four weeks earlier when I'd come with Tommy, it was my second day in Thailand and I was heading to Pattaya. I spent the morning thinking about what to do next. The dream was still haunting me, would Connor send someone to Thailand to get me or would I be safe if I stayed out of England? I could never be sure.

On the twenty-eighth, the day before I flew to Thailand, I made the usual trip to the pub in Borough Market, to pick up the order Tommy placed for the month. They must have seen the newspaper story, because there was nobody there to make the exchange. I had no way of making contact with William again. If I wanted to get back into the drugs trade I'd have to find Clay, the American Tommy met in Pattaya. What choice did I have? It was the only way I knew how to make a pile of money fast, the only way I could get even with Terry Connor for Tommy's death, and the only way I could be sure he wouldn't come after me.

CHAPTER FOUR

A respectable family

It was only four hundred baht per day, but I could be near to my daughter and I was helping to take care of my family. Every morning I would go to my aunt's house at six a.m. and we sat with huge baskets filled with freshly picked flowers. We worked until midday, weaving and lacing the petals into garlands for the hotels and businesses near Buriram. What we produced was very beautiful and by mid afternoon it was finding its way onto pillows in local hotels, to the mirrors of cars as good luck symbols or as offerings at the temples and spirit houses.

I don't think Papa really needed the money, his business was going very well. He bought a new Hyundai and was planning a small extension to our house so Dao and I could have more space. We were sharing a room with my younger sister, Pim. Dao was nearly four years old and liked to run around a lot. Pim was growing up too and wanted some privacy. My family laughed when I said how nice it would be to have a room just for me, Ghai and Dao, but he still came to talk to me and I knew that he was watching over both of us. Whenever I felt sad or troubled, he would come and tell me he was there for us; he would make sure nothing bad could ever happen to me or to Dao. If only someone had been looking after Papa in the same way, things might have been very different.

We knew something was wrong the first time Papa was called out in the middle of the night. He started work many years ago as a *tuk-tuk* driver on the streets of Bangkok and after only a short time he made enough money to buy a proper taxi. He told me the secret of his success was that he could speak a little English, so once he got a *farang* customer and he treated them well, they would be keen to use him again. Papa organised guided tours for *farang*, showing them the sights of Bangkok, where they could shop, and he got a commission from the owners of the businesses they visited. Many *farang* recommended Papa to their friends and soon he had more business than there were hours in the day. He bought a new taxi and hired a driver for his old one. A few weeks before it all went wrong, he bought a huge luxury van called a Toyota Hiace Commuter. It had eleven seats, air-conditioning, DVD player and Karaoke machine, and Papa started to learn a few words of Japanese. The van cost him one million baht. I had to write the number down and show it to him to make sure I understood how much he paid. I thought only people like Thaksin or the King might have one million baht, I could not imagine how one of my own family could pay so much money for something. My family was admired and respected in the village. People who used to sneer at me because I had no husband would smile and stop to talk to me and to Dao. I brought shame on my family but suddenly we had the one thing that can wash away all the shame in the world in Thailand. We had money. One day I heard two women talk about me in a local shop and I knew my past was being quietly forgotten.

"Little Dao is such a pretty child but her mother has no husband," the first woman said.

"Her husband was killed when the wave came to Khao Lak," the other replied.

"Are you sure they were married?"

"Yim's family are well respected here, her husband was killed when the wave came."

My family did not even have to pay to have this new story about my life. Big money buys respect and if there are some inconvenient truths, they are simply ignored.

One phone call changed everything. It was the middle of the night and Dao noticed the commotion first. Papa raced from the house and Mama shouted at him to call the police. When he did not respond she cried out.

"Please, please be careful."

Chin was a kind and gentle man, he had been friends with Papa for as long as I could remember and took over the old taxi when Papa bought the second. He had driven for Papa for three years, until that night. It was the following day that we heard what had happened. Chin woke to hear the windows of the car being broken and went out to investigate. There were two men with long metal poles that they were using to smash the windows of the taxi. As Chin arrived to challenge them, the larger man turned and struck him inches above the left knee with the pole. His leg was badly broken. The men said nothing, they turned to their own pick-up truck and pulled out two petrol cans and a glass bottle with a rag stuffed into the top. It was also full of petrol. They emptied the fuel through the broken windows of the car and then lit the rag at the top of the bottle. As soon as the flame took hold, the man threw it towards the taxi. Had Chin been on his feet he might have been turned to ashes with the car, even the men themselves were thrown to the ground as the car exploded. Chin said later that when he finally looked up, their truck was disappearing up the road. All he could do was drag himself back to his house to phone Papa.

Nobody wanted to talk about why it happened, but some people said it was a couple of young men who were high on *yaba*, a pill that makes people crazy. Maybe Chin had upset them on a taxi journey sometime and this was their revenge. When Papa came home two weeks later with a long angry cut on his face and with clothes that were torn and dirty, we started to think maybe something was terribly wrong, but Mama insisted it was just a silly fall and had nothing to do with the night the taxi was burned.

We only learned the truth the day of Papa's funeral. He was very happy to receive a three day booking from some men who came to play golf in Isaan. He charged two thousand five hundred baht plus fuel for each day and slept in the van each night. They wanted to visit Khao Yai and Buriram and then Papa was to take them back to Bangkok at the end of the trip. He stopped sending SMS messages on the very first day but we thought maybe he had no money on his phone. On the second day the policeman arrived. Papa's body was found in a ditch next to the road between Nang Rong and Prakhon Chai. There was no sign of the van or his mobile phone. The police said it was obviously a simple robbery but there was no trace of the four golfers who hired Papa for the trip. We knew he was due to pick them up from the reception area of the Orchid Hotel near Ban Bua but the hotel had no record of four men staying with them at the time Papa disappeared. Mama too, said it was probably a robbery. A one million baht van was a prized possession in our province. But at the funeral people were starting to talk, either they did not know that Pim and I could hear them speak, or they did not care too much.

"He had enough warnings, he should have known they would do something terrible eventually."

"I don't know why he was so stubborn, they were offering him a good deal if he would just agree to stick with the one taxi. He was too ambitious, too greedy. He should have taken what they offered him."

"He should have done what he had to do to take care of his family. Now they'll have nothing."

The sympathy was genuine, but the attitude of the villagers was already changing towards us. We were no longer the successful business owners to whom the other villagers looked up. In just a few short days we had become a family of women and children with no one to take care of us. Except for me and my four hundred baht per day job, making garlands with my aunt.

Everybody in the whole of the village knew the story, except me. The queue in the local 7-11 was twice as long as it should have been, because the cashier was offering minute-by-minute updates, just like on TV. My papa was treading on the toes of another taxi business from a nearby town. The owner believed only he could ferry rich tourists around the area. Initially he offered my papa a job, he wanted to buy his taxi and pay a monthly salary. When he heard about the luxury van, the man suggested they buy the vehicle together, fifty-fifty. Papa said no and ignored the threats he received on a daily basis. The attacks on Chin and Papa himself were supposed to make him back down but he would not. Instead he went to the police. We heard later, but everyone else in the village seemed to know that the senior local officer was on the payroll of his persecutor... everyone except Papa. The day after he went to see the policeman, Papa received the booking from the four men. Three days later he was dead.

Another way to make a living

I heard about many girls who went to work in the bars of Bangkok, Phuket and Pattaya. Some left our village just as I left to go to Khao Lak. Some came back with money, but they did not have the respect of the villagers. Even if they could buy land and buffalo, everyone knew how they got their money and they failed to get a husband. People would nod and smile but when they passed, everyone would talk about them and the terrible things they had to do with *farang* to earn so much money. They had done things no good Thai girl would do, things no Thai man would ask them to do. They were strangers in their own village.

Only Jum left for the bars of Pattaya and returned to the approval of the rest of the village. That's because she brought Claus with her. He may have been quite handsome once and he was not as fat as many *farang*, but Jum was twenty-four years old and Claus was seventy-six. Jum was away for three years and only met her new husband about six months before they both returned to the village. It was easy to imagine that Jum did many things no good Thai girl would do before she met Claus, and probably quite a few of those same things afterwards. But Jum managed to wipe the slate clean with one simple marriage ceremony. She was not living off the money she saved from having sex with *farang*, she was not getting a monthly payment from a man living far away with another family. Jum snared her man and brought him home. Two or three times a year they went to Switzerland, his home country, for a couple of weeks and when they returned it was with presents for all of her family and friends. Claus bought many *rai* of land and built a very beautiful house for his new bride. Jum got herself a living breathing ATM machine who took care of her and her whole family and when he died, everything he owned would pass to her. In my village, that buys you all the respect you could ever want.

It was a life I never imagined for myself, there was never any need. I was one of those girls who would smile and then chatter behind my hand as one of the girls from Pattaya passed by. We said how shocked we were and then giggled at the thought of what they had to do for that fancy phone, that brand new motorbike or the Levi jeans which were probably genuine rather than a copy from the local market. They made merit by taking care of their families, for sure. But by doing things no good Thai girl would do.

Thai Kiss

It was almost time to eat. My mama had been at the market all morning and was about to cook dinner. There was plenty of food for one good meal and when Papa was alive she would have cooked it all. I saw her look at the food and then at her purse then divide the food in two. She prepared only half and wrapped the rest so we could eat it in the morning. When I went to sleep that night, I could hear my mama crying very softly in the next room. The following morning I went to see Jum in the big house on the edge of the village. A taxi had already taken Claus to the airport - he was going back to Switzerland for a few days. I knew Jum would be alone except for her cousin who always came to stay when Claus went away. The man opened the door before I even knocked. As he stepped out of the way, he stared as though he was wondering what I was wearing under my dress. Jum gave a big smile.

"Yim, what can I do for you?"

"I want to know about the City, how I can make money for my family."

"Are you sure?" she asked.

"One million per cent," I replied.

CHAPTER FIVE

Pattaya – Take Two

I still wasn't certain that a flight to Thailand was the smartest move but putting six thousand miles between me and Terry Connor had to be a positive thing. Then again, Tommy was never shy about his affection for the country, it was a pretty obvious place to come looking if anyone wanted to find me. And they'd have worked out that Thailand was where we sourced the merchandise. Maybe I was keen to get back to something familiar, somewhere I'd had a lot of fun, somewhere I'd been with my best mate. Maybe I just wanted to get laid.

I knew that the only way I could get even with Connor was if I had money, the only way I could make enough money was by dealing and the only person who could help me with that was Clay. He'd introduced Tommy to our supplier in London and if I could find him, I was sure he'd help me too. I had a pretty good idea where to look, but there was no rush. When the supplier failed to show at Borough market, days after Tommy died, I was left with ten thousand pounds in a TESCO carrier bag. It was tightly bound up in brown paper, so I had no idea how much money I was carrying until I unwrapped the parcel. I reckoned half of it was mine, Tommy and I were partners after all, the other half was his. The day before I set off for Heathrow Airport, I went to see Maggie, the girl he'd been living with for the previous three months. I gave her half the cash and told her to split it with Tommy's mum and sister. She was a nice girl and I trusted her to do as I asked. On reflection it was a pretty smart move, it meant she owed me one, big time. Suddenly I needed her help. My partnership with Tommy worked because I did the legwork and he found the clients, I wouldn't even know where to start. The only way I could get things off the ground again, was if I could get in contact with our old customers. There was no way I could start from scratch, I hadn't the faintest idea how to set about it. I'd not heard from Maggie since I arrived in Thailand, so I called and told her I needed Tommy's address book. I knew he kept it on his laptop and that must still be in the flat they shared. She was clearly pretty grateful for the cash but sounded a bit evasive when I asked whether she had been to see Tommy's mum and sister. I should have pressed her on it but all I could think of was getting my hands on those addresses. I told her there were loads of people who'd want to know Tommy had passed away, people we met at the football ground. I said they might even want to help her out a bit, knowing she was on her own. That seemed to do the trick and she promised to find what I was after and send it on to me. There wasn't much I could do until I heard back from Maggie. I needed to find Clay but I planned on taking my time. I still had twenty-seven days left on my visa. My plan was to try to locate the American then get to know him gradually. Diving in might put him off. So, I had nearly four weeks to relax, unwind and have some fun. Thanks to Tommy, I knew my way around and I also had five thousand pounds in my hotel safe, still wrapped in a TESCO carrier bag.

Walking Street

On our first trip, Tommy and I arrived around lunchtime, I could still smell Noy on my skin from that morning in the Nana Rose. We'd booked his usual hotel, the Siam Palace near an area called LK Metro. It was a short walk to the beach and the light breeze was a pleasant contrast to the close, humid air of Bangkok. An LED display on the reception desk told me it was thirty-two degrees outside, five less than it had been in the capital. Our rooms were basic but comfortable enough. The bed was firm, the shower worked and there was a wide screen TV. Tommy had given me ten minutes to unpack and be ready for our first day in Pattaya. I threw most of my stuff into a drawer, hung up a couple of shirts and a pair of trousers and just had time to grab a quick shower before he was knocking at the door. I was keen to see the legendary Walking Street. There are stacks of videos on YouTube and Tommy never stopped talking about it, so I convinced him it was a good place to start.

The easiest way to get there was along Beach Road. Coming from a seaside town like Brighton, I imagined it'd be much the same, only hotter. It was the first of the many surprises

Pattaya had in store for me. I'm guessing when the top travel companies do their Thai photo shoots they don't rush their best photographer to Pattaya beach. I'd seen all those idyllic pictures of miles of empty sand with the occasional supermodel carefully massaging sun tan oil into her latest lover's back. The stretch of sand we were looking at was narrow, grimy and packed with deckchairs shaded by umbrellas advertising beer, banking and insurance products. Dozens of Thais were strolling around offering massage, manicures, steamed prawns, carved wooden frogs, pashmina shawls and fresh coconuts to anyone rash enough to take a seat. It was a million miles away from what I expected, but I liked it.

Brighton hasn't got a lot to shout about by comparison. At least Pattaya has sand. My home town has pebbles that could easily double as lethal weapons should the need arise. The locals are so embarrassed by what looks like a builder's stockyard, they call the rocks that cover the beach, "fat sand." We stopped for a couple of bottles of freshly squeezed orange juice and resumed our pilgrimage to Walking Street. There's another stark contrast with the promenade at Brighton. I'm sure it's been known to happen occasionally, but in general you don't get offered a shag or a blow job every thirty yards or so back in England. It was two in the afternoon and the beach was lined with girls, all of whom had their own opening line.

"I want go with you."

"You want I make you happy?"

"*Boom-boom*?"

Tommy flashed his dazzling smile and declined with a polite shake of his head. I just gawped and looked like an idiot, not quite able to believe what I was seeing. Some of the girls were truly stunning, others looked like they had been waiting there for a long time, maybe decades. Others looked chillingly like Miss Oval Eyes from Nana Plaza and so I quickened my pace, hoping Tommy would too. They were all completely unfazed by our lack of interest, mainly because there were plenty of guys who were very interested indeed. Most, it must be said, were old enough to be my granddad and if you did see a younger bloke he had that look about him that suggested he might have been in Thailand for a while. It either meant cash was running a bit short and he was rooting round in the bargain bucket for a girl, or to be kind, he was more experienced with these things and had none of the inhibitions of a newcomer to Thailand. I was sticking with my bargain bucket theory for the time being.

I'm not claiming my encounter with Noy was a great romance but at least we had a couple of drinks together first, we had a chat, played a few games, had a bit of a conversation. At any rate, that's what she told me we did, I can't actually remember. This was way too clinical for me, wandering up to a girl on the street and saying "How much darling?" Still two days earlier I was adamant I'd never pay anyone for sex.

"Come on," I said, "show me Walking Street, it's got to be better than this."

"I'm guessing it'll be pretty quiet mate," Tommy warned me. "I've never been there in daylight before."

Quiet was definitely not the word to describe Walking Street in early afternoon. Shithole is a much better word. It was impossible to match the place with what I saw on YouTube. The trademark arch was there at the entrance, but after that it was unrecognisable. The go-go bars were all closed, their un-illuminated neon lights looking eerily sad as though they'd been extinguished out of respect because someone had died. A few Thai men on motorbikes were brandishing laminated cards offering us the massage of a lifetime with a soap-covered beauty. Apart from that it was pretty desolate. A couple of restaurants were open, mainly serving western food to the guys who made the trip along Beach Road without finding someone who took their fancy. The only other activity was around the pharmacies and convenience shops that lined the street. I was certain if they were going to turn this place into the world famous hub of the Asian sex industry by nightfall they'd need to bomb it flat first. Tommy found us a table at a restaurant overlooking the street and within minutes plates of fried rice arrived with a couple of surprisingly appetising looking chicken and pork dishes. I wanted a beer but I knew how the evening would kick off, so I stuck to Coke and watched the older blokes around me, knocking back beer after beer and wondered how the fuck they were going to still be standing at nightfall.

Lunch took about twenty minutes, in which time I managed to turn down four opportunities to buy a counterfeit Rolex, two from the same guy who clearly forgot we told him to get lost a few minutes earlier. The pirated DVDs were pretty tempting, at least more so than the weird embroidery, manicure sets and hand-stitched bags offered by a couple of tired looking ladies wearing strange conical hats.

"Akha tribeswomen from up north," Tommy said, eager to reinforce his credentials as the expert on all things Thai. I was momentarily confused, where I came from, "up north" means Manchester, Liverpool, even London for the locals who didn't get out much. It took me a few seconds to realise he meant northern Thailand. We also had to admire the guy who spotted we were football fans. He rushed up and, seeing we both wore blue shirts, suggested a little wrist-band bearing the word Chelsea, would fill a yawning gap in our wardrobes. We declined but he misinterpreted our reasons for saying no. The man quickly turned his little cardboard sheet over to reveal his second offer, an identical band embroidered neatly with the words Fuck Chelsea. Maybe in a couple of years we could come back and get something with our team on it, Brighton and Hove Albion. We decided not to count on it.

After we finished lunch Tommy was keen to fit in a massage before returning to the hotel. We retraced our steps along Beach Road, noticing that quite a few of the prettier girls had disappeared. A sharp turn at the Pizza restaurant on the corner, took us into a place he called Soi Post Office and Tommy was grinning all the way to the door of Paradise Massage. We'd passed plenty of shops where the girls were dressed in some sort of traditional Thai costume, they all seemed prim, proper and professional. The girls looked up hopefully from their street-side vigil, as we crossed the threshold of Tommy's chosen shop. All wore skimpy shorts and skin tight t-shirts with the words "Welcome to Paradise." Tommy spoke to the lady behind the counter and, with him nodding smugly, I followed a girl called Woo up the stairs to the second floor.

Thai Kiss

Tommy said some massage places offered "extras", but Woo was clearly a top-notch masseuse. I could feel all the tension fall away as she worked on my shoulders and my back. I was a bit self-conscious when she took away the towel I put round my waist, but could see the point as she got to the top of my legs and my buttocks. She was really getting into the muscles, particularly at the top of my thigh where I had an old football injury. It was an almost spiritual experience. I decided all those stories about massage shops being a front for selling sex were obviously rubbish. She signalled for me to turn over and then started on my legs again. Maybe she was getting careless as she did the inside of my thighs because her hands were now making the briefest, tantalising contact each time she came close to my groin. I was sure it was accidental but it was so difficult to control the response. I failed.

"Oh my Buddha, what happen?" she exclaimed.

I opened my eyes, expecting to see her staring at my erection in horror. She was looking straight at me with that coy, mock innocent look you see in the movies. Then she put her finger in her mouth and sucked on it very slowly.

"One thousand baht," she said. It was a statement not a question. I fell at the second hurdle too.

After Dark

I chose to give Noy some cash after our night together but Woo simply took advantage of me when I was vulnerable. I still wasn't convinced I wanted or needed to pay for sex. Tommy talked about the night-clubs on Walking Street. Insomnia, Lucifer and Marine were favourite. I was determined we should try our luck at one of those instead of buying a girl out of a bar. They look like any western night-club but most of the girls are up front about the fact they want a cash gift. It might be to "help study Business at university" or so they could go home and visit the family because "mama sick", but it was still paying for it. The first night I thought I'd scored a freebie with a girl from Bangkok, but I think she was less than impressed when I didn't put my hand in my pocket the following morning. It all got a bit confusing as to what the rules of the game really were. So I decided to put my ego aside. If I was going to pay for it anyway I might as well give myself the widest possible choice. I loved the atmosphere of the go-go bars and there was no confusion as to what was on offer. I don't know any guy who doesn't like endless rows of beautiful, naked women. For a couple of pounds you could buy the girl a drink and they were always good fun, even if they weren't that great at English. If the conversation dried up, you could always resort to a silly drinking game and it was laughs and smiles all round again. If you wanted a girl you simply paid the bar a few baht and she'd trot off to your hotel and give you the night of your life. No games, no wondering whether you had said the wrong thing and messed up your chances and no doubt that after a load of chat, you were definitely going to get your leg over.

On a two week trip it wasn't that much more expensive than Greece or Spain and the women were extraordinary. No fat slappers thinking a short dress and a few Bacardi Breezers turned them into Miss Universe. Pattaya offered a steady stream of gorgeous little brown bodies to choose from and then the next day, you could choose someone else. The only thing I struggled with was the number of old blokes in the bars. There was surely no way the girls could want to be with them. Maybe they had plenty of cash but it was really grim watching these young ladies playing up to them. Tommy and I both joined a web forum called Pattaya-Dream. After my first night in town I made my first post:

"Put the lady down granddad:
Nothing worse than seeing some fat old bloke groping those poor girls. They should be listening to the Archers or something, instead of mauling bar-girls. These ladies don't want to be jumped on by someone old enough to be their granddad, they want someone close to their own age, that they can have a laugh with. Come on you old bastards, put the lady down and go have a nap."

The post was really popular and you could guess the age of the contributor from his reply. The younger members were pretty much in agreement with me and a few had stories about what the oldies were getting up to on their pensions. A member called WelshDragon reckoned the girls might prefer an older man:

"Let's face it, these girls are after cash and quick. Most blokes of 35 and over can only get it up once a night and then it's over in no time. That's got to work for some of these girls."

Then someone called Checkbinman, tried to make the case for the wrinklies:

"The girls can have all the young fit Thai blokes they want and they have got more in common with them than with morons like you. These girls want men with *jai dee*, men who will show them respect. They like older men who know how to treat a lady."

Pretty harsh, I thought. He'd never have called me a moron to my face. Still I guess they have to try to justify what they're doing somehow. It's obvious the girls are going to want a bloke who makes them laugh, who takes care of his body and can give them a good time in bed. Still I was pretty happy to have got the forum going with my first post, then the moderator closed it down:

"There's absolutely nothing anyone can post on this subject that hasn't been said before. Let's agree they are fascinating, delightful, delicate creatures and as men we are unlikely to ever understand them fully. Maybe it's better to think of it as a mystery we'll never solve."

I tried to remember that saying about sarcasm and wit.

Pattaya – without your wingman

The go-go bars are great after dark but the best place for a beer earlier in the day is one of the open air café style bars where you can watch the world go by. That's to say, leer at the endless stream of gorgeous Thais and the occasional, usually Russian, western girl. There were lots of young guys like me, here for the beach, the bars and the women but it was the sheer number of old guys I couldn't get my head around. Anyone over forty looked old to me, but plenty of these guys were sixty and above. It struck me that maybe I'd be the same when I got to their age. I had no idea what they were like when they were twenty-five. There were plenty of younger guys on their own too and that looked a bit sad when I was there with Tommy. Imagine not having a single mate who'll go on holiday with you. Then there were the blokes who were old and on their own. They had to be the saddest of the lot.

Now I was back in Pattaya for my second trip and I was in category two, the bloke with no mates. I still did the go-go bars and played a bit of pool with the girls but it wasn't the same. When you're with someone else you can be nonchalant and pretend you're there for a beer and a chat, that the girls are secondary. When you're by yourself, you either stare at the stage like a sad act, or pull out your mobile phone and pretend that your friend's been delayed but will be joining you later. It always took me a couple of drinks before I could get into the swing of things in a Thai bar, but once I got over that bit, the problem was stopping. Tommy always said I had a terrible speech defect, I simply couldn't say no.

"You buy me drink?"

"OK."

"You buy drink for my sister?"

"OK."

"You buy drink for my friend, first day in bar?"

"OK."

"You buy drink for *mamasan*?"

"OK."

"Ping-pong, only one thousand baht."

"OK."

"You pay bar, we go *boom-boom*?"

Well, you get the idea. I know the response often left my head as "No thanks love, now bugger off I've got my eye on number 32 over there," but then I'd look into those deep brown eyes and the word would just pop out of my mouth...

"OK."

I still had ten days to run on my visa but the cash in the safe was running down a little faster than I expected. It was time to decide what I was going to do next. That meant finding Clay and seeing if I could re-establish some contacts with a supplier in London. It also meant lighting a fire under that little bitch Maggie. I had given her the five thousand and practically begged her to find Tommy's address book for me. I'd heard nothing. I had to appeal to her better nature, I sent her an e-mail saying if I got the information I'd send her another grand.

Secret Service

"Can't really talk about it my friend. You know, government work." The tall thin, blond man tapped the side of his nose in a conspiratorial fashion but politely declined to say what he did for a living. I was starting to wish I'd never asked. I suppose it's one way of conveying that he has an important secret, but I spent a lot of time studying the body language of poker players. I knew the nose touch was a classic "tell" for someone bluffing or lying. Not sure why I bothered really, I only played poker on-line so that was another waste of time and effort.

A smiling server passed me another chilled Singha as I sat quietly in my usual seat on the corner of the bar in Dream, near LK Metro. I liked to have an uninterrupted view of the bar's front door and the clear escape route through Dream's tiny kitchen to the adjoining soi. If Connor's men came after me, I was sure I'd be able to spot them and high tail it out of there. I'd read all about securing your exit.

Dream was aptly named because the experiences claimed by most of its customers didn't occur in their waking hours. There were about a dozen regulars, mainly ex-pats but a few who made several trips a year. Between them, they defeated Saddam Hussein virtually single-handed, served as Special Ops in every conflict from Vietnam to Libya, smuggled drugs, cigars and people from Cuba to mainland USA or had recently retired from a successful gangland career in one of London, New York or Sydney. One guy said he used to be a taxi driver and all the other customers were pretty sure he must have been into something really heavy with a cover story like that.

Getting to meet Clay was even easier than I expected. It would have been better if Tommy had introduced us when we first visited Pattaya, but he said the American had gone back to California for the couple of weeks we were there. It was only after we returned from Thailand that I realised we never visited the bar where they met. It was Dream, in a narrow *soi* off Soi Buakhao. When I asked the baht bus driver to take me there I agreed a hundred baht fee. He drove thirty yards, then turned a corner and stopped. I was learning the ropes… slowly.

Thai Kiss

Lots of bars in Thailand have football memorabilia because the owners are ex-pats still yearning for a stale meat pie on the terraces, watching their favourite team on a Saturday afternoon. Tommy told me the owner of Dream was a mad keen Liverpool fan, so it was easy to get chatting to him. It took me about four days to be accepted as a regular. It's not hard, you buy the girls a few drinks, so they are bound to recognise you next time you stop by, and you ring the bell a couple of times. Every bar has a bell above the counter and pulling the rope indicates you are willing to stand a round of drinks for everyone present. The secret is to do it when the boss is there but otherwise it's not too busy. Carl, the owner, was in the middle of explaining to me how Liverpool was on the cusp of returning to it's former glory but a team like Brighton could never make it in the English Premier League. He had a habit of emphasising every point he made by jabbing his huge, sausage-like fingers in my direction. I'd accept his arguments or he'd shove them down my throat. There was an American voice from the next barstool. I turned to see a thin, nut-brown guy who looked to be in his early sixties. The shirt and shorts he was wearing must have been white when he bought them but hundreds of trips to the laundry turned them a dull shade of grey. He'd seen some action in his time, but looked like there was still plenty of life in him yet. The contrast with Carl couldn't have been more stark, the Yank was built like a greyhound, the Liverpudlian appeared to have been roughly hewn from a large slab of cooking fat, that was slowly melting in the heat.

"I know a guy from Brighton, used to come in here a lot. Carl, you remember Tommy, terrific guy."

Carl made the introductions.

"Paul this is Clay, I'd steer clear if I were you, he'll only get you into trouble." It was an affectionate jibe, the men were clearly friends.

"Tommy was my best friend, he talked a lot about this place, that's why I came to take a look."

"That's awesome man," said Clay. "He was a hell of a guy, we even did a bit of business together."

"Yeah, he told me. We were partners."

"You fell out then?" the American asked.

"No mate, he died." I didn't want to say I knew he'd been killed, it might have scared Clay off. I ordered another beer and gestured to Carl that the two men should join me. It took a couple of days to build a bit of trust, apparently Pattaya has loads of westerners who work as volunteer policemen and they've been known to befriend the local villains and get them to incriminate themselves once they've had a few too many Singhas. I didn't push things with Clay at all, but he talked a bit about Tommy.

"He showed me a picture of that sister of his, Molly right?"

"No mate, her name's Sally."

Then he came out with some odd story about how Tommy always liked to clink beer bottles together by striking the top of your bottle with the base of his own. Do that just after the top has come off and it makes the beer in the lower bottle overflow. I told Clay he must have picked that habit up in Thailand because I never saw him do it. Dreadful waste of beer. There was something a little unnerving about the way he was looking at me. Clay's eyes were really light blue and it felt like he was looking right inside my head. Then he'd get all jittery and start glancing round the bar as though he was looking for someone. Finally he asked me how Tommy got the scar on the back of his hand. It was only as I pointed out Tommy didn't have such a scar that it clicked. I was being tested… and I passed.

I ordered another couple of beers. Clay hit the top of my Singha with the base of his bottle and as beer flowed down my hand, the American started to explain how he got Tommy started. I assumed he must have known William, the huge Jamaican, or Mark, the guy who made the deliveries to the Brokerage in Borough Market. He shook his head slowly, then laughed and I flushed with embarrassment at my naivety.

"It's like those movies you see about terrorists, Paul. It's all based on a cell system. I connect to the person who supplies me and to the people I pass the stuff on to. I have no idea about anyone else in the chain. It's more secure if the police arrest anyone. They simply take that link out of the chain."

"So how did you put him in touch with William? I guess that wasn't his real name."

Clay laughed again. "I think you can be pretty sure about that. I just took Tommy's mobile number and sent that on to the guy who supplies me. I have no idea what he did with it, but I guess he must have passed it on to someone in London. They'd have made contact only after they checked Tommy out a bit first... they'd need to make sure he wasn't with the cops."

I remembered the photos William produced in the pub that day, Clare, my mum and Tommy's little sister. Yes, they definitely did check people out. Clay looked genuinely surprised when I explained how open we were about the exchange every month, same pub, same method. Tommy told me William said it was called Hide in Plain Sight. If you do things in the open, people don't suspect you are doing anything wrong, it just looked like two mates meeting every month for a beer after a trip to the supermarket. Skulking around a dark alley was sure to attract attention. Clay looked impressed and I felt I'd got a tiny shred of my credibility back.

I tried not to sound scared when I asked him about whether he felt the need for any sort of personal protection given his line of business. Clay laughed.

"If I had a gun, I'd probably end up shooting myself. Those things scare me shitless. If you think you need one, you'd better learn how to handle it first. There are a couple of shooting ranges in Pattaya... one on Beach Road."

I'd checked for myself on the internet that morning. I already had the addresses of two ranges and I'd read a load of articles about them in the local press. Most were about the ex-pats who decided they'd been double-crossed by a scheming Thai girl one time too many, or they'd run out of money, or had come to this particular paradise and decided it didn't really measure up. They went to their nearest Pattaya range, hired themselves a gun and then blew their own brains out on the floor. It was the second most popular way for an ex-pat to kill himself, the first was diving from a condo balcony.

I mentioned this to Clay, hoping he might suggest an alternative way of learning to use a gun, after all I never knew when Connor might come to call.

"You could ask Gordon," Clay said. "He can sort something out for you on the quiet... lessons and equipment. I'd have to put a word in for you though, he's very cautious about who he deals with."

The American gestured over my shoulder to one of the ex-pats who was sitting at the corner of the bar with a copy of a week old Sun newspaper. It was the taxi driver.

"So Paul, you want to get started in the business again?" he asked.

"Definitely."

"OK, give me your mobile phone number."

CHAPTER SIX

Kiss

One million per cent. That's how sure I was when Jum asked me if I wanted to go to the City to make money for my family. We spent many hours together over the following days. She told me what to expect if I worked in a Pattaya bar. She explained about the different places I could work and how I should choose, depending on whether I was willing to dance, how much skin I was willing to show, how much money I wanted to earn and how quickly I wanted to earn it.

"A lot of money, quick," was my reply.

"Then you should work in a go-go bar. You are very beautiful and many men will be interested in you. In a go-go bar you will get much more money each time you go with a *farang*. I have a good friend who is the *mamasan* of a bar called Kiss. Her name is Nook and she will take care of you very well. If she knows you are my friend she will watch out for you even more."

Jum explained I would have to dance, I could earn more money if I did that naked and I would have to approach men and ask them to buy me a drink. If they were interested I should ask them if they wanted to have sex with me. I practiced dancing in my room at home, it felt OK until I took my clothes off, then I just felt silly and self-conscious. I could not believe girls like me did such a thing. I was still certain I had to go to the City for sure, but if Jum asked me again, I could not say one million per cent.

Jum phoned later that week to say she was going to Pattaya. She would take me to meet her friend, Nook, and I could decide for myself. I told Dao I had to go away for a little while and that Grandma would take care of her but I promised to phone every day. I packed my bag and went to sleep knowing Jum would arrive early the following morning. Claus gave Jum big money for a taxi to drive all the way to Pattaya… eight thousand baht. Everybody knew Claus was a man with *jai dee*.

That night Ghai came to see me in my dream. He held me in his arms and told me I had to be brave and strong, I had to do the right thing to take care of our daughter.

Thai Kiss

The first time

The other girls said the first time was the worst for sure. After a while, I would get used to it. I might have to give the man encouragement and maybe do some things to get him excited, but once he started I should close my eyes and wait for it to be over. Most of the time it would not take long, then I could shower, dress, collect my money and go home to my own bed. That is why it is so important to pick the right customer first time and that is where my friends in the bar could help. There was always someone they trusted, a regular who was kind and gentle and had *jai dee*. They would help me choose the right person for my first time. And I knew Ghai was watching over me to make sure nothing bad happened. I thought if I agreed to go with a bad man, then Ghai would find a way of telling me, of letting me know I had made a mistake and I could find a way out. I was sure of that.

It was Pan who chose my first customer for me. She had only been at the bar for six months so could still remember her first time very well. It was bad for her, but two nights later she met Preben, from Denmark. He was kind and the more nervous she became, the kinder he was. He bought her a pair of shoes from a stall on the way to the hotel and told the receptionist they did not need to take her ID card. He said she was an old friend so there was nothing to worry about. It made her feel better somehow, that he trusted her even though they had done no more than play a few games of Jackpot and shared a couple of drinks. Preben massaged her feet, then they watched the end of a movie on TV before he took her to bed. He was kind, gentle and generous, which is all a girl can ever ask of a customer. Preben was in the bar again the night we decided I should go with my first customer. Pan introduced us and then moved to the other side of the bar.

As we walked to his hotel he stopped by a street stall and paid four hundred baht for a new dress for me. I already had my purse out as we walked into reception but he waved away the young man at the desk and said I was an old friend. I knew it was going to be alright. Ghai did not come to warn me I was making a mistake. I did exactly as Pan instructed and imagined that I was somewhere else. He tried very hard to please me first and I tried very hard to pretend he succeeded. That seemed to make him happy. I could not compare what happened with the time I had been with Ghai, it did not feel like the same thing at all. It felt a little bit like when I was sick and the doctor had to check inside me. Now I know more about men and I am not sure whether the doctor really needed to do that, or if it was because he wanted to. When Preben was finished, I waited for a few minutes, exactly as Pan said, before I went to shower. When I came back to the bedroom he was already looking for money in his wallet. He gave me the two thousand baht he promised and then said I should have something for the taxi. I thought he had made a mistake when he gave me another one thousand baht. Pan was right, Preben had *jai dee*. An hour later I was back in my room, hoping Ghai would come to talk to me, to tell me I was brave, that I had done the right thing for my family and for our daughter. But Ghai did not come and it was some time before I fell asleep. I cannot remember all of my dream but I know Ghai was there. I could see him, but every time I moved towards him he drifted a little further away. I saw him in the street but as I got close, the crowd moved between us and when they cleared, he was gone. I had to be patient, Ghai would come to me when I needed him.

The Russian

Many of the girls at Kiss had worked in other bars in Pattaya or Bangkok, some had bad experiences with customers, or friends with stories to tell. Most of the complaints were about "cheap charlies", men who expected the world in exchange for one lady drink or who tried to avoid paying the money they agreed before they left the bar. Some customers did not want to shower or were rough with the girls, but we kept a list and made sure any girl knew what to expect from someone who paid bar before. Many *farang* are surprised we remember them when they come back after a long time, they think it is because we are sweet and friendly. It is because our lives may depend on it.

None of the girls spoke of really bad experiences, my third customer agreed two thousand baht when we left the bar but only paid me one thousand because he said I was a starfish. Pan told me later *farang* say that if you do not move around enough during sex or maybe do not make enough noise. I bought a bottle of Jack Daniels and we spent our day off drinking whisky while she showed me how I should wriggle around and what noises I should make. I wondered if I could do those things with a customer without laughing the way I did when Pan showed me what to do. The next time I went with a customer I wriggled a lot and made lots of noise, it finished very quickly so I think he was happy and he gave me three thousand instead of two thousand, so I got my money back.

When the bar was not too busy, we had competitions to see who had the worst customer.

"I asked him for money for the taxi, he gave me one hundred baht and asked for fifty change because he knew how much a motorbike taxi should cost."

"He was so fat, I could not find his dick for five minutes. Then I had to go on top or I think he would have squashed me to death."

"I turned on the shower in his bathroom and he looked shocked, I don't think he ever used it before." The girls all laughed and reminded each other the Thai word for bad smell is "*men*".

At that stage none of us had ever met Roman, the Russian who came to the bar when I had been working for about six months. It was the first time he had ever been to Kiss. Pan gave me a lot of advice, she always had new ideas about what ladies should do with a customer. Her latest tip was that *farang* like to be kissed on the neck. This was very difficult with Roman, as he did not appear to have one. His head was completely shaved and he had a vicious looking bird tattooed behind his left ear. The bird's claws touched his shoulder, because his head looked like it was attached directly to his body. He liked me straight away and bought three lady drinks very quickly. In the same time he drank three beers and three large vodkas. He was still nice enough, but was getting louder and more drunk. Then he told me he wanted me to go with him.

"Come to my room? I give you three thousand, short time."

Thai Kiss

Roman was not a handsome man, his face looked as though someone had grabbed his ears from behind and pulled very hard. This was not that important, but he was drunk and I was thinking he did not have *jai dee*. But this was three thousand baht. That was big money, I could not refuse. I should have realised something was wrong as soon as we left the bar. He almost dragged me to the corner of the street and pointed to a motorbike parked next to a battered old truck. I could see he was drunk and did not dare ride side-saddle as I would have done if a Thai was in front. As we got on the bike he reached behind and put his hand between my legs. Then we rode off along Second Road.

I gave thanks to Buddha that we got to his apartment in one piece, he nearly came off the bike twice and crossed a red light almost into the path of a baht bus coming from one side. I thought I had made a mistake but Ghai did not come to warn me. He had not spoken to me at all for many weeks, not since before I went with Preben that first time. But he would come to me if I was in any danger, for sure. He did not come. We arrived at the apartment block and Roman took an age to find the key to the door. I thought maybe I should run away but he paid bar for me and if I ran maybe the *mamasan* would be angry. The door opened and he grabbed the back of my top and dragged me into the lobby. I reached for my ID card but Roman pushed me past the desk towards the lift. The man on reception was left standing with his mouth open, shaking his head. He did not want to confront the Russian. All the way to his apartment Roman grabbed at my breasts and talked loudly in his own language. I had no idea what he was saying. He wasn't hurting me but this is not how people behave in Thailand. Sexual things happen behind closed doors not in public. I never met a Russian before, maybe that is how all women are treated in his country. When we entered his apartment, I turned to explain I could make him happy, but he should be more gentle. That's when he slapped me across the face.

"Shut up whore. I'm paying you to fuck, not talk."

I think it was about an hour and a half later that the Russian finally finished with me, his words ringing in my ears.

"You are a filthy little whore," he told me. "I paid for you and I can do whatever I like. Understand?"

As I scrambled towards the door of his apartment, he grabbed me again, I thought the whole thing was going to start over. Then he sneered.

"You mustn't forget your money. Three thousand I think, yes?"

I nodded meekly, the money was suddenly less important than getting out of the apartment.

"I don't think that was worth three thousand. You are a whore but you are not a very good one. I will give you what I think you deserve."

He raised his hand again and I was certain he was going to strike me. I looked down to see a hundred baht note in his hand, but my eyes were drawn to the huge signet ring on the third finger of his left hand. It was a very elaborate design, an eagle taking off and the initials RS. I instinctively touched my own cheek where I am sure the ring already made contact several times. I took the note and he moved aside.

As I stepped out of the lift on the ground floor, the same man was on the reception desk. When he saw me, he appeared to find something incredibly interesting on his computer screen, as though he thought that if he hunched over enough, I would not be able to see him. Maybe that was for the best, my top was torn and I was desperately trying to hold it together so nobody could see my bra underneath. There was blood on my skirt which came from my lip and maybe a little from my nose. I was feeling very shy, I always wore shorts underneath my skirt but in my hurry to get out of the apartment, I left them behind. The Russian ripped my panties as he pushed me onto the bed, so they were nowhere to be found either. I was naked under my skirt, which is all I could focus on as I stumbled through the lobby into the street. How could I get a motorbike taxi or a baht bus with nothing on under my skirt and my top torn like this? I was so ashamed. I started the long walk home.

Sonthi

Nobody was interested in the "who has had the worst customer?" competition after that night. I would always win and nobody wanted to be reminded of the story. We all knew that every night we ran the risk of meeting a man like Roman, but saying it out loud made it seem a little more real. The bruises and the cuts healed quickly but the thought of what he said and did that night stayed with me much longer. I could not push it from my mind. I recalled that as the apartment door closed behind me all I could hear was his laughter. It was a picture that came to me many times in the weeks that followed. I tried to summon up an image of Ghai, hoping he would talk to me and tell me it would all be alright, but he never came.

Every night before we went to work, Pan and I stopped in Soi 15 to get some food. The street vendors laid out plastic tables and chairs and it was very popular with ladies from the bars. One week after the incident with the Russian, we were finishing our food as a man walked over to our table.

"Pan, how's it going. Who's your friend?"

Pan introduced me to the man, who was very good looking and appeared very athletic.

"Yim, this is Sonthi, he is a famous Muay Thai boxer in Pattaya and he has a motor-bike taxi too."

Pan started to giggle and was playing nervously with her hair. She was eager to make a good impression but I could feel his eyes on me. He ran his hand down a scratch on my arm that had not fully healed since my night with the Russian.

"Who hurt you?" he asked. His hand was still stroking my arm.

I did not want to tell the story but Pan was very keen to explain how she looked after me ever since the Russian treated me so badly. She offered a few details about what happened but spent most of the time talking about how upset I was and how she barely left my side because she was such a good friend. Sonthi asked about the Russian so I told him all I could remember.

"He said his name was Roman, he lives in the brown apartment block where Soi seven crosses Third Road. I only remember that he had a green motorbike with an eagle painted on the side." I paused because I thought I was going to cry again.

"Did he wear a ring?" Sonthi asked.

That's when I remembered the huge ring with his initials and the eagle.

"Yes, a ring with RS and a bird. Do you know him?"

"Not really, but I know who he is," Sonthi said. "He wants to be in the same line of business as me, but he is no more than a fool and a bully. A beautiful girl like you should not be troubled by a man like that."

I was flattered and Sonthi's words made me feel a little better. I had never seen a Russian man or any other *farang* wanting to work as a motorbike taxi. Maybe he wanted to fight Muay Thai. Sonthi was obviously not afraid of the Russian even if I thought him the most terrifying person I had ever met in my life.

"I'll speak to him." Then Sonthi got on his motorbike and disappeared.

The following night, Pan and I were eating *somtam* papaya salad, and *tom yum* soup, when I noticed a motorbike parked close to our table. The bike was green and had an eagle painted on the petrol tank. It belonged to the Russian. I could not have been more scared in my life. The terror was rising in me and I felt I was going to suffocate. Then Sonthi's voice broke in:

"Yim, it's so nice to see you again. I have something for you."

Everyone else at the tables was smiling, particularly Pan, and I started to take in the tall, handsome Thai man who was standing in front of me.

"The Russian wants me to apologise on his behalf," Sonthi said. "He asked me to give you the money he agreed to, and the same again as a tip."

Sonthi dropped six thousand baht next to my plate with a huge smile. Somehow, he convinced the Russian he should pay me. Suddenly, I understood how Sonthi made his point.

"He also wanted you to have this, but I think you might prefer to sell it than keep it. I cannot imagine it has good memories for you."

That is when Sonthi dropped something else on the table. It was a gold signet ring, with a very elaborate design. It was an eagle taking off combined with the initials RS. The ring was still attached to the bloodied stump of the finger of its recent owner.

Sonthi was enjoying the fact that all eyes were on him.

"He was such a generous guy," he said as he twirled a set of keys in the air. "Can you believe it? He's leaving town, but he said I could use his apartment until the lease runs out in three months time, and he gave me his motorbike. Don't you just love *farang*?"

Thai Kiss

CHAPTER SEVEN

The holiday from hell

Maggie finally called me to say she'd found Tommy's address book. The promise of another thousand pounds prompted a major change of attitude and she was very eager to help. Apparently she discovered a bunch of other stuff too, it was in a folder called Albion, one of the nicknames of our favourite football team. I told her that I wanted to contact some people we'd met at the stadium so I guess she thought that might help too. She sent everything in an e-mail, so all I had to do was find an internet shop where I could log in. Locating one was never a problem, the tricky part was the line of bar-girls waiting to Skype with their recently departed customers. The last time I used a computer for any length of time in one of those places, I heard one girl tell four different guys they were the only one for her. As I finished my lunch in the Siam Palace and started to head off to an internet shop, I thought about Clare and how it had all gone wrong. It was never perfect, I knew she saw me as reliable rather than the man of her dreams but I still hadn't really got over how it ended. I spent nearly three years hiding the fact that I was a drug dealer, waiting to save enough money to put down a deposit on a house for the two of us. I was well on the way, but I decided that we should do something special; she was looking bored and I was desperate to inject a bit of life back into our relationship.

That trip with Clare was still painfully fresh in my mind. We'd never been away together before, so I decided we'd do it in style. None of this package tour rubbish where you get bussed around and bossed around by some pimply kid, weeks out of college. I discovered that by booking months in advance I could get us business class flights for only about a hundred quid more than economy. Car hire was pretty cheap and the four star hotel in Puerto Banus was only about a hundred and twenty pounds a night. The whole thing was going to cost me about two grand but Tommy and I had a really good month so the money was not going to be a problem. I even chose a top-notch restaurant for dinner on our first night and checked that they served lobster thermidor, hoping Clare might get the hint. She looked really thrilled when I told her we were going somewhere warm and to take her passport. After I explained that we were flying business class and staying in a four star hotel, she took me by the hand, led me to the bedroom and said thank you in the nicest possible way.

It was when we got to the airport that she started to look uneasy, the final destination was still a surprise but as she looked at the departure board she was starting to narrow it down. I asked if she was OK and she insisted it was just a headache. As we approached the boarding gate Clare's agitation was obvious, but she carried on insisting it was a headache and a mild fear of flying. She'd looked forward to the business class flight but barely uttered a word while we were in the air. Admittedly, it was not all it's cracked up to be, the crew looked like they were serving their notice rather than our meal and it was hard to see how marginally better food, a tiny bottle of champagne and a curtain justified the extra money. Clare was deathly silent and I was trying to work out what had gone wrong.

Clare relaxed a little by the time we got to the hotel and I'd almost convinced myself the problem really was the flight. She'd never mentioned a fear of flying before but maybe even she didn't realise how much it affected her. We ate a late lunch by the pool and settled down to one of Clare's favourite pastimes… people watching. This is where I developed Murphy's Rule, which comes in three distinct parts:

Part One – there's often an inverse relationship between a person's physical appeal and their willingness to show their body off in public.

Part Two – the larger a man's stomach, the more likely it is that he'll be wearing a football shirt with the badge of his favourite, usually British, team.

Part Three – the more alcohol people consume the more Parts One and Two are likely to apply.

Clare liked it when I pointed out things like that. It was almost as though her pet dog had done something very clever. I was only a hospital porter but sometimes I could say things that made it sound like I had a brain. She'd long since told me I should say I worked in hospital administration when I met new people. On no account should I admit I was a porter.

"So are you ashamed of me then?"

"No don't be silly, it's just that people can be so judgmental," she'd reply.

"Doesn't sound like the kind of person I'd want to spend time with anyway. If they don't like what I do that's their problem."

"Oh don't be so ridiculous."

Lots of conversations ended like that. At the very least they'd be ended by Clare; she always had to have the final word.

The waiter brought us more drinks and Clare settled back into her sun lounger. I stole the odd glance at the gorgeous Scandinavian girl a little further along the row. She was wearing a huge pair of sunglasses, a massive sun hat and a rather demure white one-piece swimsuit. Very little flesh on show, which made her even more alluring, it sent the imagination into overdrive. We spotted the girl and her friend as living examples of Murphy's Rule Part One. The second girl wore a tiny bikini bottom, revealing acres of orange peel flesh and when she turned over she had to shovel her bared breasts back into position with her hands. Clare was fascinated by the larger girl, which gave me a degree of licence to surreptitiously letch over Miss Sunhat. It was almost a hobby. Clare loved to point out chubby, unattractive girls or the fashion disasters you see on every British High Street. It was as though she was trying to reaffirm to herself that she was far more attractive than the people she was pointing out. It couldn't be that she was fishing for compliments. I told her how fabulous she looked every day and I meant it. She worked on it - great makeup, great dress sense and she tried really hard to take care of her body. Sure she was carrying a few extra pounds but that just made her look sexy. Clare spent ages with creams and potions and I doubted there was another woman within fifty miles of Brighton town centre whose skin was softer, more moisturised or freer of unsightly hairs and blemishes than my Clare. Of course now she was in Spain and Miss Sunhat would give her more than a run for her money. It was time to go to our room and clean up before dinner.

"I saw you looking at that Swedish slut."

"We were both looking at her." I knew who she was talking about and was pretty proud of my attempt to feign innocence.

"Not the fat bitch, the pretty one. You know very well who I meant."

"Come on, you could barely see her under that sunhat. I was looking at her mate, same as you were," I responded, apparently unconvincingly.

"Bullshit, she's just your type. All pretty and sweet and so fucking thin its ridiculous. Bet she hasn't eaten anything for days."

"Don't be daft. She's not my type… you are."

The words were barely out of my mouth before I realised what I'd said. I didn't like pretty, sweet, thin girls, I liked girls like Clare.

"Jesus Christ, thanks a lot!" she exclaimed and slammed the bathroom door shut.

An hour later she had yet to emerge and I assumed the depilator, moisturiser, after sun and God knows what other creams were taking a bit of a hammering. I finally plucked up the courage to tap on the door and proffer a glass of champagne, from the half-bottle I liberated from the mini-bar. I tried to convince myself that by the time the hotel bill came through on the credit card the exchange rate might have moved to about five euros to the pound, in which case the champagne was reasonably priced. If not I'd just been mugged. Still these were desperate times, I had to get Clare to relax.

I could have saved the cash. As I opened the door she gave me a dazzling smile and was looking straight into my eyes not at the glass I was holding out to her.

"I'm really sorry, it was the flight, the excitement. You know… everything."

"It's fine, no problem," I replied.

"I know I can trust you, I know you'd never cheat on me. You know I love that about you."

It was one of the few times she ever used the word love. She'd tell me what she loved about me but never say she loved me. I suppose I should have been grateful. My mates at the Albion were always complaining about their girlfriends, how they were constantly whining.

"So do you love me?"

"You never tell me you love me."

"Susie's boyfriend is always telling her he loves her, why don't you?"

I never told Clare I loved her because I thought she'd probably not say it back. I sent her cards with those dopey bears on them with cute messages inside. She always smiled when she read the card but she never really said anything about them.

Everything appeared to be back on track. Clare looked relaxed and happy and once she had a glass of champagne inside her, I had my fun, sexy, chatty girlfriend back again. The plan was to have dinner and then find a club. First, though, we had to explore the legendary port, or "Puerto", of Banus.

The taxi dropped us at an automatic barrier which blocked the way to the port. When we looked quizzical, the driver wearily jerked his thumb in the direction we were heading as we came round the roundabout. It wasn't immediately obvious that this was the entrance to party town but there was a steady stream of holiday-makers heading towards a corner bar and then onto the street beyond. Many were doing their best to demonstrate Murphy's rule in all three parts, with the bit about alcohol kicking in despite the fact that it wasn't even nine p.m. yet. There was a fair smattering of chic and elegant couples, mainly European, mingling uneasily with the slappers falling out of their dresses, the boys on the pull and the odd group of older men who told their wives, truthfully or otherwise, that they were there for the golf. My first reaction was that this wasn't my idea of a millionaire's playground, until I saw what they charged us for a vodka tonic and a small beer in the corner bar. Then the barrier opened and a bright red car pulled slowly onto the strip. The speed at which it was travelling was a nod in the direction of good road safety, but was mainly designed to ensure that, as the crowd parted to let it pass, they could get a good look at the driver and his passenger. The car was an open-top Ferrari Scuderia 16M. I had seen a second-hand one on offer on the net a couple of weeks before. A snip at a shade under two hundred thousand pounds. The man was at least sixty and looked as though the car was stretching all of his driving skills even at a tad under four miles per hour. His companion was about twenty, possibly Russian, and could barely fit her impossibly long legs under the dashboard. While the driver was visibly enjoying the attention and pushing his chest out, the girl did look a little self-conscious. Her body language was screaming:

"Oh come on, look at the car. You'd do it too for a car like this… and you should see the yacht. You'd definitely do it if you saw the yacht."

The Ferrari made its slow progress down the strip and then turned towards a gate that barred the way onto one of the piers where the boats were moored. I visited Brighton Marina a few times so had seen some pretty impressive bits of kit but this was extraordinary. A sumptuous sun seeker with a huge deck and a massive engine caught my eye, then behind it was another gin palace which could have taken the first boat onto its deck with room to spare.

By the time Clare and I finished our third round of drinks she was getting a little tipsy. We decided to go for a pre-dinner stroll. I stopped briefly to get some cash from an ATM and had to wait as two very pretty English girls were retrieving a card. Judging by the accents, they weren't short of a few quid themselves, but as they turned towards me one said,

"I'd do anything to get on to one of those boats and I mean… anything."

I caught her eye and she paused briefly as though I might be able to offer a ticket. I smiled, shrugged and offered a weak, "Good luck girls."

They both giggled and tottered off down the street in search of their multi-millionaires.

When I found Clare again, she was staring at one of the more modest motor boats. It can't have cost the owner much more than three quarters of a million. She looked at it, then back at me several times. It looked like she was assessing the trade she'd made. I have him, so I'll never have one of those. Then she actually shrugged. I was desperate to tell her I had well over a hundred thousand pounds stashed away, I wasn't dull and boring. Every day I took chances to make a future for the two of us. Maybe we wouldn't have a Ferrari or a million dollar boat but I could give her plenty. I knew how she'd react if she found out how I made the money. Her brother's brush with drugs had torn their family apart. I was certain she'd blame the dealers and by implication she'd blame me. I had to stick to plan A. Wait until I had enough cash to help us buy a house and then play the "Guess what? I won the Lottery," card.

Clare took me by the arm and led me back along the strip to the restaurant we'd chosen. She said she didn't fancy the one that served lobster. We both liked steak and this one let you cook your own on a hot stone. Clever bastards these Spanish, they charged you the earth and you still had to make your own dinner. Clare was pretty quiet during the meal but seemed comfortable enough to just sit, eat, sip her wine and watch the world go by. I used the phrase later on to describe what I thought was a pretty good evening. I didn't think too much about it at the time when she repeated the words, but they came back to me after she'd gone.

"Yes, that's what we're doing," she said wistfully, "watching the world go by."

The wine was taking affect and it was Clare who suggested we skip the club. It looked like another early night and I was bracing myself for one of her headaches and a chaste good-night kiss. As we slipped under the duvet it was Clare who reached for me, there was no headache. It wasn't lobster thermidor but it was definitely the next best thing.

Clare was up as soon as the sun started to show through the windows of our room.

"Come on lazybones, it's back to work in two days, we have to make the most of this while we can. What's the plan?"

Tommy told me all about the beach bars that lined the front at Puerto Banus. They all had restaurants, access to the beach, a huge terrace with sun loungers or massive two person beds which could be opened to the sun or shaded at your command. Flunkies were on hand to deliver overpriced food and drink and the young, the beautiful and the rich were out in force. I was determined Clare would have everything I could afford that weekend. I couldn't buy her a boat but this was within reach. Mentally I readjusted the price of the weekend to about three grand but I never mentioned how much old cousin Beattie left me in her will so my cover story was still intact.

Clare ordered white wine and sushi, more because it was trendy than because she liked the taste of raw fish. I ordered beer and a burger. I brought a football biography called He Shot, He Scored and she brought her Kindle. I'm pretty sure she still preferred reading real books but the Kindle let her read crap chick-lit novels without anyone else being any the wiser.

The weekend was turning out pretty good after a rocky start. Clare had been really nervous about the trip, particularly when she realised it was to this part of Spain but she settled down after she got a few glasses of wine inside her. Finally, it seemed as though she was enjoying herself… that is, up until they started clearing the plates from our lunch.

"Please check if that couple would like anything else."

As the instruction was given, Clare looked up, froze and dropped her Kindle.

"My God. Clare, is that you? You look fantastic."

I turned to see a tall dark haired man who looked decidedly Spanish but was speaking with an unmistakable London accent. He was wearing an open necked white shirt and an expensive gold chain. Clare looked like she'd seen a ghost. The man turned to me and offered his hand.

"Simon… Simon Turner. Pleased to meet you. Clare and I are… old friends."

"Paul," I mumbled. "Paul Murphy."

Clare was still regaining her composure when Simon braced himself on her chair and bent to kiss her on the cheek.

"Simon… nice to see you. How are you keeping?"

"Fantastic Clare, couldn't be better. I meant to keep in touch but I've been so busy. It's been crazy since I left England."

A queasy feeling rose in my gut as the jigsaw pieces started to drop into place.

"So now you work here?" Clare asked.

Turner snorted like a pig as he laughed then paused for dramatic effect and looked round at the beach bar. It was as though we were being invited to remind ourselves of the stunning restaurant and its views of the Med, the high-spec furniture and the teams of attractive waiting staff serving ridiculously priced refreshment to the over-privileged. He looked back at us and smiled as he waved his hand in an expansive gesture.

"I suppose you could say I work here. I'm a partner, I own it with a couple of friends. I still have to put in a few days a week... keep an eye on the hired help and all that."

Clare looked like she'd been slapped. Simon explained he had some urgent business to attend to, but there was something about being his guest in the restaurant that night and how he couldn't wait to see us again. I nodded dumbly and stared at Clare.

Clare spent the rest of the day in a trance. She didn't even have to tell me; Simon was the guy who walked out on her the week we started seeing each other. He was the bloke who left her with the note, "Off to Spain to make my fortune, will be back for you when I'm rich." Well now he was rich and I suddenly realised why Clare never spoke about him. It wasn't because she'd got over him so easily, it was because she hadn't got over him at all. All that crap about being a nervous flyer, she was perfectly relaxed until she saw we might be going to Spain and then freaked when she saw the destination was Malaga. She knew Turner was only a few miles down the road near Marbella. There wasn't much doubt in my mind how he'd made his money either. This was a guy who left England two years before with nothing, suddenly he had a fancy beachside business catering to the young, rich and beautiful. There is only one thing that makes you that much money that fast... drugs. I'd also bet every penny of my precious savings that he was an enthusiastic user of the nose candy himself. He was smooth for sure, but he looked a bit jumpy, there were a few nervous tics when he spoke and he was constantly looking around as though he was searching for something or waiting for a man in a blue uniform to feel his collar. I'd seen it all before so I knew, the guy was a huge coke head. Turner looked like he was overdue for a fix. To Clare it probably came across as nervous energy but I knew it meant he was into drugs, up to his balls and beyond.

We were due for dinner at Turner's restaurant at eight p.m. and Clare disappeared at around five to get ready. She hadn't shown much interest in the hotel's beauty salon and spa before, taking one look at the price list and dismissing it as ridiculous. When she got back from the appointment she looked incredible and I knew, at that very moment, that I'd lost her.

Dinner was a nightmare. Turner was charming, attentive and dripping with gold. He even brought a date, his mother. She'd met Clare before and went to great lengths to explain how hard it was to be a rich man in Spain.

"There are so many gold diggers in Puerto Banus you know. Girls who'll do anything to meet a nice, successful man like my Simon." I'm pretty sure she glanced at me at that point, just to demonstrate the contrast. "He needs to find an English girl, who will love him for what he is, not what he has."

Clare gushed and bubbled and giggled, hanging on to every word her ex-boyfriend, or his mother, uttered. I barely said a thing, there was no point, I was defeated. As the meal was drawing to a close, Clare said she wanted to find the ladies room and Simon insisted on showing her to the facilities attached to his private office. They were gone an awfully long time, making the awkward silence between me and Mrs. Turner even harder to bear.

It was a short taxi ride back to the hotel and Clare was lost in thought. Only as we closed the door on the hotel room did she speak.

"Paul, we need to talk."

"I know… just go." I walked into the bathroom and waited for about twenty minutes until I heard the hotel door open and then click shut. That was the last time I saw Clare. She left me because I was dull and boring. She left me for a drug dealer.

There were times when I thought about how I could win her back, how I wish I told her I was making money for our future together. Other times, I decided I deserved better than that, I deserved someone who'd love me for the person I am. All I knew for sure was that I was sick of being at everyone else's beck and call. I was going to get the business up and running, I was going to get some serious money behind me and then I could start calling the shots for a change. I'd sorted out my contact with Clay, all I needed was that address book from Maggie and I'd be on my way. I found a familiar looking internet shop just off Soi Buakhao and hoped it would be the same girl on the desk as last time I was there.

The delivery boy

I didn't know much about computers but no dealer can function without a decent smart phone. It took me a few minutes to work it out, but eventually I managed to copy the address book onto my iPhone. This was perfect, I even recognised some of the names, there were people who'd know me and would jump at the chance of a reliable supplier. I had their phone numbers and their preferred location for delivery. This was going to be a piece of cake. I could organise the deliveries before I left Thailand. Hopefully, Clay's mates could ship the goods over and I'd be back on the plane in a few days, before Connor even realised I'd been back in England. I'd be able to live in Thailand most of the time. If I could get myself a recruit to do the deliveries in England, and I had a few names in mind, I could run the whole thing from Pattaya. I was heading for Easy Street.

I checked through the rest of the stuff that Maggie sent me and most of it was junk, the only thing that looked important was a spreadsheet called Accounts. I reckoned it would show who paid what and how much Tommy charged for the merchandise. This was important stuff if I was to get the business going again, but the file was locked with a password. I thought it must be something he could remember easily. He was a fanatical Albion fan and he seemed to use up all the memory space in his head with useless trivia about the club. He could list the team that nearly beat Manchester United in the 1983 FA Cup Final even though he was three months old when the game was played. Every manager since the early 1950s tripped off his tongue without a moment's hesitation. I listed all the possible combinations and started to work through them methodically. Favourite players with their shirt numbers, managers and the years they joined and left, every combination I could think of that had an Albion connection. I was planning on using the team name with the years they were promoted. I keyed in Albion and before I could add the number 2009, I accidentally hit the return key. The file started to load. The password was just Albion. Good old Tommy, charming, loveable but utterly clueless about anything remotely technical.

It took me about ten minutes to get to grips with the spreadsheet and once I had, I found myself staring at the screen in utter disbelief. The file gave a list of deliveries, virtually all of which I recognised. I'd made them myself.

It showed the name of the contact, the quantity and a price. The next column was presumably the amount of money I'd been given for each delivery. I never opened the envelopes, so had no idea how much money was in them. Occasionally part of the price was settled by receipt of another drug and there were more columns to show how those were sold. Towards the right of the page was the profit on each deal. It was the final column that made my stomach lurch and all the things that Tommy used to say to me came flooding back.

"We're partners mate, sharing the spoils."

"Everything we make I'll split with you, we'll keep it nice and simple."

He never actually said I was getting fifty per cent of the action, but he definitely made it sound that way. I had no complaints about the money I was getting because nobody ever told me how much the deals were bringing in. Tommy was always talking about how much he paid for the pills, courier costs, the incentives he had to pay to his suppliers. I just thought I was making a pretty good return for a few hours work, but I was taking all the risks. I met the courier, I stored and split the pills and I made the deliveries. All Tommy did was make a few phone calls. So how come he was giving me only ten per cent of the cash. That's what the spreadsheet was telling me. I had over a hundred grand deposited with Anwar. Tommy would have nearly a million. I thought he was my best mate but he was laughing at me right from the start.

I started to turn it all over in my mind. All that time he was playing me for a fool. But now I had his address book, the contacts knew I was trustworthy, I'd been delivering the goods to them for years. I'd no idea how much money could be made out of this racket. It hurt to think that Tommy treated me so badly but this could be the best thing that ever happened to me. I'd taken all those chances for years and it got me a hundred thousand quid. Tommy just sat on his arse the whole time and died a millionaire. Now I had the means to do precisely what he did, apart from dying, of course.

I picked a name from the contacts list at random and dialled the number. It was picked up straight away.

"Yes?"

"Is that Viking?"

"Nobody of that name here."

"I worked with Tommy, I'm just........."

The call disconnected. The next six calls were variants on the same conversation. I tried all sorts of opening lines:

"I'm Paul, I did Tommy's deliveries."

"Tommy's gone but I can help you."

"I've got some great gear I can deliver for you."

They all got the same response. I guess I needed some sort of code word, or they'd heard Tommy was dead. Whatever the reason, nobody wanted to talk to me and nobody wanted to deal with me. Then I noticed a name I recognised; Marvin. I'd met this guy, he wasn't just a customer, he was a mate of Tommy's. I called the number.

"Hello."

"Marvin, it's Paul... Tommy's mate."

"What the fuck do you want?"

"I want to help you. Tommy's gone but I thought we could start doing some business again. I can get all the same stuff for you. Maybe a bit cheaper. What do you think?" I asked.

Marvin laughed.

"The delivery boy wants to do me a deal. You're on Fantasy Island mate. People only dealt with Tommy because they liked him, nobody's going to deal with his bag carrier. You could do a buy one get one free offer with loyalty card points and you wouldn't get anyone to touch you."

"But I was his partner, it was my business too."

"Not what he told me pal. Anyway, be a good boy and delete this number won't you? And if you have any other numbers you should bin those too. Understand?"

"Marvin," I pleaded, "I reckon Connor is after me, I need a bit of help here."

The man on the other end of the phone snorted.

"Connor? I doubt he even knows you exist. The way I heard it, they weren't even trying to snuff Tommy. It was all a mistake. Be a good boy and go back to carrying bedpans at the hospital. Don't bother me again."

The phone went dead.

An hour earlier the phone book was my route to untold riches. Now it felt like every name in there was having a laugh at my expense. So, I could go back to the hospital and have nothing to fear from Connor, he wasn't hunting me down, he didn't even know about me. Even if he did, why would he be bothered with a messenger boy. I should have been elated that I wasn't in danger but I was gutted. I'd done all the work and Tommy took virtually all the money. I guess he was the one who paid the price in the end but he was supposed to be my best mate. I had five days left on my visa and a shade over a thousand pounds in the safe. There was still more than a hundred thousand in my account with Anwar, but what could I do with that? It was enough for a big deposit on a decent flat in Brighton but what would I do with my life? I could push old people round a hospital in a wheelchair until it was my turn to be pushed, I could save a bit every month and every couple of years I might be able to afford to come back to Thailand, maybe. I could find a nice girl like Clare and when she got bored she could trade me in for a bloke with better prospects. I had five days to make up my mind. I needed a drink, maybe several.

CHAPTER EIGHT

Regular check-ups for your Thai lady

"I don't understand *farang*." It was not the first time I said this to my best friend. "They smile and tell us they love us, then they spend all their time trying to find out if we have really stopped working."

Pan put the dinner plates in a bowl, we'd wash them later, and I poured two more shots of JD and topped them up with Coca-Cola. A movie was due to start on TV at any minute. Pan and I paid each other's bar-fines earlier that evening, we were close to our target for customers for the month, so could afford a day off. As a special treat I bought a half litre of Jack Daniels.

"Do you remember that man from Finland?" I asked. "He was the first one who ever sent me money, his name was so difficult to say. He thought if he sent me ten thousand baht every month, I would go back to my village and wait for him to visit. I picked up the first payment from Western Union in Pattaya and two days later he sent me an e-mail asking why I was not in my village. How was I to know that Western Union lets them check these things?"

Pan looked shocked. "How did you get out of that one?"

"I told him I was very ashamed."

"You did what?"

"I told him that before he rescued me, I had to borrow eight thousand baht from a money lender who kept my ID card until I paid the money back. Then, I said, the moneylender sent a girl who looked like me to collect the money and it just about cleared my debt. I said I was very sorry but I could not tell him in case he was angry. I promised him I really had gone to my village, I said he could speak to my mama if he did not believe me."

We both knew no *farang* ever wants to speak to a Thai lady's mother. They have been told it is all part of the trap we set to get them to marry us.

"What did he do? Surely he knew you were lying."

"Oh he believed me and the following month, he sent me twenty thousand to make up for the money I 'lost'."

"How did you pick that up?"

"My cousin looks like me and has a name that is nearly the same. The man in the Western Union office near my village was looking at her, not the card. After the first month, he did not even bother checking her ID."

We raised our glasses and drank a toast to gullible *farang* and lecherous cashiers, then Pan wanted to share her favourite story.

"I had a customer once who bought me a Blackberry. I was so happy, I spent hours checking all the things you could do on it. That's when I saw there was a tracker that would show him where I was."

"That's not so easy to get around."

But Pan had it all worked out too.

"No problem," she said. "The tracker tells him where the phone is, not where I am. I noticed it straight away while I was back in my village. I phoned to tell him we should SMS in future because voice calls were too expensive and he agreed. Then I gave the phone to my little sister. If he sent a text to the phone, my sister copied it to me, then I replied and she sent that on to him. We did that for a month, then I sold the phone and told him someone stole it."

"What did he do?" I asked.

"He sent me money for another phone."

We raised our glasses in another toast to men with more money than brains.

"You know, they spend hours swapping stories on how to catch us out," I said.

"How do you know what they do?"

"I'll show you tomorrow on the internet. Remember that big Australian man who paid bar for me for two weeks, he was always looking at a web site called Pattaya-Dream. There are thousands of them on there, writing things about us and posting those pictures they say they will never put on the internet. I read it sometimes and think they really don't like us very much."

"How did you get to read it, your customer can't have liked that? Pan asked.

"I didn't look at his computer. I went to an internet shop and joined the site myself."

Pan looked amazed, I took a little bow.

"I am sexyfarang," I told her. "I even post to the site, sometimes."

"No... what have you posted?"

"I once told them I bar-fined a lady from Kiss called Yim and it was the best night of my life. For two hundred baht I can do an advertisement for you too, if you like."

Pan stared at me as though I was crazy, but I think she was a little bit impressed.

"So what else do they say?"

"Many things, they suggest buying us webcams so they can see where we are calling from or getting Facebook accounts that show where our posts are made. There is even a company in Pattaya where they can pay to have us followed and offer us money for sex."

"It's unbelievable, why don't they trust us?"

We looked at our bar-fine tickets, lying on the table next to the nearly empty whisky bottle. When we looked up and caught each other's eye, we both collapsed in helpless giggles.

A husband to take care of me

The first time I saw Wolfgang in Kiss, he was already very popular with the girls. He liked to buy lady drinks and played games with us for money. The hostesses brought buckets of ping-pong balls for him to buy and he let us throw them to our friends. Each bucket of fifty cost one thousand baht and each ball was worth twenty baht to the girl who caught it. We told him he had *jai dee*, but the reason we liked Wolfgang was his money and that he liked spending it.

We tell every man he is handsome. When a Thai lady looks in a mirror she sees a nose that is too flat, skin that is too dark, lips that are too big, teeth that could be more straight and white. Then she looks at her body and she wants bigger breasts, to be less fat and she wants new feet. Every Thai lady hates her feet, because when we were little and ran around at home, we had no shoes. Maybe *HiSo* ladies in Bangkok like their feet, but if you come from Isaan that is not possible. When a man looks in the mirror he always sees a movie star and when we tell him he is handsome, we are saying something he already knows. Some men know they are not quite as good looking as others, but they will think they are funny or smart or charming or kind. When we say they have *jai dee*, they can look at the other men in the bar and tell themselves that is why we are happy to be with them. This is the most important skill when you work in a bar, to decide what a man wants to hear and then tell him exactly that. Maybe they know we are only saying what they want to hear, after all what else could we say. One night, I met a man called Bill:

Me: "Hello, what your name?… you handsome man."
Man: "My name Bill, I not so handsome, I fat… *poompuy*."
Me: "You only little bit, but Thai lady like *poompuy* man."
Man: "Really?"

Then he smiled and bought drinks for me and for my friends. What did he expect me to say? Maybe, "Yes, you very fat but I only want your money anyway." Sometimes I do not understand how they can be so stupid and still have so much money. Pan told me once that is why there are Thai ladies, to help deal with the problem of *farang* having too much money. Our job is to make sure they have much less.

Wolfgang had *jai dee* and I suppose he was quite handsome too, or he might have been twenty years before. He came from Frankfurt in Germany and I think he was an important man, because he had big money. But he also had a wife. Many *farang* tell us they are not married; maybe because they want to pretend for a little while they are not. I think it is also because they know many Thai ladies want to marry a *farang* man so he will take care of them and their families. *Farang* think maybe we will try a little bit harder to be good to them if we believe they might marry us. I knew Wolfgang would never marry me. I saw his wallet when he was in the shower, and the picture of a very beautiful German lady with two young girls. He already had a family. He came to Pattaya to have fun and to relax, not to find a wife. He had lots of money to spend and we were very happy to help him.

Wolfgang did not really understand Thai ladies; he visited the club maybe ten times but never took the same lady to his room twice. My friend Dah spent one night with him and he gave her an extra thousand baht as a tip. She was sure he liked her a lot, so she was very excited when he came back to the bar the next night. Dah was looking forward to another good payday. This time he bought her a drink but went with a different lady. It was a big loss of face for Dah. Everyone thought she did not take care of him, otherwise he would want to see her again. But then we realised Wolfgang was a butterfly, he just wanted as many different girls as he could get. When he chose me, I thought it would only be for one night so I was surprised he came back and asked for me again. He gave me an extra thousand baht every time so that was OK with me. Then one night he told me I could stop work and he would pay for me to go home to my village. He did not tell me he loved me, he did not promise to marry me, he simply said I was too nice to be working in a bar and I should go and take care of my daughter. Wolfgang agreed to send me thirty thousand baht every month. I was so happy I could go home and be with Dao and the rest of my family. I waited until the first payment appeared in my account before I left, I heard sometimes *farang* say they will send money but it never comes. I was very happy when I saw the money in my account. Every few days we exchanged SMS messages and I looked forward to the next time Wolfgang came to Thailand, I would make sure he knew I was very grateful. It was two days before the second payment was supposed to arrive in my bank account when the SMS message arrived. It said:

"Delete this number you greedy little whore and leave my husband alone."

The money stopped and one week later I was back at Kiss. I never saw him or heard from him again. I learned when a *farang* says he will take care of you, the promise will last until he changes his mind. I knew some ladies who married *farang* and the promise lasted many years and for some, all their lives. For me it was less than four weeks, for others a *farang's* word was good for less than a day.

There were also customers like Brian from Wales. He sent a SMS to me before every trip to say he was coming to Thailand to see only me. I knew he would pay bar for me for six whole days. He told me he loved me, that he wanted to marry me one day and that he was saving enough money to get us somewhere nice to live in his home country. I nodded and smiled and said I wanted that very much because I knew we would be very happy together. Why would I tell him anything else? He stayed in nice hotels and was happy to take me shopping for clothes once or twice. I tried to get him to buy me gold one day, but he pretended he did not understand and walked very fast past the shop. Brian was quite a nice man, it was good that he did not want *boom-boom* all the time, so I was happy to have him as a customer. In my heart I hoped he would never ask me to marry him. I knew I could not trust him.

When he first came to Pattaya, he said it was for only one week each visit and, after our first time together, that he only wanted to see me. But I knew that was not true. A few days before we met on his previous trip, I got a call from my friend Bok. She used to work in Kiss but then moved to Paris Agogo near LK Metro. She recognised Brian from Kiss and when she called, it was to say she had seen him at her club. He even bar-fined her. Then a few days later, he changed hotels, came to see me and pretended to have only just arrived in town.

I think my lies are no worse than the ones he told me. I would like a *farang* man to take care of me and my family, and then I could leave the bar. If someone asks me to marry them I will have no choice, I hope it is someone I can trust, someone who loves me and treats me with a little respect. The last time I saw Brian, he was counting out the money he was giving me for the week we spent together. The first time I went with him, we agreed he should give me two thousand five hundred for "long time", that means all night. This was his fourth time with me and the money in my hand was exactly six times two thousand five hundred baht.

"You should probably give me a discount," he told me. "But that's OK, I love you very much so I'm happy for you to have the money. Soon we can be together properly and you can come to live with me in Wales. My mates are going to be so impressed I've got a stunning girl like you."

Brian told me he was flying home later that day but as he handed me my fifteen thousand baht, he put a much bigger wad of baht notes back in his wallet. I wasn't paying much attention when he promised to come back for me, or when he said something about how one day we would be married and I would not have to go with bad men anymore. I was thinking of the first day of our holiday when he told me about his long flight, when really he just took a baht bus from LK Metro, and of the fifteen thousand baht that he carefully counted into my hand and the thirty or forty thousand he put back in his wallet. I did not really believe he would ask me to marry him but if he did, what could I do? There would be some financial security for me and my family, I would not have to sell myself to strangers, instead I would be selling myself to the same man every night. One who thought he could lie to me and I would never find out. I would be a toy doll who could be shown off to his friends and whose value could be so carefully measured in baht notes.

Protection

Kiss Club has a clock card system just like a factory. If I did not arrive on time, the *mamasan* would cut my pay. One night I was late and, in hurrying, nearly bumped into a man standing by the bar. I think, in other countries, the sight of a policeman is very reassuring, it makes people feel safe. That is not the case in Thailand. When I saw the tall, fit looking man next to the bar in Kiss it was not a surprise to see Winai, the manager, looking very worried. They only ever called in to say a girl had been hurt, that a *farang* had made a complaint or, more likely, the man was there to collect money from the bar. Selling sex is not legal in Thailand, in some districts ladies cannot dance naked and there are strict laws about when bars must close and who can work. The police are not too worried about any of those laws as long as the owners make a monthly payment. Many of the girls told stories of the bars where they worked before and of the owners who decided they would not pay. Then suppliers stopped delivering beer, windows were broken and staff stopped turning up because they were told it would be safer to work somewhere else. Some owners were attacked in the street, but the police would do nothing about it. If they still did not pay, fights started in the bar, men ran up big bar bills and then walked away. When the police were called they would not respond. Then the owner realised, if he did not pay he would lose his business.

The name of the man at the bar was Mongkut; he was an Inspector in the local police force. As I walked by, he turned and put an envelope in his breast pocket. It was then that I almost bumped into him. He was not ashamed of what he was doing, he smiled and I could feel his eyes on me as I ran up the stairs to the changing room. I hoped he was busy or that he did not like me, I heard sometimes he told the owner that he wanted a girl and she was made to go with him for no money. It was a relief to hear him call out to Winai that he was leaving.

There was a fight that night, but I knew it was nothing to do with the police. Pan told me it could happen but I never saw it before. One of the newest arrivals in the bar was a girl called Ling. She was only nineteen and very beautiful; she also looked quite innocent, which many *farang* like too much. I could not understand why they wanted a girl for sex then chose one who looked like she would not know what to do. It was one of the many things I could never understand about *farang*. We told Ling she would have to work hard to get men interested in her, but that was not how things worked out. Customers took one look at her and that was it. She barely spoke English but that did not matter either, the man looked, she smiled and the baht flowed from his wallet. She didn't have to try at all and that was the problem.

When I first came to Kiss I was in awe of a girl called Cat. She was so confident, so sure of herself and she never had a problem finding *farang* to pay bar for her. She was always in a good mood, she wore nice clothes and almost every night, she left with a customer. I knew that if I was to make the money I needed to make, I had to be like her. At least that is what I thought. It was Pan who explained the truth.

"Cat has worked here for eight years, she makes more money than any of the other girls," she told me.

"So why does she keep working? She must have plenty in the bank."

"*Yaba*," came the reply.

I knew about the little pills even when I was at home in the village. Sometimes a man went mad and smashed up his own house or crashed his car or threatened to kill his neighbours. Everyone shook their heads and said, "*yaba*." It is Thai for crazy medicine. Cat liked *yaba* too much, her husband sold it when he could get the supply and her brother got into a lot of trouble with the police back in Isaan because he sold it too. When either of them needed money, they did what all Thai men do and turned to the woman in their life to pay. Cat earned a lot of money, but she spent a lot too and after eight years in the bars she was no closer to finding a *farang* to take care of her. Pan thought it was because as soon as a western man found out she liked *yaba* he would run. I still looked at the *farang* web site, Pattaya-Dream from time to time. They shared stories about girls taking *yaba* and how everyone should avoid them. When Cat found a good customer, she did everything she could to keep him. That was what caused the fight.

"You stupid little slut, you know he was mine, everyone knows he was mine."

Ling said nothing, she just smiled her usual smile, it was what she always did when she was nervous. Cat took it as defiance and launched into her rival. Fists rained down on the smaller girl and she fell to the floor. It gave her the chance to put a metre or two between her and Cat who was panting heavily from the exertion. The bar was not due to open for another ten minutes so there were no customers yet. Most of the girls just looked on in horror, nobody wanted to stand up to Cat. Some were smirking, enjoying the spectacle and relieved they were not on the end of the onslaught.

"I did not know, he asked me for bar-fine so I said yes, I did not know he was your customer." Ling found sanctuary behind a table and plucked up the courage to defend herself, in words at least.

"Don't lie to me you little shit. I have seen you sucking up to other girl's customers before, smiling that little girly smile. Someone needs to teach you a lesson."

No-one else saw Ling do anything wrong, she smiled all the time. It was a mask so people could not see what was really going on in her head. She wasn't smiling this time though because as Cat moved forward again she, like all the rest of us, saw the knife. It looked like an old piece of wood but as Cat turned it over and over in her hand, she pressed something on the side and a blade suddenly appeared from nowhere. Half a dozen of the girls screamed and, on instinct, I stepped forward to try to reason with her.

"Ladies should stick together, we have to help each other, not fight."

I only saw her arm move at the last minute and then I felt a sharp sting. All I could think of was that there was a lot of blood for a sting that was not much worse than one I got from an insect bite when I was a little girl. How could there be such a lot of blood? It was my last thought before I passed out.

Pan told me everything later after they stitched up my arm. The injury looked much worse than it really was and when I fell some of the ladies thought I was dead.

"Winai is completely useless, he is supposed to be the manager but he sat back and watched the fight. He and the boys thought it was funny. Then they saw your blood."

"Did they really think I was dead?"

"You fell really hard and there was blood everywhere."

"So did Cat stop going crazy at least?"

"No, she still had plenty of fight in her and started lashing out again with the knife. Bapit, that cute new waiter is in a bed down the corridor and he has much worse injuries than you. It took four of them to stop her."

"Is Bapit going to be alright?"

"I think so, but Winai told Cat not to come back to the bar again. You may have made an enemy."

"But I didn't do anything, she attacked me."

"Cat was pretty scary before but now she has no work and many people are looking to her to take care of them. She will want to blame someone else. Just be careful that's all."

Cat would have no problem finding another job, but I hoped she would not want to settle any old scores. I was afraid Pan might be right and Cat would think I was, at least partly, to blame.

Pan went back to work and I waited for a doctor to say it was alright to leave. He smiled as he told me the owner of Kiss had already paid for my treatment. I was supposed to be happy but I knew I would be paying it all back out of my monthly salary, plus interest. Pattaya was suddenly a much more daunting place. Seeing the policeman made me remember what could happen if they don't get paid for their protection, but they were not the only people to fear, even the other girls could be dangerous if you said or did the wrong thing.

The doctor gave me a quick check-up and said it was alright to leave, so I headed for the door on unsteady feet. I think I was still a little shocked by what had happened, my legs did not want to do as I told them. It took me ages to get to where the motorbike taxis usually parked outside the hospital. My heart sank as I saw who was waiting there. Aun was a pest, none of the girls liked him and we all tried to avoid using him. He always said things about what we did for work and why we should try the same with a proper Thai man, instead of a fat, ugly *farang*. He said that we probably did not know what sex should be like, but he would be happy to fix that. The only time I ever used him, he tried to touch me as he helped me put on the helmet, then as we rode along he started to run his hand along my leg. As I saw him ride away that day, I hoped he would crash, then I went to the temple to make merit after having such terrible thoughts. He was the last person I wanted to see and there were no other motorbike taxis around.

"I know you, you're that little prick teaser that works in Kiss right? You look like you need someone to take care of you. I could take care of you real good."

He laughed so hard that spit landed on my shirt. He held out the helmet with a sneer and looked around as if to say, 'You don't have any choice, do you?'

"No thanks, I am going to walk, I don't need a taxi."

"Don't be stupid, I know where you live."

He managed to make that sound like a threat too. Then he stepped closer, looking around as though he was checking whether there was anyone else about. There wasn't. I was sure he was going to attack me there and then. He was looking me up and down like a starving man wondering what he was going to eat first. I backed off a couple of steps... that's when we heard another motorbike approaching. Aun stepped back, waiting for it to pass. We both knew, by the sound of the engine, that it could not possibly be a taxi bike. It sounded like an expensive machine, so neither of us expected it to stop.

"Yim, are you OK?"

I never thought I could be so happy to see the bike with the flying eagle on the side. It was Sonthi.

Aun stepped away as he saw who was on the bike and in a matter of seconds he suddenly looked smaller... and afraid... exactly like me a few minutes earlier.

"Is Aun bothering you?"

Aun stared at me like he was pleading for me to say everything was OK. I said nothing.

"Sonthi, I wasn't doing anything really, I promise, she looked like she needed help so I was trying to help but maybe she is still a bit confused so she didn't understand and if I'd known she was a friend of yours, well anyway, you know what I mean, I wouldn't have done anything, I really wouldn't..."

Sonthi looked at me with an eyebrow raised as though he was asking a question. I didn't say anything, I just kept looking at Aun with as cold a stare as I could manage. His motorbike was the only thing between him and my saviour. Sonthi kicked the stand away and watched Aun's bike crash to the floor.

"What do you say?"

"Sonthi, I am sorry for putting the bike in your way," Aun replied hoping that was what the bigger man wanted to hear.

"To the lady."

"I am sorry, I was really trying to help, honestly."

Sonthi stepped forward.

"OK," Aun said, "I am sorry if I frightened you, it won't happen again. It really won't."

"How much did you make today?" asked Sonthi.

"One thousand."

"Show me."

Aun slowly turned out his pockets and held up one thousand four hundred baht for Sonthi to inspect. Sonthi smiled as he took the money and then turned to me.

"Dinner?" he asked and nodded towards his motorbike.

I started to think about all the things that happened to me the last time I rode on that bike, but I wanted to get away from Aun as quickly as I could.

Sonthi spoke quietly as though he did not want me to hear, but it was unmistakable.

"Never speak to her, never look at her, don't even think of her again. If you do, I will know and I will come and find you. Do you understand?"

Aun babbled something incomprehensible but it was pretty clear he understood. I was very confident that as long as he thought Sonthi was looking out for me, he would never trouble me again.

I've ridden side-saddle on a thousand bikes, sometimes I did my make-up as we weaved through the traffic, I could perch on one in my sleep. This time though, there was a bandage on my arm so it felt perfectly natural to put my other arm round the big, strong Thai man in front. I did not have such a good reason to rest my head on his back but I was very tired and I was sure he did not mind.

We did not sleep together that first night and the fact that he did not seem to expect it made it even easier the next time we met. It was nice to be with a man who spoke my language, it was nice to be with a strong, fit, handsome man that other girls obviously wanted. It was nice not to worry about asking men for money. Most of all it was nice to feel so very safe. It was three weeks later that we saw Cat again. She had started work in a beer bar on Beach Road and was standing outside as Sonthi and I walked past. She looked at us twice as we passed, the first with recognition then with what I was sure was grudging respect. Because of Sonthi, there was nothing to fear from Aun, and now I knew there was nothing to fear from Cat either.

Thai Kiss

CHAPTER NINE

The visa run

It was the time difference I could never get used to. I'd have some breakfast and then decide to phone a mate back in England, only to get a load of abuse for waking them up in the middle of the night. I only wanted a chat and I wasn't getting any sympathy. They thought I was just here for a party, they had no idea what I was going through. There was a bit of sympathy that my best mate was dead, but blokes aren't very good at that sort of thing, they think you should shrug it off. Especially if they've never been there themselves. The only familiar voice I could rely on was my mum. She thought I was still upset about Clare so I could rely on a sympathetic ear, even if I couldn't tell her my plans to be a mega-rich drug dealer were in tatters.

There was an easy way of sorting out the time difference, by getting back on UK time. No expensive flight to worry about, I decided to spend the last week of my trip getting to bed about five a.m. and getting up around one in the afternoon. It meant a lot of drinking, a few little pink pills courtesy of my new mate Clay and the diverting company of nine or ten gorgeous Thai ladies who assured me I was the most fascinating, sexy, desirable man they ever met. Obviously the bullshit meter was going off the scale but it was still nice to hear. I was having to find a few new bars of course, because the girls don't like it if you bar-fine them and then try to shag their best mate the following day. This was explained to me at great length by the lovely Mon, she sounded exactly like Clare apart from the dodgy English. I suppose, even if you're paying for it, you're supposed to pretend that there's more to it than just a business transaction.

There were two days left of my trip when I bumped into a guy called Ronny from Newcastle. He was a regular in Starbar and based on a bit of idle chat over a couple of beers, I decided he was probably a nice enough bloke. We'd caught a few Premier League football matches together over the weeks and whilst we didn't support the same teams we hated the same ones. That worked just as well.

"What you up to tomorrow Paul?" he asked.

I tried to remember what was on my busy schedule and paused for a few seconds before replying.

"Fuck all."

"Great, it'll cost you about ten thousand baht but it'll be a hoot. Just bring your passport and meet me here at nine in the morning."

"Passport?"

"Trust me."

I still had a bit of cash left over and was intrigued by the offer. When the alarm woke me up at eight the following morning, I'd changed my mind. I still needed a good five hours sleep if I was going to stay on UK time, invaluable given that I was about to get on a plane back to England. But I needed to pee, so I headed for the bathroom. By the time I'd splashed a bit of water on my face I was almost awake and the thought of the mystery trip was starting to appeal to me. I jumped in the shower.

The sliding doors of the minivan opened to reveal Ronny, in the clothes he was wearing the night before, Mai from the Starbar where we usually watched football, and two cool boxes that appeared to be laden with food and beer. Mai was a legend at Starbar. Her name is the Thai word for no and it was generally agreed that the only time she ever said no was when she said her own name. Wherever we were going, the plan appeared to be that I was going to be the third wheel, the alternative of course was that they wanted me to join in with whatever they were going to be doing, which was actually even worse. Then another head poked out from behind the door.

"This is Sin," Ronny said with a raucous laugh. Sin gave me a smile that indicated she knew what I was thinking and she was more than up to the challenge. She crooked her finger and beckoned me towards the van and I started to walk. It would've been rude not to.

I didn't have the vaguest idea where we were going. The Thai driver pulled a curtain at the front so he was completely screened from his passengers. Ronny and Mai took the three-seater bench immediately behind him and Sin took my hand and led me to the back row seats. She cracked open a can of Singha for me and offered a small polystyrene container filled with rice and beef. I took the beer but declined the food, which she munched on happily for the first fifteen minutes of the trip. She knew my name already, but we still went through the other compulsory pleasantries.

"Where you from?"

"How long you stay?"

"You come alone?"

"You have Thai lady?"

We were twenty minutes into the journey so by Thai bar standards we were old friends, which is probably why she thought it was a reasonable next step to unzip my shorts and root around until she found what she was looking for in my counterfeit Calvin Kleins.

"Sin still hungry, little bit," she said as she bent over and took me into her mouth. That was the point I realised I wouldn't have liked the beef she offered me anyway, it obviously had way too much chilli in it. After the initial surprise, I settled back in my seat to enjoy the experience.

Sin was extraordinary, we spent the trip eating, drinking, occasionally sleeping but otherwise fooling around like randy teenagers. Based on the noises coming from the bench seat, Mai still hadn't learnt to say no either. I was really disappointed when the minivan drew to a halt, I'd no idea whether we were at our mystery destination or back where we started. As the sliding door opened I could see that we were at a fuel station. Ronny confirmed we had an hour to go. After a quick trip to the men's room, we were given ten minutes to stretch our legs while the driver filled up with LPG and the girls cowered behind a bus because they believed there was a fifty-fifty chance the minivan was going to explode into a ball of flame. It's what happens when you go overboard with the Health & Safety stuff. The driver gave us the thumbs up and Sin, once again, beckoned me to join her on the back seat of the bus.

At first I thought the Friendship Market was our final destination. Ronny explained we were in a town called Aranyaprathet and the girls loved to go there for cheap shopping. I wasn't sure how anything could be cheaper than the markets I'd already seen in Thailand, but I was assured this was where you could go for a bargain. Not, of course, if you are a six foot three inch *farang*. The stallholders were Cambodian and were aiming for Thai customers, not people like me. I gave up after trying on a great leather belt and finding that it got barely three quarters of the way round my waist. Then Ronny explained that wasn't the point. We each gave our girl three thousand baht and they disappeared to the stalls with looks of unbridled glee. Ronny and I hired a golf buggy to ensure we could visit every corner of the vast market. We decided to take turns to see how fast we could do the perimeter of the site. In our minds, it was the souped-up version of the thing you do as a kid, racing your mates round the supermarket with a shopping trolley.

"I'm not complaining mate, that was the best bus journey of my life, but did we really come all this way to go shopping? The cost of the minivan has got to be more than anything they save."

"No," Ronny replied. "One more stop mate, I'm doing my visa run. That's why I told you to bring the passport. The border is a couple of miles down the road, get the thing stamped and it's another thirty days in Thailand."

"I'm alright mate, I'm off home in a couple of days, I don't need the stamp."

"So what you going back to then? Wife and kids, great job, hot girlfriend? Tell me what you've got back there that's better than here."

I started to open my mouth, but I couldn't think of a single thing to say.

Ronny's phone beeped and we set off again, at breakneck speed, to meet the girls. They were literally jumping up and down with joy. We loaded the golf cart with jeans, belts, shirts, bed linen and pillows then headed back for the minivan.

"Ronny, I'll come over with you mate. I fancy a new stamp in my passport but I've got a flight booked and everything. I'll just keep you company."

Ronny smiled. It took about an hour to make the crossing, have a quick beer and then get back to the girls who stayed on the Thai side of the border. Neither owned a passport.

Soon it was time to head back to Pattaya and as I turned towards the van, Sin was crooking her finger in my direction again.

We made it back to Pattaya in time for a few more drinks in Starbar and then Sin took my hand and led me back to my hotel. It was like being hit by a whirlwind, she was the most amazing woman I'd ever met. She had an insatiable appetite for everything in life, totally fascinated by anything new, always laughing and smiling and couldn't get enough alcohol, food and sex. I was completely smitten. Even as I reached into my wallet for her money, she smiled at me again.

"You want say goodbye, or maybe *boom-boom* one more time?"

She might as well have asked me to run a marathon.

"Sin, I'd love to, but I need a rest darling."

"No problem, next time we go pharmacy first." Then she brushed down her skirt and stood up. There was four thousand baht left in my wallet and I gave her the lot. I'd already spent the best part of the ten thousand Ronny warned me about the previous day, so this was my most expensive twenty-four hours in Thailand yet, but it was worth every penny. Sin gave me a long and lingering kiss and then bounced out the door looking like she was ready for another twenty-four hours of non-stop partying. I collapsed on the bed as my phone beeped to say there was a message. It took me a couple of minutes to find it. My guard was right down the night before. I knew about all the things you must do when you take a girl back to your room. Phones, wallets, cameras, anything of value goes straight in the safe... you never know if they've slipped something in your drink. My wallet was on the bedside table, nothing was missing. The phone was with my passport in the pocket of my trousers, lying in a heap on the hotel room floor. The SMS was from Ronny, it was just a smiley face, so I sent one back to him. Then I looked in the passport and there was the stamp from the day before, giving me leave to stay in Thailand for another thirty days.

I looked back at the phone and decided to make two calls, the first was to my mum in Brighton. I told her I wasn't coming back yet but I'd see her as soon as I could. She told me the hospital wouldn't hold the job open, I told her that was fine. I'd no idea what I was going to do next but it wasn't going to be pushing stiffs to the mortuary every day. There had to be something else in life. Then I phoned the travel agent and tried to rebook my flight for a month's time. Apparently it was a fixed ticket, I thought about it for a full three seconds before I told them to cancel it. The cash I brought from England was gone but there was still over one hundred thousand pounds just waiting for me to collect. I was planning on getting some sleep then I'd get a taxi to Bangkok. Anwar had given me the address of the guy I needed to see. I could withdraw enough to tide me over until I decided what to do next. First I needed some sleep, a lot of sleep.

Reality strikes

It was an awesome twenty-four hours. I could hardly wait to get back to Starbar and find Sin again. I wasn't kidding myself that it was love or anything, I'd read all the stuff on the forum at Pattaya-Dream and I'd even picked up a couple of books about the bar scene at the airport. They all said the same thing, fall for a bar-girl and you are well and truly stuffed. I was sure that was true, but I'd made a real connection with Sin. I wanted a few more days with her. Back in Britain, having a different girl each night is every bloke's dream but I'd been doing that for a while now. I fancied getting close to someone, spending a bit of time getting to know them and now I had a whole month on my hands.

I put on my smartest trousers, a newly laundered shirt and a hint of the after-shave I picked up at duty free on the way in. What woman could resist? Especially given that I'd be offering a cash incentive. Ronny texted to say he was picking up Mai at nine and was hoping we could take the girls to dinner. I was there at a quarter to the hour. The bar was only a simple horseshoe shaped counter alongside about twenty others that looked exactly the same. Starbar always was a bit busier and the girls looked like they were having more fun. There was even a really good pool table between it and the next bar. It looked like the same bloke, Phil, an Englishman married to a local woman, owned that one too. He was definitely living the dream. Apparently he'd been a schoolteacher back in England and chucked it all in to come to Thailand. I suppose he was quite handsome once, but he still had that way about him. He peered at you over the top of his glasses as though he was at the front of the class, you'd put your hand up and he was hoping you weren't going to say something stupid. I found it quite intimidating until I got to know him a bit better. I'd seen the way he and his wife talked, the little looks and smiles they gave one another. Either she was the best actress in Thailand or she really cared about him. Maybe there was something to it after all, maybe you could find yourself the perfect woman. You might have to get used to the fact she'd been with a few blokes, but if you got past that one then it would probably be alright. I'd briefly dated a girl back in the UK who was famous for screwing around. I didn't really have a problem with that as long as she didn't do it while she was seeing me. Unfortunately, my sense of humour got in the way. I left a message on her mobile one time and she never forgave me for it.

"Hello this is Tracy, leave your name and number," was the greeting.

"It's Paul," I replied, "I think you said I was number forty nine, I didn't realise you were keeping a register." She stopped answering my texts and I reckon she probably hit fifty within the week.

Starbar was packed, a busload of Japanese had just arrived and Puy, the owner's wife, slipped a couple of hundred baht to the driver. Almost every stool was already taken and the drinks were flowing like water. I'd barely sat down when one of the tour party rang the bell and a free Singha was placed on a coaster in front of me. I was trying to play it cool but I was looking out for Sin, she was nowhere to be seen. The only other bloke at the bar was huge, Asian and looked a lot like the other recent arrivals. They'd clearly already been drinking because the one who rang the bell dropped his trousers and was cavorting around the pole that marked the centre of the bar. The girls played along but they told me they hate it when a customer does that. Still the guy's mate rang the bell again, so I don't suppose anyone was going to tell him to get down. The large Asian guy who was already at the bar didn't look that impressed, but there was a girl draped around him, so the newcomers weren't going to spoil his fun. Then I saw Sin, rushing back from the toilets where I guess she was sorting her make-up. I gave her a wave but she didn't seem to notice. When she got to the edge of the bar, she jumped straight into the Asian guy's lap and they all fell about laughing. Then she spotted me, it looked like she took a second to place the face, then she gave me a huge smile and a shrug and went back to pawing the big guy.

One of the girls placed another free Singha in front of me and gave me one of those million volt smiles.

"He Korean man, very rich, he have *jai dee*. He like Sin and Lek too much, he like two lady every time."

I was close enough to see him peel two one thousand baht notes off a wad he'd taken from his pocket and he slipped one into each girl's cleavage. It clearly wasn't their fee for the night, it was just his insurance policy to make sure there wasn't a way in the world they'd think of going with anyone else. I knew I was beaten, I was getting used to it. There was no *checkbin* to settle, but I left a hundred baht for the girl with the smile and headed back towards the street. Sin gave me a little wave and another shrug, then turned back to the Korean. I started on the long walk back to my hotel.

It wasn't such a big blow, I had no illusions that Sin was going to be the love of my life, but I thought she really liked me, that part of her enthusiasm from the previous day was because she was happy to be with me. Then I thought of queuing up in the supermarket every Saturday with Clare; I could never believe how miserable the cashiers usually were. We used to say "It's a shitty job, they might as well do it with a smile on their faces, the time might pass a bit quicker." I guess the same applies for bar-girls. Sin obviously decided that if she was going to have to sell sex she might as well throw herself into the job. I cast my mind back to the twenty-four hours we spent together, there was no doubt she was having fun. Looking back though, it was easy to see the times when she really lit up. It was when we sent her shopping with her mate and a wad of cash, it was when she and Mai were chatting, knowing we couldn't understand a word, it was when I handed over the four thousand in the morning and didn't ask for change. It was a living; all she wanted was the cash. Who can blame her? Like half the population of my country, I spent most of my life worshipping professional footballers. They say they love your team, they kiss the badge and pretend they'd die if they weren't with your club. You somehow manage to scrape together sixty quid to buy a shirt with their name on it, a shirt they probably paid a Thai factory worker a couple of quid to make. Then the first day you proudly wear it in public they announce they always dreamt of playing for the team that just offered to double their wages. And they are off, saying they'll always have a place in their heart for your team. It's a modern miracle, how footballers get put on a pedestal and are worshipped like Gods and bar-girls are called whores and worse. And don't even get me started on footballer's girlfriends. I was only fifty yards down Beach Road and I was feeling better already. I was pretty proud of how I'd managed to rationalise the whole thing. Whoever you are, it's all about the money. I couldn't blame Sin for picking a ridiculously rich Korean over me, I could probably cope with the footballers too if they weren't so fucking hypocritical. And what about me? I came to Thailand to get a drug trafficking business up and running, so I could make as much money as possible. I wasn't any better.

"Where you go?"

"Make you happy?"

"Where your hotel, sexy man?"

I'd hit the massed ranks of the Beach Road choir singing their favourite tune. Eleven offers of sex in barely one hundred yards was possibly a record even for Pattaya and three of those were from the prettiest, most feminine men I ever laid eyes on. I hurried on my way and, minutes later, I was looking at the Walking Street arch.

Fuck it, I thought. One more beer can't hurt.

Thai Kiss

CHAPTER TEN

Leaving Sin behind me

I'd read about Kiss on the forum at Pattaya-Dream. It was apparently fairly new but already one of the most popular go-go bars in Walking Street. The usual line of "hello girls" held out placards to make sure you were in no doubt about what was on offer inside… girls, cheap beer and more girls. A couple of squat, muscular Thais stood ready to open the door should you decide to enter. They smiled at all the customers in a way that said, "Welcome, as long as you spend money and behave yourself." I imagined anyone who caused trouble might end up leaving by the back door. I was still getting to grips with the local geography, but it only took me a moment or two to realise that the bar backed straight onto the sea. I looked at the two Thais again and concluded that wouldn't bother them too much.

"Welcome, welcome sexy man. Free blow job with first drink." I was relieved to see it was one of the girls making the offer, the doormen were looking at me as though they were wondering whether I could swim. I knew I was going to behave myself and my pockets were full of the cash I'd intended to lavish on Sin. I was pretty certain I'd be allowed to leave the way I arrived.

I took my life into my hands and allowed a tiny hello girl who looked to be in her mid-teens to lead me by the hand into the bar. Tommy once explained the younger girls were only there to bring the punters in. Once they made their eighteenth birthday, knowing how much money the go-go girls earned, it was assumed they'd move inside and start going with customers. It was a crude form of apprenticeship, giving the bar a steady flow of new dancers, who were used to the scene and could probably speak enough English to get by with *farang*. I was barely through the door before being handed over to two hostesses anxious to pounce on the new arrivals. They were wearing smart dresses that showed a hint of cleavage and an enticing amount of thigh, their name badges said Tip and Toy, and in seconds a place was found for me opposite the middle of the stage. The girls stood on either side of my table and Tip started the small talk.

"What you drink?"

"Singha please," I replied, wondering about the offer they'd made outside the bar. Tommy and I visited a place in Soi Cowboy when we were in Bangkok. They were completely open about the fact that blow jobs were available. The customer didn't even have to leave the room, he was simply led to a corner where the lower half of his body was obscured by the corner of the bar. One of the girls would disappear from view, the guy would start to smile and a small brown head could be seen bobbing up and down. There was no way I'd go for that in a public place but I was intrigued as to how they were going to go through with the offer. Tip returned with my beer and another small glass filled with some sickly liqueur.

"Hey, I never said you could have a lady drink," I protested.

"Not lady drink," Tip said as she put the glass in front of me. "This your blow job."

Well, I'd ordered Sex on the Beach in Brighton once and it came in a tall glass with an umbrella, I couldn't blame the Thais for reworking the idea. The girls looked like they were relieved that I saw the funny side. I guessed some customers might've taken exception.

"OK ladies, drinks for you."

Tip and Toy managed a perfectly synchronised hop and handclap and then both disappeared to the serving area. It gave me time to take a look around. The central stage was heaving with girls who could have dropped straight out of a lingerie catalogue. Most bars have their fair share of plain women who are just making up the numbers, Kiss was clearly an exception. My fellow members of Pattaya-Dream were constantly asking where they could find a ten as in "ten out of ten" and how much she might cost. I'd not discussed prices yet but this was clearly the place with the maximum choice. There were also plenty of hostess girls, who seemed to fall into one of two categories. Some, like Tip, were a little older and might have been dancers before, but maybe childbirth meant they weren't so flat round the stomach any more or their breasts were fighting a losing battle with gravity. They had a better chance of getting a bar-fine if the guy didn't see too much of their bodies before he paid for their company. The younger girls, like Toy, were maybe too shy to undress in public and were trying their luck as hostesses first.

There was plenty of activity in one corner of the bar and I noticed the staircase for the first time. Then my eyes were drawn to the ceiling, which was made entirely of glass. Seated at one of the stools around the stage, drinkers could admire the dancers in front of them and get a worm's eye view of the girls dancing on the stage upstairs. Tommy told me about bars with two floors, it was all coming back.

"They put the younger ones upstairs," he told me.

"What, underage?" I asked him warily.

"Don't know to be honest mate, they dance in the open so probably not. They're just making sure the punters know what they're going to get. Older experienced ones downstairs, jailbait on the top floor. Stick them in a short skirt and the blokes on the ground floor get quite a view through the glass ceiling."

"They're all legal though right?"

"I reckon so, but I'm not sure even the bar owners can be certain. The girls have ID, but it could be fake or borrowed. Next time you bar-fine a girl, take a look at her ID. Nine times out of ten you wouldn't know it was the same girl. They all got their cards back in their villages, no make-up, hair tied back, not smiling. It could be anyone."

I was wondering how I was going to get by without Tommy's little pearls of wisdom.

At that moment, another tour party of Japanese arrived, maybe it was even the same lot from Starbar. They made straight for the staircase without giving the girls on the downstairs stage so much as a glance. It reminded me of one of the few times Tommy tried to flex his intellectual muscles. Our conversation tended to stick with three subjects, football, women and hospital managers who were, in Tommy's view, useless, overpaid parasites. It was an unusual opening gambit and another subject close to his heart… hardcore pornography. Tommy was an expert, a connoisseur you might say.

"I think it tells you a lot about national character," he once announced.

"Sorry Tommy, what does?"

"Porn, of course." He looked at me as though I was an imbecile and he'd finally lost patience with my failure to keep up.

"Porn does that?" I paused to let it sink in, then nodded as though the connection was obvious now that he'd pointed it out.

"Of course it does. Russians are pretty scary right? You get the impression they take what they want and you don't want to get in the way. You watch their porn and that's what its all about. Never looks like the girl has much say in it as far as I can see."

I was bowing to his superior knowledge and the fact I knew he'd clearly done a thorough investigation.

"The USA is all about 'bigger is better' and their porn is just the same. Fake tits and huge dicks. Everyone is built like a body builder, even the women."

Tommy had the basis of a first draft doctoral thesis here and was clearly warming to his subject.

"Then you've got the French, they are all class and sophistication, so chances are they do the business on some bit of antique furniture, or there is a nice painting on the wall. The Italians are obsessed with religion so half their stuff is priests, bishops and naughty nuns."

I was genuinely stunned at the hours of painstaking research Tommy must have done to develop these fascinating theories.

"And the Japanese, they love schoolgirls. Go onto one of those free tube sites and key in schoolgirl and the first fifty movies you get, three quarters will be Japanese."

"So what about the British?" I asked, thinking I could catch him out.

"There's not so much about, but most of what I've seen is embarrassed, useless looking blokes and women calling the shots."

That conversation took place on our first night in Bangkok, eight weeks earlier. I was anxious to hear more of Tommy's grand theory but a couple of young Thai girls had appeared demanding lady drinks. I grinned at them self-consciously and nearly knocked my drink over as I shifted across to make room for them to sit, then I mumbled OK, without really making eye-contact with either girl.

Tommy just smiled, I didn't have to comment on his theory, I'd proved it.

Tip and Toy were back by my side and as we raised our glasses in a toast, they slid onto the bench seat alongside me.

"Paul, England, Four weeks, Yes alone." I said as rapidly as I could.

"What you say?" Tip, who was clearly the leader, asked. Toy smiled vacantly and massaged the inside of my thigh.

"Nothing… it's a little prayer," I said.

There was a pause as the girls looked at each other, each seeking a signal they'd picked a dud and should gulp the drinks and head for the hills. After the Japanese, there weren't too many new customers coming in but plenty of hostesses were waiting to pounce on those that did, so they decided to press on. Tip launched into her opening routine and neither girl could see why I thought it funny that the first four questions she asked were the standard.

"What your name?"

"Where you from?"

"How long you stay?"

"You come alone?"

I was chuckling as I repeated the answers I'd already given, and the girls did indeed sling back what was left of their drinks.

"OK, one more," I said. Tip and Toy still hadn't worked out whether I was a loon, but I was buying drinks. They looked at each other uncertainly, then Tip shrugged. There weren't too many spare customers, so their options were limited. Both girls turned to me and smiled, they were willing to take the chance.

"And tequilas, two each," I called after the disappearing Toy. I decided I was going to get very pissed indeed. We played Rock, Scissors, Paper to decide who was going to drink the tequila and I lost three of the six games. Each defeat was greeted with a squeal of triumph from my opponents. A very pleasant buzz was building in my head and I tried to work out whether I should offer to take both girls back to my hotel. I'd never had a threesome before and I wasn't sure I was up to it to be honest. I liked to try to give a girl pleasure even if I'd paid for her and I always thought there were so many things you needed to do to one woman to get the required result. I'd never be able to cope with double the effort. Other girls noticed that I was happy to buy drinks and plenty stopped by to try to join the party. The *mamasan* also came by regularly to check whether I was happy and if I'd buy her another tequila. My speech defect was kicking in again, courtesy of the alcohol, and I couldn't manage much more than yes and OK, whatever was being asked.

"You want lady tonight?" the *mamasan* enquired.

"Maybe," I replied cautiously, proud that my word repertoire had increased by fifty per cent and that I managed to show even token resistance.

"One lady or two, you choose. I think you have big power so two lady no problem. Tip and Toy can go with you... they very happy go with you."

I was really missing Tommy by now, the girls were great, I knew I'd be taking one home, but it was much more fun to have a mate, someone to banter with in your own language. Another bit of Tommy wisdom was drifting back into my mind. He told me I should always take my time choosing a girl to bar-fine.

"It's sod's law mate. I can guarantee it. Even if you've checked out most of the girls in the bar, the second you agree to a bar-fine and she is off to get changed, you'll see another girl. No matter how hot your chick is, this one will be better and she'll give you a smile that says, 'You should've been patient, then you could've had me'. Happens every time, I promise you."

"Is that right?" I asked, wondering when he was going to run out of go-go bar philosophy.

"Absolutely, there is only one sure-fire way of meeting the hottest girl in any bar."

"Which is?" I was intrigued.

"Bar-fine someone, anyone, then she'll be along within a couple of minutes."

"So you want me take care you?" It was Tip, bringing me back to the present with a gentle squeeze to the top of my thigh.

"Maybe."

"Toy too?"

"No, just one lady, OK... I pay bar for you."

Tip repeated the little hop and handclap and Toy smiled graciously. I slipped two hundred baht into Toy's hand as a tip and she left to get my *checkbin* at the same moment as the Japanese tour group came down the stairs. This time each had a young Thai girl in tow. Tommy was right about their preferences. He'd also given me the inside track on how to tell a Thai girl's age.

"Rule of thumb mate, they all look about four years younger than they really are. Girl looks twenty six, she's thirty." He'd been right up to now, Noy looked eighteen but swore she was twenty-two. Using the same arithmetic, the line of girls escorting their Japanese customers from the bar were nineteen at most.

Toy returned with my bill and I pulled a wad of baht notes from my pocket. Including the bar-fine for Tip, I was paying about three thousand baht for a couple of hours of great fun with two gorgeous women, with more to come. Tip asked for two thousand but said she had to leave after a couple of hours to take care of her daughter. I was a bit disappointed, I wanted her to stay all night, but it would have been mean to change my mind simply because she was a mum.

"This my friend, you give her tip?" Toy knew I was about to leave and she was trying to get as much cash out of me as possible in the interim. I turned to say I wasn't going to give money to someone who'd bowled up as I was going out the door.

"My name Ling, please to meet you." Tommy's prediction had come true. I was staring at the most exquisite face I'd ever seen, if she'd arrived before I offered Tip the bar-fine, I'd have been going home with this one instead. The girl smiled and I dumbly handed her the three hundred baht in my hand. She popped up on tiptoe to give me a chaste peck on the cheek, then gave a deep *wai* before she turned and disappeared into the crowd.

As I tried to hide my disappointment, I felt a tap on my shoulder and braced myself for another request for a parting gift. The hand belonged to another stunning Thai girl, not quite as bewitching as Ling, but a comfortable ten by any standard. As expected she had her hand out.

"Sorry love, no more tips," I said.

"I not want tip, you drop money."

I looked down, instead of an open, eager palm, the girl was holding three thousand baht in cash and pushing it in my direction.

"Your money mister. It fall on floor."

117

I was dumbfounded, the forum was full of stories of how girls rip you off and this one was handing over what must be about a week's salary for a go-go dancer. She pushed the money into my hand, turned and disappeared into the crowd. She didn't even wait around to see if I'd give her some cash to say thanks.

Tip returned and exchanged a few words with Toy. Maybe they discussed my encounters with the other girls because Tip grabbed my hand and started to drag me from the bar. I barely had time for one brief exchange with Toy.

"Night Toy, great to meet you. See you again."

"Night night mister Paul, see you next time. You not forget me *kaa*"

"That girl who gave me money back, what's her name."

"Her name Yim," Toy replied. Tip flashed an exasperated look at her friend and pulled me ever closer to the door.

CHAPTER ELEVEN

A week's salary

I have never stolen anything in my life, but when a *farang* does not take care of his money I think it is not stealing. Many times I have been in a hotel with a customer and he has left things out when he is in the shower. It would be so easy for me to take a few thousand baht, he would never even notice. Some spend more money in one night than I can earn in a month, a few thousand baht made no difference to them. I saw the *farang* with Tip and Toy, but I did not go to him like the other girls. I did not like it if ladies tried to steal my customers, so I would not do it to them. Anyway, my mind was not really on my job. My daughter was sick and my mama took her to the hospital that day. Mama promised to send me an SMS when they got home safe. I was not allowed to carry my phone with me, there was nowhere to put it, so it was in my locker. If I went to check too often the *mamasan* would fine me for being lazy. It was more than two hours since I last looked. I was on my way to the changing room when *mamasan* told me to get on stage, many girls had already gone with customers so there were not enough girls to dance. I went up the stairs at one end. As each song finished, the girl at the other end of the stage stepped down and another joined behind me. The girls in the middle shuffled along to take up a new position, hoping to catch the eye of a nearby customer. I had to endure twelve songs before I could check my phone. I felt like everyone knew I was in a hurry and were conspiring against me. The *mamasan* could easily have picked someone else to fill in, the DJ was definitely playing all the longest songs he could find and as one track changed, my heel got stuck in a loose tile on the stage. Before I could free it the girl behind slipped past and took up my position for the next song. I would have to dance for three extra minutes at least. I even started to blame Pan and that really old Swedish guy she was with all evening. Had she still been around, I could have asked her to check my phone, but there was nobody else I could trust to go to my locker. He paid bar ten minutes before I went on stage and they were on their way back to his hotel. Everything was against me.

Finally it was my turn to leave the stage and I had to pass the *farang* who was drinking with Tip and Toy. He was searching his pockets for the money to pay his *checkbin*. I saw the money drop to the floor and my heart leapt. It was definitely two, possibly three thousand baht. It was more than one week's salary, or the commission on fifty lady drinks, or the amount I hoped to charge a customer for a whole night at his hotel. And he would not even know it was missing. I bent down to pick up the money, he still did not notice. I hoped that Ghai might come to tell me what I should do, but he had not spoken to me since my first night with a *farang* customer. I turned towards the spirit house that was set on a shelf above the cashier's table. I had brought a flower garland and bottle of Sprite to make merit that evening but my mind was still no clearer as to what I should do. I knew I could not steal, but this was not stealing surely, he lost the money and I found it. Then I saw another *farang* look at me and smile, one of the waiters too was staring at me, they both saw me pick up the notes. I had to do the right thing, or maybe I was just so afraid of being caught doing the wrong thing. I tapped him on the arm. All that mattered then was getting to my locker to check my phone, I put the cash into his hand and he said something, I can't remember what it was. Then I pushed past Toy and raced to the changing room.

There was one SMS: We are home safe, she is fine and we both love you very much.

The morning after

Tip was a delight. We chatted as she got dressed and she finally admitted to being thirty-two. Her eldest child was a daughter of fifteen, the youngest was just six. She worked to keep three girls in school and, ultimately, out of the go-go bars. Two marriages ended with her being traded in for a younger model. Tommy warned me these stories were often made up to encourage a customer to pay a little extra. I didn't really care, she was sweet, sexy and affectionate. I tried again to encourage her to stay until morning, but she was adamant. I went back to sleep within minutes of Tip leaving my room.

I loved that feeling in the morning when you were half asleep and half awake. It was like you could have a bit of input into your own dreams. I was conscious enough to be trying to recall the night before, but sleepy enough that my sub-conscious was enhancing the story line. It wasn't Tip that was at the forefront of my mind. First it was Ling, the young girl with the amazing smile. Tip was great, but if I'd just been a bit more patient, it could have been the most exquisite girl I'd seen since I started coming to Thailand. I was half dreaming of what might have happened had she come back to my room. Tip could not have been further from my mind, all I could think of was this extraordinary looking girl, this doll-like creature, so perfect she hardly looked real. Ling barely said a word to me either, she just smiled. I could have looked at that face all day long. Then, in half sleep, I felt a tug on my sleeve and turned to see another face, another smile and a girl handing me three thousand baht. I wanted to reach out and touch her, take the girl's hand and draw her towards me. I wanted to know how a beautiful girl like that could sell herself in a bar, but then pass up the chance to pocket such a windfall.

I'd only seen her for a few seconds but the picture in my head was like a photograph. Her hair was up, held in place with a couple of flower-covered combs. It was easy to imagine her tugging them gently and shaking her head to let long black hair tumble to her waist. I suspected a nose job because she didn't have the flattened bridge or slightly flared nostrils that so many Isaan girls save hard to have corrected. Her eyes were huge, with eyelashes just long enough to be noticed, without looking like exotic insects that might make their escape at any second. Her lips had that slightly puckered look, some might say they appeared to be in mid-kiss. I could spend hours trying to find the words to describe them but there was only one phrase that captured it. The girl had blow job lips. There was no other way of putting it. She'd been too close for me to get a really good look at her body but as she disappeared into the crowd, I got a fair idea. Tommy was always on about the leg ratio.

"She can be gorgeous mate, but if her legs are shorter than her body it's a non-starter for me." I'm pretty sure he actually worked out the ideal proportions, and he'd measured quite a few in his time. I'd stopped listening by then, in those days I had only one criteria... would she let me?

Now I was getting a bit picky too. This girl had long, long legs, even Tommy might have approved.

I really wanted to see her again.

"One girl per bar mate, that's the rule." Tommy's words were coming back to haunt me. I knew if I went back to Kiss, I couldn't ignore Tip and I certainly couldn't bar-fine another girl. Plenty of blokes did it, but it's like etiquette in golf. You have to have some standards, they couldn't lock you up for it, but it wasn't right. I can't deny Ling popped into my head more than once as the day went on. Any man might want to spend the night with her and that was the point. I wanted to shag her and then tell anyone who'd listen that I'd had the best looking chick in Pattaya.

It took me a while to remember the other girl's name. I was pretty sure it was Yim. You'd not chuck her out of bed either but there was something else about her. She was so much more than just a face or a body, there was a purpose to her, a bit of inner determination. I wanted to know about her, how she came to work in a bar and what sort of person passes up the chance to make a week's money in five seconds. I planned to go back that night and see Tip again, if I stayed long enough I could probably get to see the other girl too. Then I could get it out of my system.

The doors to Kiss had been open for a little more than five minutes and I was already back in the same seat as the night before. The girls were still milling around a little aimlessly, as though they weren't quite ready for the night ahead, when I heard a piercing cry from the other side of the bar. Toy rushed to my side.

"Mister Paul, you not forget. You come back see me."

"Sure Toy, great to see you. Drink?"

Toy was back in minutes with Ling in tow. If anything she looked even more dazzling than the night before. Sober, I was able to truly appreciate this was female perfection in one small package. A waitress was summoned to bring more drinks.

"Where's Tip?" I asked.

"She not tell you?"

"No, what should she tell me?"

"She have customer come today, he take her holiday for two week. She not come back bar for long time. I think she not come back until number six next month."

I took the opportunity and lied.

"Wow, I come to say hello to Tip."

"She say she sure you come back, but she say it OK if you go with other lady. We big family here, you choose another lady because Tip not here, but she want you be happy."

Both girls pushed their breasts out proudly, suggesting they were perfectly placed to take on Tip's responsibilities in her absence.

"Alright ladies, let's have more drinks."

Toy signalled to a passing waitress to get another round. I was trying to get my head around this latest lesson in bar etiquette. I knew you weren't supposed to take more than one girl from the same bar. It was all about the Asian concept of face. Pick a different girl the second time and it was a kick in the teeth for the first one. Yet Tip apparently knew I was coming back but had a better offer from another customer. What about my face? She'd even lined me up with her friends and given them permission to go with me. I guess that was probably the opposite of losing face, her mates thought she was the Queen of Sheba, handing over her old cast offs. I decided to count my blessings and go with the girl I was daydreaming about for most of the past twenty-four hours.

"One thing Toy, last night there was very nice lady. I think you say her name Yim. She found money I lost. I want to buy her a drink to say thank you. Is she here?"

"Not sure," said Toy, possibly feeling her grip on the proceedings slipping away. Ling looked a little surprised too, I doubted most guys ever looked at another girl once she sidled up to them.

"Can you check?"

"Sure, no problem," Toy said, as she wandered off. Ling and I just looked at each other, exchanged smiles and sipped our drinks.

Telling the truth for a change

I did not tell Sonthi about the *farang* and the three thousand baht I picked up from the floor, I knew he would be angry. When I first met Sonthi, some of the girls said he was a bad man, that he only went with Thai ladies so they might take care of him and give him money. He never asked me for anything. I did not love him, nobody could take Ghai's place in my heart, but he made me feel safe and secure. It was like when I was back in the village and people nodded and smiled because my family had money. In Pattaya they did the same because they did not want to make Sonthi angry. He was kind to me and he wanted little in return. We met on my day off and sometimes he picked me up after work if I had no bar-fine and he was not asleep already. I never asked him where he was or what he was doing. He liked that. He always wanted sex when we were alone, but I was used to the ways of men. He had a very beautiful body and worked hard to please me but most times I just wriggled and made the noises I learnt for when I was with *farang*. That made him happy. He asked me about my customers, whether they were rich, if they lived in Pattaya or might want to send me money. I told him there were some who gave good tips but that was all. Sometimes he became a little impatient about that but then he would smile and say he wanted people to be good to me. I was not sure that I believed him. He would be angry enough that I had thrown away three thousand baht. Worse, everyone knew he hated *farang* and would not have wanted me to do anything to help one.

I did not expect to see the *farang* again so it was a big surprise when Toy said he wanted to buy me a drink.

"I wanted to say thank you, you are very good lady," he told me.

"It not my money, what else should I do?" I said, as though the thought of keeping it never occurred to me.

"Well, are you hungry?"

"*Nit noi*... little bit."

"Have dinner with me, to say thank you."

"You have to pay bar," I told him.

"No problem."

It was the light streaming through the window the following morning that woke me up. I was still fully clothed and Paul was lying next to me still asleep. I knew almost nothing about him, only that he was from England, liked football and his best friend had died. He came to Thailand to decide what to do with his life. He seemed quite sad and lonely. We ate dinner at Sea Zone, one of the big restaurants in Walking Street and he made me talk all the time. Sometimes we tell customers new stories about ourselves, it gets boring saying the same thing all the time.

"I am from Cambodia and should not be in country, I hope you will not tell police."

"My father was famous politician but there was big scandal and my family was ruined. Now I have to work bar."

"No I not have baby, I was virgin until I came to work bar three weeks ago."

I did not really want to lie, but I thought my life was very boring. Sometimes I told them things to make it sound more interesting. Some things I learnt from the ladies at Kiss, others I just copied from daytime TV shows I watched with Pan. With Paul I tried something completely new, I decided to tell him the truth and maybe my life was not so boring after all. I told him about Khao Lak and Ghai and my baby daughter, then about my papa and how he had been killed, and how I came to Pattaya to earn money for my family. He just wanted to know more and more. I told him about the things that happened in the bar, about the fight between Cat and Ling and about the men we had to be so careful about. I even told him about the Russian and how Sonthi taught him a lesson, with only one tiny detail that was different. In my version of the story, it was Pan who went with the Russian and Sonthi was her boyfriend.

Paul asked me to go back to his room, but when we got there he wanted to carry on talking. I forget what I told him last, but I must have fallen asleep. I had customers before who did not want sex, maybe they couldn't, I did not care as long as they paid. I decided Paul must be like that, and when he woke he would give me some money, then I could go home.

"Stay with me today?" His voice broke into my thoughts.
"OK."

"I go shower." Paul was gone for about ten minutes and smiled at me as he came back into the room with only a towel around his waist. He was quite handsome and very strong looking. I think he did some exercise, but not enough because he was *poompuy, nit noi.*

"Now your turn," he said, throwing me a towel.

He paid bar for me for two weeks and I discovered he did like sex. Not too often and he never asked me to do anything I didn't want to do. So it was fine, he was kind and gentle and wanted me to enjoy it too. I wriggled and made noises and he believed I did enjoy it just as much as he hoped. That, after all, is the most important thing.

Paul even asked me one time if he had made me happy. That is what we say when we mean orgasm. I said yes, but he asked me if I was sure. I had to lie.

I said, "one million per cent."

Sonthi didn't mind at all. His only concern was when I told him the two weeks was up and I had to go back to the bar the following night. Paul was taking me out for a special dinner to celebrate our last evening together.

The other Pattaya

I tried to remember the conversations I had with Clare and the other girls I dated back in England. Nothing really stood out for me but maybe it was my fault. I perfected the art of nodding, smiling, looking surprised or astonished and throwing in the odd "Really?", "That's awful" or "That's amazing", depending on the gist of what they were saying. If I'd only just met them, I'd be wondering whether I could get them into bed and if I'd known them a while, I'd let them get on with it and hope they wouldn't mind me watching the football when it came on TV later. It all sounds a bit shallow but I'm sure when I did listen it was so incredibly dull. They all had pretty cushy lives with a nice job or a cheque from the government every month to ease the stigma of unemployment. They were all looking for a bloke to take care of them and their only goal was to get married and have kids. Nothing really bad ever happened in their lives and all they wanted to talk about was what their mates said or did, what was on the TV or where I'd be taking them next time we went out. The ideal holiday was a Spanish beach and if you could get by without having to eat any of the local food then that would be perfect. They had no idea what went on in the rest of the world. Maybe I was the same to some extent, but Thailand opened my eyes to new places, new people and something other than pie and chips for my dinner. I'd always liked reading, I just hid it from my mates, and I liked a good documentary on TV or on YouTube. My trip gave me the chance to see how other people lived, not have some TV presenter give me their take on it all. Thailand was like a different planet in many respects and the more you found out about it, the more there still appeared to be to uncover. I could feel the place getting right under my skin.

Yim was extraordinary. I'd simply wanted to know what kind of girl passes up the chance to pocket a week's salary without anyone being any the wiser, but the more we talked the more fascinating her story became. I'd never met a girl like her, she'd been through more in the previous eight years than most English girls will experience in a lifetime and the more shit that was thrown at her the more determined she was to find a way through it all.

"So why you not take the money, no one would have noticed?" I asked.

"I not steal, only bad girl steal and then pay for that in next life. I do good thing for you and something good will happen to me or to my family. That is karma."

"You really believe that?"

"For sure, one million per cent," she replied with a look of total certainty on her face. "Would you steal from me, Paul?"

"No, of course not."

"Then we same same, *chai mai*?

I guess she was right, I was somehow thinking because she was poor she was more likely to be dishonest. It's a road I'd travelled myself, dealing drugs because I couldn't make money honestly. It was pretty humbling stuff, but I was still sure she'd spin me all the stories about being in the bar for only a few weeks, hating Thai men because they were useless and denying she had children. I reckoned that might be true in her case. Tommy told me how many Thai mothers have a thin brown line running from their naval to their groin, it's a product of childbirth. Sometimes even the younger ones never quite get back the perfect stomach they had before. Yim showed no sign of ever having had a child. Her belly was flat and tight and a uniform shade of dark honey. She continued to surprise me.

"So you ever have Thai boyfriend?"

"Sure, I have boyfriend I love very much but he die many year ago."

"You still think about him?" I tried to hide the pang of jealousy that struck when she said she'd loved the guy.

"Every day, because he father of my daughter. I think she, then I think him too. He very good man, but he not here now."

It was so matter of fact, she didn't have an ounce of deceit in her. She was simply telling it like it was.

"How did he die?"

"He die when the wave came to hotel where we work together."

"The wave?"

"Tsunami, many people die. You not see on TV in your country?"

I suddenly felt stupid not to have made the connection. This girl lived through one of the most infamous tragedies of recent years and it ripped her life apart.

"Yes, of course I see that. I just never hear anyone call it the wave before. So you come here to work bar to take care of daughter." I was quietly congratulating myself on my growing grasp of the strange hybrid language used by the girls and their customers.

"No, first I go home and my family take care. My papa had good job and big money. I do little bit work but he pay for me and my daughter. No problem."

"So what happened? Why did you come here?"

"Man kill my papa, because they have fight about business. Then family have no money, so I come work bar."

"When?" I could barely believe what she had gone through.

"Two year ago now, long time."

Yim talked about her life the same way girls at home talked about their humdrum existences, but she'd really been through some terrible stuff. Left a single parent at barely eighteen and now having to sell sex to foreigners because her papa was murdered. She took it all in her stride. Clare once went into a two day depression because the woman in front of her in a department store got the last jar of a particularly sought-after rejuvenating skin cream. I couldn't even begin to contemplate how the average English girl might cope with the life Yim was forced to live. There was no state system to fall back on either. If you wanted your kids to eat, you found a way of making money. Yim turned to the option chosen by most young, beautiful but poor Thai women and she never once uttered so much as a word of complaint. This was the hand she'd been dealt and she was going to play it as best she could. She had no real expectation of any great reward, only that her daughter might avoid the same path and she might come back to a better life next time round.

I was awestruck.

I paid her bar-fine for the next two weeks and I barely let her out of my sight. Occasionally I'd pay bar for her best friend too and we'd go on day trips or out for dinner, but Yim and I always returned to the hotel alone. I was a little nervous the first time I suggested we take Pan out, in case Yim thought I wanted a more intimate end to the evening for the three of us. She dealt with the issue in typically direct fashion.

"Sure you can bar-fine Pan, but you try *boom-boom* her and I cut off your cock. Understand?"

"One million per cent," I replied, trying to mimic her accent.

A new Pattaya opened up for me with Yim. Before, my days followed an identical routine. Late to emerge from my room, I'd go for a massage, then some food. If I was feeling energetic, I might do a couple of laps in the hotel pool. More often I visited an internet shop for a couple of hours, did a bit of reading, or grabbed a manicure and pedicure on the beach. After an hour's sleep I'd head out to the bars. Dinner was a burger, a kebab or a bit of Thai barbecue picked up from a street vendor, then I'd embark on getting as pissed as I could. Usually I found a girl to come back to the hotel, and in the morning I'd have forgotten her name and where she came from, assuming I ever asked in the first place.

We still hit the go-go bars at night, Yim had lots of friends in town and it was good for her to show up in their bars with a *farang* with a bit of cash in his pocket. I wasn't looking to get pissed and laid any more. I knew who was coming back to my hotel that night and I was enjoying her company. We went to the cinema and she was thrilled we could have the VIP seats. In one theatre, that was basically a double bed where we could stretch out in front of the movie and have drinks and snacks served to us as we watched. Yim taught me about Thai food and we were soon regulars in a seafront restaurant in nearby Naklua. I loved being the only *farang* in the whole place. One night we took Pan and drank a bottle of Jack Daniels in the private room of a karaoke bar. The songs were all in Thai and they all sounded the same to me, but the girls were having the time of their lives. My reward was the occasional little smile from Yim, the way she tenderly touched my hand and how she always made sure my glass was full of JD, coke and fresh ice.

I was part of the new generation when it came to women. We laughed at the images from our granddad's era. Men came home from work and expected their dinner to be on the table. If they wanted their teacup refilled they rattled the saucer with a spoon, without raising their eyes from the evening paper, and a dutiful wife silently responded. We bought into the whole equality thing, women were no longer subservient and if you were really lucky they might just offer to pay their way. To an extent life with Yim was a throwback. She told me her role was to take care. She chose my food, made sure my plate was replenished and tidied my clothes away when I left them lying around the hotel room. My side of the deal was to pay the bills. I should have felt a little guilty but I loved every minute of it.

My Mum was always proud of her fruit bowl. Not just that we had one, but that it was always full. We couldn't stretch to much more than apples, oranges or bananas but it was certainly one up on the neighbours. Occasionally she would buy us a couple of peaches, we'd look at them for a while before she gave permission to dig in. They seemed impossibly exotic. Yim loved fruit and most days she would prepare a plate for us to nibble on as we relaxed after an afternoon at the shops or at the beach. She introduced me to Mangosteens, Rambutans, Longkongs and Raghams. Western fruit sellers worry more about what fruit looks like than how it tastes. Thai fruit invariably appears as though it has recently been expelled from the digestive system of an animal. If you can get past that, it tastes amazing. Peaches suddenly seemed a little dull. Yim would carefully peel each fruit and remove the stones, then present me with a selection. But there'd be a little warning shot across the bows in case I thought she was too much of a doormat. I should say *korp khun mak kap…* thank you very much. If I forgot, the plate would be withheld until I remembered my manners. The message was clear, she would take care of me, but she wasn't going to take any crap.

Like many Thai women, Yim could appear to be the picture of innocence. Going without a bra in public was inconceivable, she always wore what looked like cycling shorts under her dresses and while holding hands in public was permitted, even the most chaste of kisses was utterly forbidden. It was the day we went to Koh Larn island that I realised I had seriously fallen for her.

Koh Larn is about thirty minutes by ferry from Pattaya's Bali Hai pier. The beaches are far more beautiful than the rough stretch of sand on the mainland and the restaurants are all equipped with full-length sun loungers for their guests. You don't even have to get up, food and drink is brought to wherever you are slumped under your umbrella. Yim daintily worked her way through the biggest plate of fresh prawns I'd ever seen, sheltered by an umbrella and a huge sun hat that wouldn't have looked out of place in a Mexican based western movie. She grudgingly agreed to join me for a swim and I already had trunks on under my shorts. I liberated a couple of towels from the hotel and, after my swim, would use one as cover as I swapped back to shorts. I'd go commando back to the hotel. I was looking forward to seeing Yim in a bikini, she'd be a real head turner compared with some of the lumpy looking westerners who were parading up and down the sand. I assumed she'd done the same as me and was already wearing her swimming gear.

I was wrong.

As Yim emerged from the changing room, the towel was wrapped firmly around her from shoulders to mid thigh. The sombrero-like hat was pulled down over her eyes so there was no chance of anyone recognising her as she made her way back to where we were sitting. Just in case, she was still wearing the huge sunglasses I bought her in Walking Street the night before.

"Ready?"

"For sure, but I not swim good, so you take care me."

"Trust me, I will take care."

We started to head for the water.

"Yim, you have to leave the towel, you need it to be dry when we get out of the water. And the hat."

I could feel her eyes boring into me from behind the massive lenses of her sunglasses, she looked like an exquisitely beautiful bug, who might just kill me if she got the chance. Then she dropped the towel.

I think I covered it pretty well. I couldn't wait to see this awesome girl in a tiny bikini, I spent the previous two hours fantasising about whether it would be white or black. It was neither.

"You not like? Yim not sexy now?"

"You are always sexy *tirak* … darling, I've just never seen your costume before."

That was true, but I had seen one exactly like it, on a postcard back in Brighton. It depicted my seaside home, circa 1902. The bathers wore costumes that weren't far short of full length and Yim's outfit was based on the same design. Flowery shorts ended half way down her thigh and the matching top had a modest, throat high round collar together with short sleeves. It was impossible to square what I was seeing with the fact that the first time I met Yim, she was wearing no more than a pair of black knickers and high heels.

"What you think?" She pouted at me.

"I think you are the most beautiful human being I've ever set eyes on." And I meant every word.

The swim was brief but fun, once Yim was satisfied that she was in sufficiently deep water that no-one could see her below shoulder height. Back on dry land, I slipped my trunks off under the towel and put the shorts back on without incident. Yim trooped off to the changing room to get back into street clothes.

We had plenty of time before our ferry and Yim wanted to visit the temple a couple of hundred yards from the jetty. She taught me how to light incense sticks and place flowers as offerings before we put two small slivers of gold leaf on the statue of the Enlightened One, the Buddha. As we knelt to pray, she looked at me very seriously.

"You can ask for things you want but not ask too much, OK? Not good if you too greedy. You know what you want?"

"Oh yes," I replied. "I'm certain I know exactly what I want."

Later that day Yim reserved a table in our favourite restaurant in Naklua. The food was fabulous as ever and she looked really happy and relaxed. There were occasional lulls in the conversation but they never tipped over into embarrassed silences. It was nice, I felt really comfortable with her. Yim recalled her brief splash in the Gulf of Thailand as though it was training for an Olympic triathlon and I finally managed to explain why I thought her costume was amusing. I asked her if she'd mind wearing the swimsuit in bed that night. She just covered her mouth with her hand and giggled silently so her shoulders shook.

As I paid the bill, I told her I wanted to look at the sea before we headed back to Pattaya.

"Yim, I want you to stop work."

"I cannot, I have to take care of family."

"I give you money every month, for you and your family. I give you twenty-five thousand baht."

I was expecting her to jump at the chance, but she didn't look that sure. I guessed it was just the matter of fact way she dealt with everything in her life.

"But you go England, then you forget me and money stop. I know this happen for sure. One million per cent."

"I'm not going to England. I'm staying here. I want to find a flat and I want you to stay with me."

There was a trace of smile.

"I stay with you and you give me twenty-five thousand baht, every month?"

"For sure, you have to give money to family and pay for daughter."

"*Jing lor?* Really?"

"*Jing jing.* Yes, really."

"You promise?"

"I promise."

"One million per cent?"

"Ten million per cent."

Yim put her arms round me and buried her face in my neck. She held me like that for a couple of minutes, the only time she ever hugged me in public. I could feel her body shuddering a little as though she was crying, then she breathed really deeply. It was a sniff kiss, the Thai alternative to a western kiss and often every bit as sexy. As we moved apart, she briefly brushed at her eyes and then she was back in complete control.

"*Rak na mak mak*, Paul," she said.

"And I love you very much too."

CHAPTER TWELVE

The Sign

Yim was sweet, smart and sexy, we always had a great time together. I found myself listening to soppy love songs and nodding at the compelling wisdom of the lyrics. Pattaya wasn't supposed to turn out this way. She loved the bar life, so we still spent plenty of time in the go-gos and night clubs and rarely got back to the room until two or three in the morning. Even then, she was always up for it once we got to bed. I used to pop the odd *yaba* pill, and even a Cialis or Viagra if I thought the old man might need a bit of encouragement. Yim never needed any help, she went off like a rocket every night. God knows where she got the energy. I kept thinking about Clare and her line about blow jobs and lobster thermidor. Yim couldn't have been more different. She wasn't even that demanding. I gave her the twenty-five thousand baht a month, as promised, and she seemed happy with that. I'd buy her a few presents from time to time and if she had a real emergency, I might give her a few extra baht, but it never added up to that much. Occasionally the odd couple of thousand for a medical bill for her family, or some new clothes for her daughter. Two months passed since our first meeting, six weeks since I asked her to move in with me. As every day went by, it seemed like a better decision, but there was an even more important choice to come. I still had the cash I saved for the house with Clare and I didn't mind sharing it with Yim for the time being, but it wasn't going to last forever. Either I needed to find something to do in Thailand or I'd have to head back to the UK. I knew that if it was the latter, I could ask Yim to come with me but I'd no idea how she'd cope with the cold, the strange food, no friends and, worst of all, being six thousand miles away from her mother and daughter. We made one trip to her village near Buriram and I met the family. They were all pretty happy to see the guy who was paying their way and I wasn't complaining. Where else in the world could you take care of a whole family like that for less than five hundred pounds a month. Dao was an absolute delight, six years old and as cute a child as you could imagine. She had perfect manners and even knew a few words of English. I was starting to feel like a proud stepdad.

We'd been back in Pattaya for three weeks when Yim said her mother was ill. She didn't need more money, she just needed to go back and take care of Dao for a couple of weeks until her mother was better. I saw her off at the bus station and headed to Dream, I hadn't been back there since the day I met Yim in Kiss. Carl was sitting at a corner barstool but otherwise it was pretty empty. He was looking fairly glum so I assumed Liverpool must have taken a hammering sometime in the last couple of days.

"Hey mate, how's it going?"

"Oh... Paul, right? Yeah it's going, I guess."

"Singha please. Where is everyone, thought I might catch Clay or one of the other guys."

"Clay's gone mate. The police got him, some little slut from round the corner set him up with the boys in brown. They got an English girl too, can't believe you haven't heard, it was in all the local papers."

"That's a bad rap. How long's he going down for?" I asked.

"It's not prison for dealing here mate. It's the fucking death sentence... for the girl too."

It was a real shock to hear what happened to Clay, but I couldn't help feeling a little rush. If I'd got involved with Clay and tried to get back in the drugs game, it could've been me that got stung alongside the American. Maybe my luck was changing, things were going great ever since I met Yim. She was always talking about signs, little things that tell you your life is picking up or slipping back. Well suddenly I was certain, I was starting to get some breaks, things were going my way. It turned out Liverpool did lose the week before, to local rivals Everton and the winning goal was, as Carl put it, "half a fucking mile offside." It would have been a long night if I'd stayed at Dream, so I headed back to Starbar, my other favourite "pre-Yim" watering hole. Sin was there, draped around a tall athletic looking Australian and Phil and Puy were behind the bar as usual, looking like they didn't have a care in the world. I wanted someone to talk to so I resorted to the easiest if not cheapest way of making friends in Pattaya - I rang the bell. There weren't many customers, so I got change from two thousand baht and Phil came over for a chat.

"Thought you'd gone home, we haven't seen you since your day trip to Cambodia. Did Sin upset you?" Phil looked genuinely concerned.

Puy came and delivered our drinks and it was impossible not to notice how their hands trailed against each other as she moved away. They didn't actually say anything, but there was communication. They really cared about each other.

"No not all," I replied. "Sin was fabulous but she has too many fans, I couldn't compete. I've got a proper girlfriend now anyway and she's the best thing that ever happened to me. We started living together six weeks ago."

"So you're staying." Phil made it a statement not a question.

"Maybe. Did you ever think of taking Puy back to England?"

Phil snorted. "I ran away... hated the place, couldn't wait to get out. Why would I want to take her back there? She'd loathe it anyway, her friends and family are here. If she ever said she wanted to go, I guess we might do a holiday, but she never shows the slightest interest."

"I'd love to stay, but what could I do?" I said. "I've got some savings but they won't last forever. I need to earn some cash." I was playing with the pool of condensation that had rolled down my beer bottle onto the bar top. Phil pushed my hands away and mopped the counter.

"Well I know a bloke who came here and opened a bar, and then he found the perfect woman. No reason you can't do the same thing in reverse."

I nearly asked him if I could meet the guy, the Singha was taking it's toll.

"So you reckon it's a good idea."

"No doubt about it mate, if she's the girl you think she is, it'll be the best decision you ever made. If she's not, of course, you'll get completely screwed."

We had another couple of drinks and Phil gave me the run down on how he set about buying the bar. There was some complication about foreigners buying Thai properties that I didn't fully understand, but he promised to introduce me to a mate of his who'd help me out. Maybe this was what I was meant to do, I'd be earning money fair and square, I'd have my own business and I'd have a stunning woman to share it all with. Yim talked a lot about fate, some things were meant to be. I'd been back to Dream and seen what dealing drugs can mean in a country like Thailand. Then I went to Starbar and saw what can happen if you find the right woman and a business you can run together. Things were falling into place in my mind. I couldn't wait to tell Yim what I wanted us to do. I saw a baht bus and raised my hand to get the driver to stop. If he'd spotted me I'd never have seen the sign and I'd still be wondering whether it was really such a good idea. Instead he just drove past and left me standing on the corner next to a boarded up shophouse with a huge painted sign that read: Bar for Sale.

Laughing out loud

"She's going to take you to the fucking cleaners mate and no mistake." Carl was congratulating me on my plan to become a bar owner, but in his own way.

"They're all sweetness and light until they've worked out how much cash you've got and how they can get their hands on it. Then it's like one of those sci-fi movies with the six foot lizards."

"Sorry Carl, I was right with you, until the bit about the lizards, run that by me again."

"You've seen the movie, you know the one. They take over the planet, they get into government and the army and stuff like that, then when there are enough of them in place, they take the masks off."

"The masks."

"Yeah, that's right. They seem OK until they're ready to take over the world, they look human - just like you and me - then the masks come off and they're all fucking aliens that look like six foot lizards."

"What... Thai girls?"

"No... in the fucking movie, but that's what Thai girls are like too, when you strip away all that 'anything to make you happy *tirak*' bollocks . Once they're ready to pounce, the mask comes off and it's a creature from another world under there."

138

"What was her name then Carl?"

"Who?"

"Your six foot lizard."

"Fuck you, you're barred."

He wasn't being rude, I'd learned to understand, that 'Fuck you' was what they said in Liverpool instead of 'Have a nice day'. Carl stalked off to the back of the bar and I tried to finish my beer without laughing. For every bloke like Carl there had to be at least a couple like Phil, enjoying brilliant relationships with Thai girls. You could see it every day on the streets of Pattaya, western men with gorgeous Thai wives and kids. Most of them had to cope with an age difference too, that wasn't a problem for me and Yim. Carl had been hurt and the only way he could rationalise it was by saying all Thai women were scheming bitches. I knew Yim wasn't like that, and if I was in any doubt at all, I'd seen the evidence to the contrary for myself in the previous couple of days. Carl's rant stuck in my mind though, mainly because it made me laugh. After that day I'd try to picture Yim as a six-foot lizard and if she did ever get angry with me, I had a new nickname for her... Liz.

Yim was absolutely fantastic when I told her about my plan. Based on Pattaya legend, she was supposed to jump at the chance of me buying a bar. I'd probably have to involve her in the legal side in some way; I might even need to put it in her name. She'd know all the ways a hapless westerner could get fleeced and she was supposed to keep it all to herself, then I'd be blissfully unaware as she and her friends and family bled me dry. That was how it was supposed to happen but it didn't. We went to Naklua again, it was our special place for celebrating but she took the wind right out of my sails.

"Paul, you crazy man, you see any *farang* bar owners who look happy?"

"Course I have; Phil at Starbar."

"He too lucky, he have Puy. She take care everything, he not have to work too much."

"And I have you. We can do this together, then you still work bar but you the boss. It's perfect."

"But *farang* cannot own business here. You need Thai person for contract. Bad for you if everything go wrong."

"*Tirak*, we can put bar in your name. I trust you. You won't cheat me, will you?"

"I not cheat you, but I not know how to run bar, I just dance and go with customer. Many thing can go wrong. You need manager and maybe manager cheat you."

"No problem, I'll get Puy to help me find someone."

"What about police? They take money from you or things will happen for sure. And mafia too, they all take money or they make sure you not have lucky bar."

Yim was really in her stride by this stage; she wanted to make sure I knew what I was letting myself in for. Wait until Carl heard this stuff, it was the exact opposite of what he told me to expect.

"Yim, I need to start earning money in Thailand, if I can't do that I have to go home sometime and I don't want that. What do you want?"

"I just want you not be stupid."

Ouch! "You want us to be together?"

"For sure."

"You want us to stay Thailand, near your family?"

"Yes, I want."

"You want maybe we have place where your daughter can come live with us?"

"One million per cent, but I think bar bad idea. Maybe you think of something else."

"Like what?"

"Not know but I think you crazy man if you buy bar."

"Phil knows a lawyer, we can go see tomorrow. If he think it bad idea then we stop, OK?"

"OK."

I'd never seen a sexier pout in my entire life. I knew I was on pretty safe ground if she was going to be happy to take the lawyer's word for it. I'd never dealt with one myself but plenty of friends knew the score. The general consensus was that the average lawyer would kill his own grandmother for a bit of extra fee income. The chances of one turning down a job were basically zero.

I was sufficiently confident of the outcome that I decided to broach the subject of what we might call the bar, assuming the lawyer gave his blessing. I'd seen this hippie type who carved incredible things out of old bits of wood, he sold his stuff from the pavement on Beach Road. He'd do a fantastic job.

I told Yim I really wanted to name the bar after my favourite team, or it's nickname at least.

"So what your team nickname?"

"Seagulls," I told her proudly.

"What seagull?" she asked.

I thought for a moment. "It's big, white bird with a huge beak and round body."

"Like many *farang*." Yim laughed, she was very pleased with her joke.

"Ha, ha, ha," I replied. When wit failed me, I generally resorted to sarcasm.

"Now that good name for bar."

"What? Ha, ha, ha? Are you serious?"

"For sure; in Thai Ha is number 5, so Ha, ha, ha is 555."

Suddenly it all clicked into place, all those posts on Pattaya-Dream where the guy thought he was being funny, they all had 555 at the bottom. It was the Thai equivalent of LOL... laugh out loud. I had to agree that 555 was a very good name for a bar. The bloke on the beach wouldn't even need a very big piece of wood.

Secrets

Paul asked me what I wanted, but if I told him he might not love me any more. It was not a chance I could afford to take.

He was kind to me and once he got his bar, maybe he would settle down a little bit. I did not understand why he thought owning a bar would make me happy. It was the life I wanted to escape. I saw the people who ran bars; they made money by getting Thai ladies to go with *farang* for money. Paul wanted me to be one of those people. They could not make good karma by doing such a thing. What sort of life would they have next?

Thai Kiss

Paul was not a butterfly, but he liked to party too much. Many nights, he wanted to go drinking, party like before and then have sex. He wanted things to stay the way they were when we first met, when I was a bar-girl and he was my customer. All that changed was that he paid me once a month by bank transfer instead of every day in cash. I could not tell him how I felt. If he left me I would have to go back to the bar and dance and go with *farang*. He thought I liked go-go bars because that is where we went with my friends when he first took me out from Kiss. I just told him I liked them so he would be happy and we could all get our lady drink commission. We only went to bars owned by the same people as Kiss, so we still got paid for drinks and ping-pong. I didn't want to drink in noisy bars any more, it was the life I wanted to leave behind. And I didn't always feel like having sex, it would have been nice if I could choose for a change, to fall asleep in front of a movie or with a book. Paul thought I wanted sex all the time, but that was the person he met in the bar, it was not the real me.

He said maybe I could bring Dao to live with us in Pattaya. I love my daughter more than anything or anyone but I swore this would never happen. I did not want her to see that place, to see what people did and know what her mother had to do to send money to my mama.

These are the things I could not tell him, because if I did he might not love me any more and then I would not be able to take care of my family.

One day, maybe I will be able to tell Paul I want to go back to Buriram, to live in my village and give my daughter the sort of life I had before the wave came to Khao Lak and everything changed. Maybe he will understand, maybe he will want to come too. For now I cannot tell him, because I don't know what he would do. I do not know when I can trust him, but until then I will have to keep my secrets.

I could not tell him that I did not want to run a bar. Nor did I tell him my other secrets. Their names were Pascal, Ralf, Oshi and Sonthi.

Paul did not know about the other men who sent me money and I was not going to tell them they should stop. One day a *farang* will say he loves a girl, but the next day he will love a different girl. Maybe Paul would be the same and if I told the others not to send me money and he left me I would have nothing. I could not take the risk.

Pascal was from Paris, he sent me twenty thousand baht every month so I would not have to work. He was very generous, because Ralf from Switzerland only sent me ten thousand, the same as Oshi from Japan. They should have been happy because they wanted me to stay away from the bars. If only one of them sent me money then that would be impossible, it was not enough to take care of my family. Instead, I could send money to my mama, my sister could go to school and I could save to buy some land in our village. Most important, I could take care of Dao.

I know telling these men I loved them was wrong, but as long as nobody found out then everyone would be happy. My sponsors thought I lived in my village and that I could not go back to Pattaya, because the memory of the life they saved me from was too painful. It is a bad lie but it was no worse than the lies they told me.

I never had to tell Sonthi I loved him. He never asked me if I was the only man in his life, he picked me up from a *farang's* hotel many times and he knew exactly what I did to make money. He did not want anything much from me, except sex occasionally and to be the devoted girlfriend when we saw his friends. I heard bad stories that he used girls for money and expected them to help him when he ran into debt but he did not do that to me. He drove a motorbike taxi, fought Muay Thai and worked security from time to time at a Walking Street nightclub. There was some talk he worked for a local mafia man too. People said Sonthi started by collecting money for an illegal lottery game but maybe he moved on and was involved in drugs. I did not ask and I did not want to know. I had many problems, I did not need any more.

Pattaya can be a frightening place for Thai ladies. If you have a man like Sonthi it is not so frightening. I gave him what he wanted in return for that. It was just another trade in a life that had so many. I also started to realise I never saw anyone say no to Sonthi. If he wanted something, he got it. I was not sad at the thought my relationship with him would end one day, just that it could only happen when he made the choice.

For the time being Sonthi was my security - the girls in the bar gave me respect, the motorbike riders treated me like a Queen and I knew if I got into trouble I could go to him for help. He was not like *farang* who do not want a girl to look at other men, he understood what I needed to do for work and he did not judge me for it. He told me he was really happy that I was living with Paul and that my days in Kiss bar were over. Either he cared about me and wanted me to have a better life or was tired of me and was happy for another man to take his place.

Two days after we finally agreed to buy the bar, Sonthi took me to dinner, I told Paul I was going to the cinema with Pan. Sonthi was fascinated by the *farang* and wanted to hear all about him and his plans for the bar.

Opening time

The lawyer had agreed that the bar was a sure-fire winner and he was delighted to help with the paperwork. Yim reluctantly signed the deeds, though she still thought it was a crazy idea. I'd heard all the warnings about her friends and family coming to get their noses in the trough but it never happened. If anything it was the opposite. They were eager to help and expected little or nothing in return. Puy introduced us to Daeng, her cousin who used to run a go-go bar in Patpong, Bangkok and we took him on straight away to handle the business side. Yim knew a couple of people who could give the inside a coat of paint and eight weeks after she signed the papers, we were ready to go. A couple of the girls who worked at Kiss were keen to join and by the time the balloons were going up for our opening party, we employed ten dancers. Yim became the *mamasan* and my job was to serve a few drinks, chat to the *farang* customers and watch over the bar area. The budget was a bit tight so one girl would serve drinks and do the cashier job. We reckoned if she got too busy that would be a good thing, we could probably afford to get someone else to help her out.

Thai Kiss

I asked Yim to stand back as I dramatically threw open the door. There were big comfortable chairs, plus a couple of sofas, a wide screen TV, a handy little kitchen area and this fantastic bath tub with a shower and Jacuzzi. Mind you, that was just the bar, the little flat where Yim and I'd be living was not nearly so fancy. The previous owner used that area as short time rooms for his customers. Like the girl but can't be bothered to take her back to the hotel? No problem, you can pop upstairs for a… massage. We had no choice, the project was more expensive than I anticipated and there was no cash left over for a separate place to live. There was enough money for six months or so, but if the bar wasn't paying its way by then it would be back to the drawing board, with my precious nest-egg all spent.

Yim started putting the finishing touches to the bar decorations.

"Yim, darling, are you alright? You look sad."

"Am OK *tirak*, I think too much."

"*Kit arai*… what you think?"

"I worry bar not good idea and you lose all money then not stay Thailand. Bad for you and bad for me too."

"Sweetheart, this is going to be fantastic, I promise. And whatever happens I stay with you. I love you."

Yim didn't reply, she turned and hurried back towards the toilets at the back of the bar.

"I go check, make sure ladies ready to dance."

I knew she was worried, afraid the bar might fail and that I'd leave her. Or worse, maybe the bar would fail and I'd want to stay, then she'd be stuck with a lovesick *farang* with no money. There was no budget for a DJ so we spent the day before loading ten hours of music onto my laptop and linking it all up to a cheap set of speakers.

It was eight o'clock, there was free food on the bar, the girls were ready, so I clicked play on the laptop and threw the doors open. There were four girls writhing on stage, wearing only bikini bottoms, high heels and their best Thai smiles, the others waited near the door to escort the customers to their tables. All our girls wore black bikinis, simply because we couldn't afford to buy them the uniforms that are so popular in other bars. Yim and I raised our glasses to toast the success of our new venture and sat back to await the stampede.

At ten past eight, four English guys wandered in and stayed for a whole hour. We sold twelve beers and the same number of lady drinks. The oldest of the group even bought a basket of ping-pong balls to throw to the girls. We were off to a flying start, I was in two minds as to whether I was hoping they'd offer to bar-fine the girls. We'd get five hundred for each girl, but the place would be deserted when the next lot of customers came in. Phil said it was the hardest part of the job.

"You need the girls to make it a successful bar, but until it succeeds the best girls won't want to work there."

Still, it was a pretty good start, we just needed to find a way of keeping the guys there, buying drinks. Soo was by far the most vivacious of the girls and she was doing her utmost. Most of the main street bars allow a bit of fooling around but draw the line at any explicit sex acts in their bars. There are quite a few exceptions of course and we were in no position to get too fussy with so few customers. Soo spent a few seconds wrestling with something in the lap of one of the English guys and then her right arm was moving smoothly up and down as though she was conducting an orchestra with only one instrument. In a way I guess that was exactly what she was doing. Her companion definitely wasn't complaining.

In the twenty minutes after the Englishmen arrived, two more customers arrived. They headed straight for the free food and ordered a draft beer each. These guys were balloon chasers... men who scoured the streets of Pattaya at night looking for a free party where they could eat for the price of one draft beer. If they were lucky someone might ring the bell and they'd get a free drink too.

Yim went over to check whether the first group wanted more drinks and I could see them shake their heads, a couple of the guys checked their watches and it looked like they were on their way. They'd been in the bar for exactly one hour. That's when I realised I'd seen them before, they were all regulars in Starbar. I put two and two together and realised Phil must have told them to come over, to give us some customers on opening night. I was a desperate man, about to lose our best prospects on our first night. I rang the bell.

"Sorry mate, great bar and thanks for the offer but we really have to go." It was the older guy.

The four men extricated themselves from the girls they were sitting with and headed for the door and I was left looking at twelve hopeful faces, Daeng shaking his head in disbelief and Yim staring at me with barely concealed contempt.

"What?" I pleaded.

"You ring bell, now you have to buy drink for everyone." Yim rolled her eyes and turned back towards the bar. She decided I was an idiot. Our ten go-go dancers and the two balloon chasers had a very different opinion, they thought I was a terrific guy. I tended to agree with Yim.

At no point during the course of our first evening did the customers outnumber the staff. It came pretty close around eleven p.m. Four gentlemen arrived who explained they didn't want a drink but were happy to pay a small fee just to watch the girls dance. I told Yim I thought no self-respecting go-go bar would allow that. She rolled her eyes again and took their money. One hundred baht each for thirty minutes and they turned their noses up at the free food.

Yim felt she had to explain the economics to me.

"First two men buy one beer, eat our food and then you buy them drink, we lose money. These men give us one hundred baht for do nothing. We make money. Understand?"

I stared at the floor like a naughty schoolboy and nodded.

The voyeurs had only five minutes of their allotted time left. It occurred to me we should offer them a discount for a second slot but I couldn't summon the courage to suggest it to Yim. She said I'd make some mistakes at the start but I guess she never imagined they'd all be on the first night.

My spirits lifted when I saw two very well dressed young Americans appear in the doorway. Close cropped hair, square jaws and impossibly straight, white teeth were the initial clues to nationality. The clincher was the buttoned-down collar shirts, done up all the way to the throat and laundered, immaculately pressed shorts. I'd spent months in Pattaya and I never saw anyone with ironed shorts until that moment. I nodded at Soo and Fon and gestured towards the door, these guys were going to be like lambs to the slaughter. As the girls approached, they hardly broke stride as they saw the guys had companions, two equally proper, if undeniably attractive young women. The four of them were a walking toothpaste commercial, with smiles that said they were never so happy to be anywhere as they were right at that moment. Soo and Fon were highly trained professionals. They made straight for the girls, knowing that was the only way the guys would be allowed to stick around. Bar-girl rule number one: fawn over the man when his woman is around and they'll be gone after one drink, make the woman feel special and he could be buying drinks all night. Or so they thought.

Oddly, they all made a little hand gesture as they crossed the threshold, it looked like the sign of the cross that my mum used to make every time I did something she thought might count against me in the afterlife. Still, four rich Americans, this had to be worth a few baht.

"Four cokes."

"With what?" I asked.

"Ice," said Yim, who'd taken their order.

"You're joking, no alcohol?"

"They trouble, we give them drink then tell them fuck off, OK?"

Now I was thinking Yim was losing it. Maybe we weren't going to make a lot of money but I couldn't see what harm this lot were going to do.

"They come save us, I see before. They come introduce us to Jesus. They tell us we do bad thing but we can come read bible with them and play table tennis and all our problem finish."

"Seriously? Bible-bashers here? What do they do?"

"They tell us we do bad thing when sleep with *farang*. Better if we work shop or factory and go church every day. They want we stop work and go learn about Jesus with them and play table tennis. They not say how we take care family if we work shop."

"So what you say when they tell you this."

"All girls say same; 'Yes, I know we do bad thing, maybe we need to find Jesus'."

"And they mean that?"

"No, not mean, but if we say this maybe they buy drink for us. Same horny *farang*, lady just say what customer want to hear."

"So you ever know a girl who went to their bible class?"

"My friend Pan go, she like very much."

"She liked bible classes?" I asked, trying to imagine the little ball of dynamite that was Pan, poring over the sacred book.

"No, she like table tennis."

I looked in the till, it was a depressing sight. Once we paid the staff, it was clear we'd be way down on the night. It was nearly midnight, the voyeurs had gone and my only customers were trying to convince my staff that almost any life was better than what they were doing. What was it about Christians that made them think they knew all the answers and that whenever they saw a brown face they were looking at some pagan savage? All the girls I met in Thailand were devout Buddhists, they might shag blokes for money but they took their faith seriously. Here they were, being lectured by followers of a guy, in whose name millions of people have been slaughtered over the centuries. They made me mad. As soon as they paid their bill, I was going to toss them into the street.

The Americans clearly felt they were making some progress. Watching them speak to the girls was bordering on the hilarious. It reminded me of a nun who taught me at school. She'd explain things with this terribly serious look on her face, as though I should be in no doubt that the flames of hell were waiting for me if I lost another pencil. When I said I understood and would never do it again, her face was wreathed in smiles. Another sinner had been saved and could be led towards the one true light. Her name was Sister Mary of Mercy and it was clearly ironic. The tools of her trade were chalk, rosary beads and a thin leather strap that she applied to the bare legs of any sinner she came across, with unconcealed glee. You have to assume the name Sister Mary of Mindless Fucking Cruelty was already spoken for when she took her vows.

Yim reluctantly took an order for another four cokes, only because the missionaries paid for drinks for four of the girls too. The bikini-clad temptresses were nodding, smiling and, for all the world it appeared they were captivated with what they were hearing. Each received a business card with a picture of a cross and that symbol that looks like a fish. My girls were seconds from conversion to another way.

Just then, the curtain across our entrance twitched and a familiar face appeared. It was the bus driver who dropped the Japanese tourists at Starbar the night I went back to find Sin. He appeared to have satisfied his curiosity and disappeared again. When the curtain moved a second time, eight Japanese gentleman, still in the sort of golf attire you only see in western TV satire, breezed into the bar. Four girls were sitting close to the door, neither on dance duty nor at our impromptu, unwanted Bible class. They fell on the new arrivals like a pack of tiny, perfectly formed wolves. The girls talking to the Americans rose as though they were one being, downed their drinks and each gave their customers a deep *wai*. As one they chorused "thank you for drink, see you next time." They rushed to the Japanese golfers to pick up any leftovers from their colleague's initial advance. The two remaining dancers threw themselves into as sensuous and provocative a routine as I'd ever seen. The men didn't stand a chance.

The looks on the Americans' faces were priceless. It was all going so well, then the devil played his trump card with a busload of horny golfers. They were left with half-finished Coca-Colas and four business cards, still sitting where the girls had left them. As they stumbled back into the street, there was no mistake as to the gesture. They were blessing themselves for all they were worth. Next stop; the hotel, for a long cold bath in holy water.

Yim returned from the party that was now in full flow in the corner of the room.

"Eight Singha, ten lady drink, two bottles JD Black Label and six coke."

I smiled at her.

"Layo, layo," she ordered. It was the Thai equivalent of "make it snappy, dumbass," but there was a hint of a smile at the corner of her mouth.

As I served the drinks, I realised that the bus driver who brought the men in was sitting at the corner of the bar.

"Drinks on me," I told him.

"Chang beer," he replied. "Puy and Phil say good luck for you."

Thai Kiss

CHAPTER THIRTEEN

Take off

Boo, our latest recruit, looked at me as though I'd lost my mind. I was only handing her a little plastic disc to attach to her skirt while she was working. I presented it as though it was an Olympic medal. To her it was no more than a numbered badge that allowed a *farang* in the corner of the bar to have her summoned to his side for a lady drink. To me it was a symbol of the success of 555. We'd been open only three weeks and the disc I handed her was number 20. There were twice as many dancers as on opening night and the cashier no longer served drinks. Our new full time barman slid a chilled Singha across the counter to me. He smiled and put his finger to his lips, he'd not be telling Yim how many I'd had. My job was simply to sit at the corner of the main counter, watch over anyone handling cash and try not to get too pissed. Quite frankly, that was the biggest challenge.

The Japanese group came back each night for a week, every girl was bar-fined at least a couple of times and word started to get around about Pattaya's latest go-go. The dancers' friends came to see if there were vacancies and we were popular with tourists and the ex-pat community alike. I joined the Pattaya-Dream forum a few days before my first trip to Thailand and they let me post adverts for the new bar. Customers showing one of their loyalty cards got a free shot with the first drink and a special price for draught beer. Yim knew a few of the motorbike taxi guys and they were doing all they could to bring customers through the door. We offered bottles of fuel to any driver who brought someone in. It occurred to me that a few of our more adventurous customers might have seen petrol as a great addition to our cocktail list, but they'd have to make do with tequila. One day, as I was handing over a fuel bottle to a particularly hot and thirsty looking driver, I realised how odd it must have looked.

"Want a cold one?" I asked him. He didn't see the joke.

Yim appeared to have relaxed a little and was obviously very proud as we counted the takings at the end of each night. Things were going much better than planned.

"They not look at me same before at bank," she told me. "Before they know I bar-girl and they look like my money dirty, they not want to touch. Now they think I important business lady and they treat me like I *HiSo*. But it still same money, same before, money from *farang* who want to buy lady." Yim shook her head as though the weight of the world was on her shoulders, then looked up at me as though I could find some words to make it all better.

"*Tirak*, you are important, if people are not good to you, they're just jealous. You're successful and soon you'll be rich. Your family will never have to worry about money again." I smiled and she covered her mouth and giggled behind her hand.

"I never hold so much money before."

I recalled saying those exact words not that long ago.

Yim put the takings for the night into an envelope. We'd take it to the bank in the morning.

As we got ready for bed, while Yim was showering yet again, I checked my phone. I scrolled quickly through the e-mail messages, but only one caught my eye. It was from Clare.

"Hi Paul, I hope you are well. I hear you are out East somewhere now. I bumped into your mum in the supermarket today. She is really proud of you, says you send her money every month. Sounds like you are doing really well. Well I'm back from Spain now, it didn't really work out with Simon. I'm still really sorry about what happened out there, I just went a bit crazy I suppose. Won't bore you with the detail here but it would be lovely to see you. Maybe we could catch up if you are over, or maybe I should save up and come and say hello. Let me know what you think, it would be really good to see you again.

Lots of love from Clare.

I pressed reply… then cancel… then delete.

The following night things started slowly, the bar was empty at eight fifteen and when the first customer arrived I was surprised to see that he was Thai, well Asian at least, I still couldn't always tell the difference. All that was certain was that he wasn't Japanese or Korean, I could always spot them. The man was immaculately dressed and while almost every customer was kitted out in designer label gear, this was the real thing, not copies bought at a tenth of the price from my own favourite stalls at Mike Shopping Mall.

I was often surprised when a Thai women said one of her own countrymen was handsome. They never looked that special, but I guess it's hard for a foreigner to tell. It's not very politically correct but they really did all look the same to me. It was like that with our new customer, he was tall, very slim and it looked like an expensive haircut. I suppose he was good looking, but he clearly thought he'd just stepped out of the movies. You sometimes caught the girls admiring themselves in the mirrors that lined the walls. I reckoned they were simply bored with dancing and didn't fancy catching the eye of any of the customers leering at them. This guy couldn't take his eyes off his own reflection. He finally decided his left profile was marginally better than his right and arranged himself accordingly.

The dancers were still doubling as waitresses until we were certain we could afford the extra staff, so Fon brought him a large whisky with coke. She was a little wary of the man, either his presence was intimidating, or she'd seen him before, or she was just not used to throwing herself at one of her own countrymen. If he was a westerner, she'd have been unzipping his trousers by that stage. I was watching it all with detached amusement, when I spotted Yim coming out of the toilet area where some of the girls were still getting changed. When she saw the man, the reaction was physical, as though she'd been slapped. Even so, she walked towards him slowly and calmly and brought her hands together in a *wai*. Her fingertips were a few millimetres above the level of the bridge of her nose, so this was clearly an important man. He gave her one of those smiles you see in the movies where one character knows he is holding all the cards and his opponent is simply working out how much they're going to lose.

Things had been going too well. I had the strangest feeling that was about to change.

Mongkut

Paul was on his usual stool at the corner of the bar counter, watching Fon and her customer. I would have to tell him not to stare, it makes people uncomfortable. Fon was certainly looking nervous and the man... the man was Thai and someone I recognised only too well. I should not have been surprised to see him, it was going to happen some time, for sure. I actually expected the police to come a little sooner. The shock was that it was Mongkut, the same man I saw in Kiss the night Cat cut me. I remembered how he looked at me, how I knew exactly what he wanted to do with me. As I crossed the bar, he gave me the same look again, I was starting to feel sick.

"Good evening sir, I hope this lady is taking care of you well. Can I get you another drink?"

"Aah, the lovely Yim, you have done so well since I saw you in Kiss. I wanted to get to know you better then, maybe I will have the chance now we meet again."

"I am pleased to offer you a drink on the house, and of course the ladies will make sure you have a good time."

He laughed. "Yes, of course, you are no longer a bar-girl, you are a successful business woman with a *farang* to take care of you."

"I own the bar."

"Then it's with you that I need to discuss a matter which I hope you will seriously consider."

"As you wish."

I knew already that no consideration was required, he would tell me the price to pay if I wanted 555 to stay open.

"You know the local police force is involved in many projects for the good of the community. I thought you might like to make a contribution."

"How much?"

"Twenty thousand baht."

"Every month?" I asked, trying my best to sound shocked.

"Every week, starting today."

I gasped, but in truth it was little more than I expected. A big dent in the bar profits but this was the way things worked in Thailand.

"Have the money ready when I get back."

The policeman grabbed Fon by the arm and pulled her towards the back of the bar.

"This lady can entertain me upstairs for a while. It really should be you, but we have a mutual friend. Taking you would be impolite on my part."

"But we have no rooms for that upstairs, it is my home."

"Excellent, then the sheets will be clean and the bed comfortable I'm sure."

Paul was moving across the bar to intervene but I got to him before he reached the policeman.

"Who the fuck is that? And what is he doing going to our room?"

"Police, his name Mongkut, I see before at Kiss. He come for money."

"What the fuck? He can't do that... can he?"

"Paul, I tell you before, this happen. I tell you but you not believe me. We pay or he make life impossible for us, for sure. One million per cent."

"How much."

"Twenty thousand."

"Every month?" Paul sounded shocked.

"Every week."

"Fuck."

I recognised the look in Mongkut's eyes as he dragged Fon up the stairs, it was like the Russian I had gone with all that time ago. I should have been used to it by now, but every time a girl left the bar with a customer I prayed for them. I prayed the man had *jai dee*, that he would remember we are human beings too and that he would give her what he promised.

Fon came back after thirty minutes, she looked shaken.

"He treat you OK?" I asked.

"I've had worse."

"Did he pay you?"

Fon shook her head and went to find a seat at the opposite end of the bar, as though she wanted to put as much distance as she could between her and the policeman.

Mongkut returned a few minutes later, he had taken his time, probably preening in front of the mirror to make sure he looked as handsome and smart as possible. He held out his hand and I gave him an envelope. I was certain he would quietly slip it into his pocket, the bar had filled up a little since he went upstairs, surely he wanted to avoid being seen taking money in public. Instead he slid the cash out and counted.

"It's one thousand short, please don't play games with me."

"I'll give it to Fon. You take money from me but not from my ladies. You go with them, you pay." My heart was in my mouth as I waited for him to react. It could have been a very stupid thing to have done.

Mongkut was weighing up his response. As he looked at me, I could see he was deciding whether he should teach me a lesson. If he grabbed my hand and dragged me upstairs I knew Paul would react, I also knew Mongkut carried a gun. I tried to look calm and poised but my heart was racing. Then he smiled very slowly.

"You are a brave woman. Out of respect for our mutual friend, the contents of the envelope will suffice for now. I will see you next week. I am looking forward to it already."

He allowed me a tiny victory, but made sure that I dreaded each visit. He also made me realise even more how much I relied on our mutual friend. He meant Sonthi for sure. I did not know another soul who had any standing with a powerful policeman. As long as I had Sonthi, Mongkut would leave me alone. If Sonthi chose not to protect me, I would certainly pay for my moment of defiance.

Invincibles

Yim was right, she warned me about the police. In return for a cash filled brown envelope once a week, they left us alone. Only three weeks before we opened, a story appeared on the front page of the Pattaya Daily News. A van-load of Immigration Police had raided a beer bar, the Australian owner was arrested for working without a permit and the staff were charged with prostitution offences. Invincibles was the fourth in a row of eight bars and the name suddenly seemed ironic. They all had foreign owners working behind the bar, the staff all sold sex to passing *farang*. In all probability, only one thing distinguished the Australian's establishment from its neighbours, it refused to make the required weekly contribution to the local police.

Yim was constantly reminding me that it was the way things worked in Thailand and we had to accept it. Business was really good since that first night and we had a growing reputation. Yim talked it through with Daeng and they agreed to put ten baht on the price of every drink. If we maintained the level of sales from the first few weeks, we could recover the money we paid the police and make a little bit on top. We were taking the pain but then passing it on. I started to feel like a proper businessman, even though I played no part in the decision. That's how big companies behave, the price of oil goes up and the petrol companies add a few pence to a gallon of fuel, your favourite footballer signs a big new contract and when you go to buy a shirt with his name on it, it's ten quid more than last year. We weren't paying the police, our customers were, that made me feel a little bit better about it all.

The only problem with the whole bribery and corruption thing is, you can't dig out the contract and check what's included and what isn't.

Until Mongkut's visit we were very careful to close the bar at exactly two a.m. That was the official closing time across Pattaya. Two days after he collected his first payment we decided to try our luck. At two-twenty, four very drunk, free spending Swedes were still in the bar. I could hear an argument in the street and opened the curtain just in time to see two policemen, dressed in standard issue mud brown uniforms, in a heated debate with the owner of another new bar across the road. The older officer clearly enjoyed the fruits of his job, the buttons on his shirt strained to contain a protruding gut. The younger policeman was immaculately turned out but was flapping around his older colleague like an excited puppy. Perhaps it was the first time he'd seen, at first hand, the fringe benefits that went with his basic pay. It was clear they were telling the bar owner he should be shut. The man eventually shrugged and began ushering the last remaining customers out into the street. The policemen weren't finished and the argument only ended when the bar owner reached into his pocket and produced a wad of notes. He counted off a few and handed them to the two officers. They turned and saw me watching, my instinct was to flee back to my barstool but I held my ground. The two officers smiled, doffed their caps in my direction and continued to walk down the road.

It was four a.m. before we closed the bar. The Swedes disappeared to their hotel, they couldn't choose between the six remaining girls, so they bar-fined all of them. They were the sort of customers we could do with every night. Yim and I retired to our upstairs room where we fell into bed and were both asleep within seconds.

Yim turned the early mornings into a military routine, no variation was permitted even when the bar was open a little later than usual. I finally swallowed my pride about the money we paid to Mongkut. Our profits were higher than before, even after his cut. Yim was quick to point out that once Mongkut realised that, he would almost certainly come back for more. Even so, the whole thing was a lot less damaging than I feared.

The alarm rang at ten and I rolled over, hoping Yim was in the mood to let her morning routine slide by half an hour or so. Actually we'd not made love for more than a week, so five minutes would probably have been ample but I was too slow and she was out and in the shower in seconds. Breakfast was always on the table at half past ten and thirty minutes after that I'd unlock the shutters and together we'd take the short walk to the bank to deposit our takings from the previous night. It was just like any other morning, at one minute past eleven I opened the internal door and then released the shutter from the inside. I nodded at the young Thai eating pineapple from a small plastic bag and turned to tell Yim we were ready to go. That was when he rushed me from behind, it wasn't much more than a really hard shove but I wasn't expecting it and landed face down. As I tried to get up, the man pulled a bandana up over his face and another identically disguised Thai was suddenly standing right next to him. A gentle push with the second man's foot was enough to send me flying again.

Yim was by the bar, I'd expected her to scream but she just looked dazed. Both men were holding knives and I was in no doubt they were willing to use them.

"Money *farang*, now. All you got."

"We have no money here. The bar's closed."

"You go bank every day, eleven o'clock. Today same same. Money now."

"We give money to manager last night. No money here."

The taller of the two men advanced on Yim and pulled her towards him by her hair. This time she screamed. The man spun her round and was standing behind her, one hand holding a knife to the side of her face, the other cupping and squeezing her left breast.

"Money now *farang*, or we fuck your girlfriend and you watch. And then..." He slid his finger along the blade of the knife.

I reached for the pocket of my cargo shorts and pulled out the envelope, then slid it across the floor. The taller man almost looked disappointed, he was hoping we'd resist, but they took the cash and ran. A motorbike started up outside the door and the machine raced down the soi. I scrambled to my feet and stumbled over to where Yim was standing, trembling.

"We have to call Mongkut, this is not supposed to happen. What the fuck are we paying all that money for?" I said, pulling her towards me so her head rested against my shoulder.

"You can try but he not care, I sure."

"You think maybe he did this?"

"No, but he not care."

"We paid so this sort of thing wouldn't happen. How can he not care?"

"Paul, you not understand. We pay so police leave us alone, we not pay to stop bad thing. These men mafia, they come back again for sure, then we have to pay them too."

"Fuck that."

I called Mongkut and screamed at him down the phone.

"What are we paying you for? Find these assholes and make sure something like this doesn't happen again."

"*Khun* Paul, you need to understand our arrangement. If your bar does not comply with local law in every respect, I can overlook that. If you attract the wrong type of customer, then that is your problem. I hope I make myself clear."

I thought I heard him call me *kwai*... stupid buffalo, as he hung up on me. We were on our own for certain.

Daeng, the bar manager, arrived at midday and came up with a few ideas to improve security. We agreed to clear the till at regular intervals during the evening and have the money taken to Daeng's room. He'd do the bank deposit the following day. If we were robbed again in the morning, our losses would be limited. Yim made a phone call and later that afternoon Noom, a young Thai, arrived to be our new security guard. Noom looked as though the best he could do if there was trouble, would be to hold my coat while I waded in and got beaten to death. At a pinch he was about five feet two but he walked with a slight stoop, which made him look even shorter. His face was thin and drawn and his habit of looking around nervously and sniffing the air made him look like a cornered rat. Noom intimidated nobody. I was assured he was a very proficient Muay Thai boxer but that remained to be seen.

I found out just how good Noom was that same evening. The bar was busier than ever, Mongkut arrived around nine p.m. and, as Yim predicted, informed us he had some new projects that required financing. He was sure we'd like to contribute. The Inspector was clearly on a whistle-stop tour of his clients as he downed his drink in one and gave Fon no more than a wistful look as he headed for the door.

As I watched Mongkut leave, I noticed a group of Thai men drinking at a table in the corner of the bar. Yim apparently spotted them as soon as they came in. Locals didn't usually frequent go-go bars so all the girls were on edge. I was a little insulted that they didn't mention their concerns to me, they clearly thought I wasn't going to be much use if it turned nasty.

No sooner had I seen them than they appeared to be getting ready to leave. I saw Yim move across to the table to take their money. That was when the empty whisky bottle hit the floor.

Noom, the new security man leapt into action... he picked up his phone.

The man who dropped the bottle was speaking to Yim in very rapid Thai. Only when he stood up did I realise how powerful he looked. The leather vest with the skull motif was a bit of a tough guy cliché and I was pretty sure he was wearing cowboy boots, but his physique was the product of long hours in the gym or hard physical labour. The man was a trained fighter. I'd no idea what he was saying to Yim at the time, but she told me later that night.

He explained the service was poor and he wasn't going to pay, that we should expect this to happen a lot in the future as he was sure other people would also be disappointed. He said our girls should be very careful when they left each night as bad things happened to whores when they were out alone. He told her we should check our electrical wiring because bars like ours often burned down. He even said that sending our takings to the manager's room during the night was a very stupid idea because he too could easily be robbed on the way to the bank.

I wanted to intervene, but was frozen to the spot. I looked at Noom, our new security man, but he was sniffing the air and looking helplessly at his phone. Yim told me later, the man concluded by saying we could avoid all those issues, if we were willing to pay for his protection. He even quoted a price. We were making more money than I ever anticipated, but the additional haemorrhaging of cash would have killed the bar then and there. We'd be working our tails off and giving every penny to either the police or the local mafia.

Just when it looked like it was going to get ugly, it did. The door opened and three more Thais walked in. I thought they must be the reinforcements, but my security man was no longer staring at his phone. He stood, smiled and walked confidently towards the door, joining the three new arrivals. The four of them closed on the corner table and the fur started to fly. The fight was over in a couple of minutes. The final act had the tallest of the three new arrivals grinding the face of the leather vested ringleader into the broken glass on the floor. Noom removed a wallet from the man's pocket, carefully consulted the bill they declined to pay and removed exactly the right amount of cash before returning it. Then our customers were unceremoniously dumped into the street.

The tall, muscular Thai walked over to the bar and smiled. I held out my hand nervously and he shook it.

"Perhaps that is worth a beer?"

"Yes… yes of course, whatever you want. Thank you, how did you know to come?"

"Noom is my cousin, he phoned to say you have problem."

"I really appreciate it, I really don't know what we'd have done if you hadn't turned up. Will they be back?"

"I think they not come back. I know this man, I have problem with him before, but he know it is not a good thing to make me angry."

Yim crossed the bar and gave the man a respectful wai? She spoke in Thai and I assumed she was thanking him too.

"Would you help us again if we had problems?" I asked.

"Happy to help you, of course. Maybe you pay me something for my time but for a successful bar like this, I think it is small money."

I knew there had to be a catch, but when the man said how much he wanted, it sounded very reasonable compared with what we were already giving the police. In a way I was being blackmailed, but under the circumstances, I couldn't help but be grateful. If we could get back to selling drinks it was a very small price to pay. I looked at Yim and raised an eyebrow, she nodded without really catching my eye, she was still traumatised by what had happened.

"I guess we have a deal." I stretched out my hand to offer a handshake.

"My name is Paul, pleased to meet you."

"Please to meet you too *Khun* Paul, my name Sonthi."

Calm after the storm

I'd settled into the routine and I'm sure my weeks were much the same as any British pub landlord. Checking the stock, ordering beer and spirits, taking deliveries, organising the staff rota, sending the girls to the doctor and checking their blood test results, bribing the police and paying off the mafia. If I ever went back to the UK to run a country pub, I'd hit the ground running for sure. The problem was that I'd got used to it all, it was what Thailand did to you. Things that were unthinkable back in England were accepted with a shrug and a nod in Pattaya. Even with all of that going on, I could convince myself I was now a fine upstanding citizen because I was no longer dealing drugs. In my mind I'd gone straight, being a brothel owner who bribes the police didn't seem odd in the least.

I was still worried about Yim, she'd never been keen on the bar idea and I was about to drag her in a little deeper.

"*Tirak*, I think we should buy a house."

I had her total attention.

"Paul, you know it same as bar, you cannot buy, you *farang*."

"I know darling, we put house in your name. Phil thinks we can even borrow some money now because 555 making good profit. We could get something really nice."

"Who live above bar?" she asked warily.

"Nobody darling, maybe we have rooms for ladies and customers."

I convinced myself that sounded more elegant than calling them short time rooms. Yim was biting her bottom lip. She still hadn't come to terms with what we were doing and I was making it worse.

"Yim darling, if we want a really nice house then we have to earn as much money as we can. This makes a lot of sense."

"I look for house, you make rooms with Daeng. Not up to me."

She agreed, a little reluctantly, but I'd expected days of argument. Maybe she was finally coming round to the fact we were making a very good living. Whatever way she looked at it, it was a huge step up from dancing in a go-go and going home with anyone who picked you off the stage. I didn't mention to her it was Sonthi who made the suggestion. He stopped by every night to make sure there were no problems and we often had a brief chat. He'd raised his fee a little since we first made the agreement but it was well worth the money. There'd been no serious trouble since that night he turned up following Noom's phone call. I often thought how lucky we'd been that he was close by when all the trouble started.

As Sonthi arrived, I was almost grateful Yim had taken the rest of the evening off. She said she was having dinner with an old friend. I was careful never to play the jealous boyfriend so I didn't ask for details. Yim was clearly intimidated by Sonthi, not surprising given how easily he dispatched the three thugs that night. She never made eye contact with him and, as far as I could see, went to great lengths to avoid him when he came to the bar. I reckoned he was what we English call a "man's man". I was sure lots of single women would go for him, but he seemed a lot more comfortable drinking with the guys. Anyway, I was really glad to have him around, he gave everyone that feeling he was looking out for them.

It was irritating that he never offered to pay for the drinks he ordered at 555. We always put a wooden cup in front of him and the girls dropped the bill into it every time he ordered something. But as he left each night he made a point of saying thanks, then he simply pushed the cup in my direction. Tonight Sonthi was ordering Black Label whisky and had a friend in tow. It might be an expensive night.

"This man is my partner, *Khun* Paul. Meet Sunan."

"Hi Sunan, nice to meet you."

The man nodded, I was trying to remember if I should be insulted because he didn't *wai*.

"Sunan saved me once from the boys in brown. We had some special packages… if you know what I mean." The men raised their glasses in a toast to one another. Yim once dragged me to see a movie called Brokeback Mountain, about two cowboys who spent way too much time together. It was all flooding back as I watched the Thais' mutual admiration society. The wooden bin was filling up as Pan, Yim's best friend and our latest recruit, bounced up to the bar. She and Sunan were clearly well acquainted. A lady drink was ordered, the chit went into the cup and the happy couple went off to find a quiet corner of the bar.

"He is a good man," said Sonthi. "We are partners. When I'm not around, you can call him. He will take care of any problem you have."

The sight of the rapidly filling bin was driving me nuts and Sonthi's admiration for his friend was making me feel a bit queasy.

"Sonthi, I need to check the stock in the cellar. I reckon we're running short of Black Label." He didn't take the hint.

"No problem *Khun* Paul, Sunan and me will be here."

I grabbed a Singha beer from the fridge, picked up a copy of the daily paper and headed for the chair in the corner of the stock room.

Thai Kiss

CHAPTER FOURTEEN

Visitors from abroad

Sonthi had given me a knowing wink as I walked out of the bar the night before. I had arranged to have dinner with Nook, the *mamasan* from Kiss; we were still friends from my time as a dancer. Had I not left, I could barely imagine what might have happened when the Frenchman turned up at 555. I was so close to seeing it all slip away.

"Who is this Sunan?" I asked.

"He works for Sonthi," Pan replied.

Pan came to work at 555 two months earlier. I was paying her more money than she earned in Kiss but Paul did not know that. I really needed my friend to be close to me.

"They are best friends now and he is a very sexy man," Pan continued with a smile. She just thought it was an exciting story, she had no idea how close my life was to collapsing around me.

"Have you had sex with him?"

"Of course, that's why he told me the story."

"How do they know each other?"

"Sunan was buying some *yaba* from Sonthi when the police arrived. He managed to get away but they pinned Sonthi to the ground, they were going to arrest him. Apparently Sonthi knows a policeman, but this all happened in the next district so that was no use. One of the officers went to call for help and Sunan came back and hit the other one with a bottle. Sonthi got away and he and Sunan are now best friends. They are partners."

"So what happened last night?"

"Well, your customer Pascal arrived drunk. He was really angry, he had looked for you all over Pattaya. He said he sent you money for two years but had not seen you for many months. He said you sent him e-mails every week right up until he told you he was coming to see you again."

"Yes, then I told him I was going to Australia and he shouldn't send me money anymore. So how did he know where to come looking for me?"

"He went to Kiss and someone told him you had a *farang* boyfriend and owned a bar."

"Oh my Buddha. Why did no one call to warn me?"

"I telephoned all our old friends in Kiss and nobody will admit they told him. Dah says she remembers seeing him, but she has no idea who said that to him."

"I don't understand, why would someone want to make life difficult for me?"

"Yim, you make many ladies jealous. You are very beautiful and you always had many customers, now you are a successful businesswoman. That is a life every Thai lady wants."

I looked at Pan and felt a little guilty. She was probably right, many ladies did want this life but I hated it. I wanted to be away from the bars, away from *farang* who thought I would do anything for a few baht.

"I could never hurt another Thai lady like that," I told her. "So Paul was definitely not in the bar when this happened?"

"For sure, he was talking to Sonthi for a while then he went to sit in that chair of his in the stock room. You know, where he goes when he is angry with everyone."

"So what are you saying about me?"

I nearly fainted when I heard Paul's voice, I thought he was still in the shower.

"Pan and I talk about the sexiest *farang* in Pattaya. You in top one hundred for sure," I said, trying to smile.

"Cheeky girl," he said, then moved to the other corner of the bar, where he normally sat to read the newspaper.

"Don't say my boyfriend's name again, or the Frenchman's," I told Pan.

She nodded.

"So why did he leave with Sunan? And how do I stop him from coming back?"

"Sunan was drinking with me while ...you know who, was shouting at us. I had to tell Sunan he was an old customer of yours."

"Then?"

"Sunan went over to him with a beer in his hand. He said a few words, I don't know what, but Pasc... the French guy calmed down a bit. Sunan did a lot of talking and... the other one... sat there and nodded. Then they walked out of the bar together."

"I have to talk to Sunan, maybe he can get the guy to stay away."

I heard Paul's voice and thought he was talking to himself, but he gestured to me to come.

"Yim, look at this. How can they put this horror show on the front page of a daily paper? These pictures are disgusting, they'd never be allowed to get away with that in England."

It was terrible but many newspapers do the same, if a body is found, a girl has been attacked or there is a bad traffic accident, they take a picture and print it on their front page. Sometimes they do something so you can't quite see the face but most times they don't care too much. This one was taken from a distance but you could still see it was a man lying on a concrete floor and there was lots of blood.

"Paul, you know they do this all the time."

"I know, but it's too much. Poor bastard chucked himself from a hotel balcony, they should show more respect. I hate the way they do this too."

"Do what?"

"The way they print the guys details straight away, his family could read it on the internet before they've been told properly. It's just wrong."

"*Tirak*, Thai people don't think about death the same way as *farang*, that's all."

"I guess so, but his family back in Paris probably thinks he's in bloody Hong Kong on business ... and then poor old Mrs Renand sees her Pascal splashed all over a Pattaya pavement... are you OK *tirak*? You look ill."

"Go toilet, I come back."

I felt ashamed. A little bit of me was glad I did not have to worry about Pascal again, but he was a good man; he did not deserve this. And I was scared, Sonthi had promised to protect me but there was no limit to what he and his friends would do. They did not use violence because they had to, but because they enjoyed it. Pascal was fifty-five years old, I think he would not have had a fight since he was a little boy. If Sunan had just told him to stay away... I don't know but surely they did not have to kill him. I splashed some water on my face and went back into the bar. Paul was still reading the same story.

"It's an odd one for sure. Normally, it's the ex-pats who kill themselves, but this bloke had only been in town for two days apparently. I guess he had a fight with his girlfriend, maybe he got ripped off or something. Makes me realise how lucky I am *tirak*. I guess not everyone can meet a girl like you."

Yaba

I told Sonthi about the business I had with Tommy back in Brighton. He was pretty impressed, although I guess I may have embellished it a bit here and there. I was pretty sure Sonthi was a supplier, he reminded me of William, our London contact. It was on one of his nightly visits that he made the offer.

"Paul, you can make a lot of money and no risk. There is no rival gang and the police will not trouble you. I make sure people know this is where to come. You make thirty per cent of price of every pill you sell."

"What about Mongkut, he's in here all the time?"

Sonthi smiled and entwined his forefingers so they looked like links in a chain. The policeman was clearly in on the deal. When did he ever have time to catch any criminals?

"Yeah mate, it's really interesting. Let me think about it, let me talk to Yim, she'd have to be onside and all that."

Sonthi gave me a strange look, I really don't think he got the bit about me talking to Yim. I guess Thai men don't worry too much about what their girlfriends think. He was obviously irritated that I didn't jump at the chance, but I wasn't at all sure I wanted to get back into dealing. Things were going great as they were, why would I do anything to fuck it all up? And I was sure that Yim wouldn't go for it. I'd pushed her far enough with the bar and then the short time rooms upstairs. They'd gone really well, a lot of the girls got one customer short time in the early evening and then another to take them home at the end of the night. We were charging two bar-fines and the girls were making a fortune. Everyone came out a winner.

"OK Paul, you think, but not too long. I give you special price, maybe next week price not so good."

"Yeah right… of course. I'll get back to you."

I wasn't paying much attention. There was this *farang* standing right in front of me and it looked an awful lot like Marco, the right-hand man to Terry Connor, Brighton's number one gangster. I remembered him as younger, fitter and a good deal more intimidating. The trademark blond ponytail was still there but his face was puffy, like he spent a lot of time drinking. He always wore skin tight t-shirts to show off his well toned abs and biceps, now they did no more than accentuate a spreading waistline. Something had changed in his life. I'd always assumed it was Marco who'd killed Tommy.

"Well fuck me gently with a crowbar … Paul Murphy isn't it? What the bloody hell are you doing here?"

Either he really was surprised to see me or he was a seriously good actor.

"Sorry about your mate Tommy, crying shame what happened to him."

"This is my bar, I own it with my girlfriend."

I nodded towards Yim. Still feeling a little shell-shocked, I was kicking myself already. I shouldn't have told him anything about myself until I knew what he was doing in Pattaya.

"Wow, you really are punching above your weight mate, that is one fucking awesome chick."

I wanted to reach across the bar and rip his throat out. I was certain he'd been involved in Tommy's death, now he was eying Yim as though she was a piece of meat.

"What are you doing here Marco, did Connor send you?"

"Connor?" Marco looked genuinely surprised, I was starting to believe it was all a coincidence. "Connor's in no position to send anyone anywhere; he can't even tie his own shoelaces… he even needs someone to wipe his arse when he takes a crap."

"You messing with me? What the fuck happened?"

"I can't believe you didn't hear about it. It was big news in England. His Bentley turned up on Beachy Head. He was sitting in the driver's seat with a bullet lodged in his brain. That chauffeur of his, Dmitri, was nowhere to be seen. They called it an attempted suicide, but it was a hit for sure. But the old bastard wouldn't die, he's a fucking vegetable now and I don't have a job any more."

"A hit that looked like something else huh?" I stared Marco straight in the eyes. He shifted a bit in his seat and looked at his beer as though it was the most interesting thing in the world. If I was ever in any doubt about what happened to Tommy, I had my confirmation.

Soo and Fon passed the bar and I called them over.

"Ladies, this is Marco, he is a very special friend from England, you make sure he has a good time. And it's all on the house. You been to Thailand before Marco?"

"Course I have mate, I know how it all works but thanks for that, you're a real gent."

Soo led Marco to a corner table, I had a very quick word with Fon and then went back to Sonthi who was still sitting at the bar.

Exactly twenty minutes later, as instructed, Soo opened the door to the larger of the two short time rooms and stepped back to let Fon and Marco go in first. It was a calculated gamble, I couldn't be certain he'd come upstairs with them, but most men found it difficult to say no to those two when they had to pay. Marco had obviously done the bar scene before and was coming back for more, there was no way he could turn down a free threesome. As Marco entered, Sonthi grabbed him by the neck, banged his head against the wall and threw him across the room. Marco was lying on the floor, as the girls closed the door on their way back downstairs.

I dropped onto one knee, my forearm resting on the other.

"What did you do to Tommy?"

"Nothing, I swear."

I stepped back and Sonthi moved forward. Marco took one look at the Thai and screamed.

"No! Don't. I'll tell you everything."

"So tell."

"It was an accident. Danny and me, we were putting him straight, just telling him the score. We told him we knew where he lived and we might pop round and pay that pretty little girlfriend of his a visit if he didn't move along." He paused, realising that was probably not the smartest thing to have said. "It was all talk we were just trying to scare him a bit, we'd never have done his girlfriend. We said he could start dealing somewhere else. All he had to do was stay off our territory."

"So how did he end up under the pier?" I asked, as calmly as I could.

Marco was eying Sonthi anxiously.

"We were being really nice to the guy, but he told us to fuck off, so Danny gave him a slap and the stupid bastard decided to run. He went off down the promenade like a bloody greyhound, so we went after him."

I could picture it, Tommy would do anything to avoid a fight.

"He went about fifty yards, then he saw Stevie coming the other way, so he turned and ran onto the pier. By the time we caught up with him he was going absolutely mental, he looked terrified."

"Of course he was fucking terrified, he hated the pier, he was afraid of the water."

I wanted to take a swing at Marco myself. Sonthi read my mind and gave the little weasel a sharp punch to the ribs, then stepped back and pulled a flick knife from his pocket. He opened the blade and inspected it like a surgeon checking his instruments. Marco looked as though he was going to cry. Then Sonthi nonchalantly started to clean his fingernails with the tip of the knife.

"Then you killed him?"

"No, I swear, he ran at us and Stevie gave him another slap. It really wasn't any more than that, but Tommy lost his balance and his head hit one of those benches. Dead as a door-nail before he hit the floor I reckon."

Marco realised he sounded a little too matter of fact about my best friend's death. "What I mean is… that he didn't suffer, he just went out like a light."

"So how did he end up in the sea, and what about the whisky." I was amazed at how calm I'd become.

"We panicked a bit. Stevie reckoned we couldn't leave him there. He thought it was obvious that there'd been a fight. Nobody was thinking very clearly. Danny had a half full bottle of Scotch with him, so we tucked it into Tommy's coat and then

Thai Kiss

slipped him over the side. The newspapers said he was probably pissed and just fell in and the coppers bought it too."

"So Connor never ordered him to be killed?"

"No never, he only told us to scare him a bit."

"But you killed him?"

"It wasn't me, I swear, it was Stevie, I never touched your mate. I'd never do a thing like that."

"You want I kill him now?" Sonthi sounded like he was suggesting that he pop out to put the kettle on. A dark wet stain spread across Marco's shorts.

I pulled out my iPhone and took a photo of him trying to cover his embarrassment.

"Sonthi knows most of the bar owners and all of the taxi drivers in Pattaya. He's going to pass this picture round. If one of them sees you, he'll phone Sonthi who'll come and track you down. Best you get out of town… now. Kao jai mai… do you understand?"

Marco's head was nodding wildly, his eyes were wide and bulging. He clearly thought this was the best idea he'd ever heard.

"Your wallet?" I asked calmly. Marco handed over a billfold that looked like it had about twenty thousand baht. I took the money.

"The beer and the girls, that was all free, but Sonthi's time doesn't come cheap and you've made a terrible mess. This should cover it."

I handed Sonthi five thousand baht but as I went to put the rest of the money in my pocket, his palm was still outstretched. I gave him another five, one at a time till he folded them in half and withdrew his hand, then I turned back to Marco.

"Sonthi and I'll be coming down in about one minute. If you aren't out of the bar by then, I can't be responsible for what might happen."

Marco fled, it sounded like he fell down the last three or four steps but as we opened the door a few seconds later, he was gone.

Yim didn't arrive until nearly midnight and she wasn't too happy to see me sitting with Sonthi, Soo and Fon. We were all a little drunk, the bottle of Jim Beam in front of us was nearly empty. I'd given each girl one thousand baht for their part in what we'd done to Marco and I was feeling on top of the world. I couldn't tell Yim what had happened, she had enough to worry about recently, she'd simply have to accept I was getting pissed with the staff. I'd gone a little way towards settling the score for Tommy and the bloke who shot Connor had done the rest.

"*Khun* Paul," Sonthi said, draining the last few drops from his glass, "You like power, little bit. But for power you need money, you need to take my offer. We work well together, I think."

"We certainly do. I need you to give me a day or two."

I raised my glass and my three drinking buddies did the same.

"*Chok dee kap,*" we said in unison.

This was starting to feel really good.

Expanding the Empire

I wasn't going to be able to fend off Sonthi for long, he was pushing me really hard. He even suggested that if I wasn't willing to sell his drugs he would have to try to find another bar owner. They might want him to provide the sort of protection he offered 555 and he didn't have the resources to cover both bars, unless I paid a lot more money. At first I thought he just meant I'd have to find someone else, a shame but not the end of the world. As Sonthi got more forceful, I started to realise that it was a threat. I had to deal drugs or he'd start to put the squeeze on us in exactly the same way as the first mafia man who came to call. He gave me a deadline of four weeks. I managed to keep him at bay because we bought the shophouse next door and were in the middle of completing an extension to the club. By the end of the month, 555 would be roughly twice as big as when we first bought it. Sonthi agreed we could get that up and running before he expected us to sell his merchandise, but it became a fait accompli. We were no longer talking about "if" we sold drugs, it was about "when."

Thai Kiss

I'd not seen Jamie Hill since the last time I went to watch the Albion play, a week or two before I did a runner for Thailand. He got in touch via Facebook and I convinced him he should bring his mates on a golf tour to Pattaya. I made all the arrangements, including picking them up from the airport and sorting out their reservations at the Siam Palace. It turned out the whole thing was being paid for by a guy called Callum Doherty. Jamie fancied himself a bit. He was always dressed like one of those guys in the menswear brochures. You could imagine him trying on a sweater by seeing how it looked draped across his shoulders and new sunglasses would have been propped on his forehead before he ever tried them over his eyes. Image was everything. It was why he called himself a business consultant. He was actually an accountant and Doherty was apparently his best client by far. I got a full briefing on the phone.

"Doherty is worth a fortune and he loves chucking his cash around."

"So he's a pretty smart guy then, I guess. Are you sure he's going to go for this sort of trip. It's a bit rough and ready."

I was feeling very nervous about hosting a genuinely successful businessman.

"Paul, he's as rough as a badger's arse mate. He made his money laying tarmac. Some say he was one of those blokes who knocked on old ladies' doors and offered to fix their driveway for fifty quid. Then he got them to sign a contract and when the job was done, he'd bill them for a couple of grand."

"You don't get rich doing that... do you?"

Jamie laughed. "No chance, he went up in the world. Now he does car parks, city centre stuff, airports, sports centres, anything like that. Don't think his marketing is any more sophisticated though. He finds the blokes who can sign the contracts and then plies them with drink, dinners, two grand a night hookers and as much Colombian marching powder as they can stick up their noses. He made a fortune off of local councils until they clamped down a bit. Still plenty of action if you can find the right councillor... or so I'm told."

I wasn't sure I needed any more crooks in my life but the extension was proving to be a bit more expensive than we thought and a high roller in the bar was precisely what we needed.

Doherty was everything Jamie promised and more. He had the build of a rugby prop forward, but I guessed he got it moving heavy machinery, he didn't look like the kind of guy who got the spandex on for a gym session. His hair was a slightly startling shade of red and crooked teeth and pock marked skin suggested he might not be first on every lady's dance card. Unless he paid them of course. Doherty spent three straight nights in the bar. One small section of the extension was finished and we gave him and his entourage exclusive access. Each night he chose eight girls to join him, Jamie and the other two guys in their private bar. The ladies of 555 were more than content to overlook their main customer's physical imperfections. Jamie tipped me off that he liked champagne and vodka, usually combined, and I needed to find someone who could provide the drugs. Our drinks supplier was thrilled with my initial order, which I was sure would last for the whole of Doherty's trip. I had to repeat it after he'd been with us one night. The man was a phenomenon.

We had to turn a blind eye to what went on in our hastily organised VIP area. Yim locked the connecting door and just sent in one waitress every half hour with champagne, vodka and condoms. When she didn't come out for twenty minutes we sent in another to take over serving duties. Sonthi stopped in around ten p.m. on the first evening and gave Doherty a large brown bag. As the Thai left the bar, he gave me a huge happy smile. He was tucking something into his pocket, I could only imagine he was struggling to find room in his jeans for all the baht notes Doherty handed him.

I was invited to join the party but it took only one look at Yim to realise that would have been a fatal error on my part. I left them to it and watched as the tab got bigger and bigger. There was a surge of panic as I tried to envisage what might happen if he refused to pay at the end of the trip. I was advancing a huge amount of credit. I had the presence of mind to make sure Jamie knew we didn't take credit cards, the men had to pay in cash. He smiled and said it wasn't a problem. My only comfort was that the men paid our girls each night and none of them could believe how much they were being given.

"I normally do five *farang* for same money," Boo declared... she was very happy to have switched to 555.

Even so, my heart was in my mouth as I presented the bill on their last day. They came back to the bar for a late lunch, their flight wasn't leaving until after eleven p.m. I handed the bill to Doherty who nonchalantly waved it away. My stomach lurched.

"Jamie, sort that for me. And give my new friend a very handsome tip, whatever you think is right, He's been an excellent host."

Jamie didn't reach into his pocket as I expected but opened a briefcase that was at his feet. The bill was equal to about three weeks of high season takings for the bar. Selling champagne and premium vodka instead of draught Chang makes one hell of a difference. Jamie carefully counted out the notes and stacked them in a neat pile right in front of me. Then he made another pile of exactly the same height and put that next to it. Finally he pushed all the cash over to me.

I thought it had to be a joke, or they misunderstood.

Doherty got up from his seat and walked the few steps to where Jamie and I sat. He looked at me intently.

"That's a one hundred per cent tip," I said, stating the obvious.

"Worth every penny, we had a blast. So how much did it cost you to set up a place like this?"

I told him.

"Could you do it again?"

"No problem," I replied, having never given the matter a second's thought.

"I want a bar like this, and you can be my partner. I'll pay you twice what you invested in this place, but I want a bar that's double the size. You and your girlfriend get to keep fifty per cent of the action. Jamie, give him the down payment, you get the rest when we have a signed contract and you've found the premises for the new bar."

Doherty shook my hand and then walked into the street leaving me to gape open mouthed at his back. Jamie was busily counting out more cash.

"Jamie, I can't do it mate. He'll be all over me if he's my partner. I don't know how to deal with a bloke like that."

"You won't be dealing with him, you'll be dealing with me. It's fun money for him, he wants to tell his mates he owns a huge bar in Thailand. He'll send a few clients over and all you have to do is give them the same experience we had for the last few days. Trust me, he won't give this another thought until he wants to come back here in a few months."

"You're sure?"

"Couldn't be more certain. I have only one question. Would it ever occur to you to try to rip him off?"

"You can't be serious, he'd kill me."

"Got it in one mate. He does stuff on a handshake, he'll barely look at the contract and I don't know a word of Thai. He'll pay me to check it all out, but I wouldn't know where to start. You play it straight by him and we're all going to do just fine. Try to screw with him and you're history."

"Jamie, I swear I'll play it straight, I'd be crazy not to."

"Good lad."

Thai Kiss

CHAPTER FIFTEEN

The promise

The money was stacked on the kitchen table when Yim returned. I guess I was hoping she'd be happy but there was that lingering thought that it might be more complicated than that.

"You crazy man, more bars, more police, more mafia. Now you have partner who carries millions of baht around in a bag. This go bad, it has to go bad. Then we have nothing, why you not happy with little bit. *Farang* always want more money, more power. You crazy man."

"So what do you want me to do, give it back?"

"He kill you if you do. Men like that not hear when you say no."

She was right in a way, the more successful we became, the more people there were who wanted to be part of it. Mongkut, Sonthi and now Doherty. Yim didn't know Sonthi was pushing me to sell drugs. The Doherty thing might keep him at bay for a bit. Instead of selling a few pills through 555, I hoped he'd agree just to sell to high-rolling punters in the new club. Better to keep our noses clean until that was up and running.

"So what do you want me to do?" I was pleading with her now.

"You have to give him his bar."

"You'll support me on this, we'll do it together?"

"If you make promise."

"Anything," I replied.

"We make bar for him, we get half. When it start make money, we sell everything, we go Buriram and live my village like proper family. You promise, then I help you."

No fucking chance, I've finally found something I'm good at. Something that gets me respect and money and you want me to live in a shit hole in the country. Not a chance. The thought couldn't have been clearer in my mind, there was no way I could give all of this up to be a peasant, swatting mosquitos half the day and night. The words, however, never made it out of my mouth.

When I actually spoke, my response was, shall we say, more conciliatory.

"Sure *tirak*, that's what we'll do. I promise."

We eyed each other warily. I had to break the ice.

"So what do we do with all this cash? It can't go in the bank in one go, can it? I'll ask Sonthi what we should do?"

"No!" Yim screamed. "You cannot tell him about this... he will want more money from us. Wait and we will tell him when we have a plan for the new bar."

I nodded, but I needed to tell Sonthi something. There had to be some incentive to get him to hold off on selling drugs through 555. I wouldn't tell him about the money yet, that's all.

Yim found an old 7-11 shopping bag and started to fill it with baht notes. I'd never seen so much cash in my life and it was mine... well, ours I suppose. She'd come around eventually, she always did, once she saw it all take shape. Then she'd realise this was the best way of taking care of her family. In Thailand, that's all that counts.

"I'm popping out."

Yim just grunted. I'd be back in an hour with a huge gold necklace, I'd seen her look at it once on the way to the bank. That sort of thing might make her realise things were going really well, we'd be daft to back out now. Jamie promised we'd be left alone and I'd get a half share in a great bar, for nothing.

Erin

I wanted to call the new bar something that made the connection with 555 clear. I toyed briefly with 666, but that was tempting fate. It was years since I'd been inside a church, but I'd seen plenty of movies where the innocent looking kid turns out to be the devil's spawn and none of them ended well. I only got one instruction from Doherty, that the bar must have an Irish connection. I vaguely remembered my mum telling me that Erin was an ancient, mystical name for Ireland and my partner was overjoyed. I told Sonthi about the new bar and he was happy to wait until it was up and running. Even he could see that a couple of nights a month selling drugs to super rich *farang* in a private room was smarter than peddling them to passersby across the bar at 555. At this point, I didn't want to get back into drugs but I had no choice. I told myself I was doing it to protect Yim and the investment we'd made.

Sonthi convinced me to use Mr Tan, a friend of his, to arrange the legal stuff. The lawyer helped find the new premises, just two sois away from 555. Giving him the contract work was the least I could do to say thank you and he was a lot cheaper than the man Phil had introduced us to when we bought the first bar. Mr Tan finalised the purchase of the new bar and wrote up the contract for me and Doherty to sign. It was all in English and as far as I could tell, it reflected everything I'd agreed with my new partner, but with a lot of legal bollocks thrown in to make it sound complicated. I guess that's how lawyers make their money.

I expected Doherty to reappear for the signing, but it was just Jamie who turned up at 555. I passed the two contracts across the bar. He didn't even bother to look at them, but slid a small attaché case across the counter. It contained the balance of what Doherty agreed to pay.

Soo, Fon and Boo were waiting a respectful distance from where the exchange took place but, as it was completed, they bounced forward and started to drag Jamie towards the new short time rooms we'd built above the now completed extension. The champagne was already chilling in a fridge in the corner of one room, some snacks were laid out and Sonthi had delivered another of his small brown packages. I made a note that the room was unavailable until morning and went to find Yim to give her the attaché case.

She was certainly coming round to my way of thinking. Yim worked really hard on the design of the new bar, she'd even started to line up new staff although opening date was months away. I knew she'd forgiven me, because I'd finally worked out the thing that was bugging her. I was no more than a boyfriend who might let her down at any time, it had probably happened to her before. There was one thing I could do to give her the feeling that I was in there for the long term. She'd told me about the way people in her village treated girls who worked the bars. Even the ones who brought home lots of dough didn't necessarily get any respect. Money helps but a nice Thai girl has a husband and a father for her kids. I knew she forgave me because I asked her to marry me… and she said yes.

The key

I liked Paul, I would be happy for him to be my husband and for him and me and Dao to be a family. There was only one problem, he was a man and men do not tell the truth. I could see in his eyes that he did not want to give up the bar, he did not want to move to Buriram. He thought a gold necklace might make me change my mind and be happy. He made a promise to leave Pattaya when the second bar was making a profit. I made a promise I would not steal from him. Everything was registered in my name, the house, the bars and the bank account. I could take it all, but I made a promise and I would not break my word. If we made the second bar a success and he refused to leave Pattaya, I would go to Buriram alone, I could not live this life any more. If he did not give me my share of the money, I would take it. There would be nothing he could do. Until he broke his promise, I would keep mine, which is why, when he asked me to marry him, I said yes.

Many *farang* liked to cuddle after sex, but it was not something I could do. I wanted to shower and be clean again. Then I could pretend it did not happen or that I was just waiting for Ghai to come to my bed. This time for sure, I could stay in the shower all day and not be clean. I knew I had to go back to the bedroom eventually.

"Why do you do this? You could pick anyone, why do you want me?"

"But you are the sexiest woman in all Pattaya, maybe all Thailand, why should I not want you?"

"You could have many girls who would be happy to go with you. Why do you make me do this? You have got everything you wanted. I have done everything you asked. I want you to find another lady."

Sonthi stretched out on the bed and started to laugh.

"Because I hate that arrogant little *farang* prick. He thinks he is a great businessman but we have steered him every step of the way. We made him a success, but he still thinks I am his servant, a hired thug to keep the nasty people away. I have given him many things he did not deserve and then I have to listen to him tell me how successful he is. I can only stomach hearing that shit if I can look him in the eye and know I can have his beloved whore whenever I want. If he was half a man he would have guessed what was going on."

"Paul has *jai dee*, he is a good man. It would never occur to him that you would arrange a robbery and set up a fight in the bar."

"Has he never seen a Muay Thai fight before? That scene in the bar was like your daughter's school play and he fell for it. Nathon made me buy him a new leather vest and he is still complaining about how I scratched his face on the floor. I was sure your man would realise after that fiasco, instead he just told me how lucky it was that I was nearby." Sonthi could barely contain himself.

"I cannot do this any more."

"You want to give all this up? That beautiful new house, all the money you are earning from the bar. Because if Paul knew about Ralf and Oshi and where you were really going when you said your mother was sick, I don't think he would let you stick around."

"I own the bar and the house and I have not seen those men for months."

"Sure, they haven't come but you still take their cash, don't you? And remember that French guy? Things didn't turn out too well for him did they? Yes, you own the house and the bar, but you know how easy it is to lose these things if you make enemies of the wrong people."

I knew only too well.

"But Paul and I are getting married. What will happen after that?"

"Same as before. You run the bars, and you do as I say. I will keep your secrets and you will keep mine, and when I call you, you will come running. Understand?"

Sonthi jumped out of bed and made for the shower. I had been dismissed, I was not expected to be in the room when he came back. He did not phone very often, maybe less than once a week, but when he did I was expected to be at his beck and call.

When I arrived at his room that day, he was looking at two handwritten notebooks which he then locked in a drawer. Sonthi was usually very careful about such things, but I saw him tuck the key into the pocket of his jeans. I could hear the shower running and his jeans were carefully folded over the back of a chair. It took a couple of minutes to open the drawer and check the notebooks. The first contained a list of what might be sales of something. Every entry had a name, a date, a place and two numbers - quantity and price perhaps. At the end of each month the prices were totalled and another number was written in the book. It was always fifteen per cent of the total. The other book had a similar list but there was no calculation at the end of each month. I heard the shower being switched off and threw the books back into the drawer. I'd only just got the key back into his pocket when Sonthi emerged from the bathroom.

A rookie error

I promised to drive Yim back to Isaan myself. She needed a couple of days of preparation for our big day and Phil was already in Buriram with Puy. They were our guests of honour and while the ladies planned the wedding, the men would go and play golf. I think Phil was humouring me, he wasn't much of a sportsman but agreed to play a couple of rounds. To be honest, part of the reason I was so enthusiastic to act as chauffeur was that I was desperate to drive my new SUV. It was the first car I'd ever owned, well Yim owned it really but that was basically the same thing. Sonthi arranged for a friend of his to paint the 555 logo on the side, with our web address and phone number. Yim was furious.

"You paint big sign for go-go bar on car and then we go see my family."

"I'm really sorry, I didn't think."

"*Farang*, never think, not with head for sure." She turned on her heel and marched back into the bar, slamming the door with more force than I thought she had in her.

I wasn't happy about being called a *farang*, and I knew what she was getting at with the rest of it. All the girls came out with the line at some stage, "*farang* only think with their dick." Now, I was suddenly just one of them. I followed her inside. She was sitting at the bar with her back to me, her shoulders were rising and falling as though she'd run a race. Her fists were clenched. She was probably imagining what it would be like if her delicate little hands were round my throat.

"*Tirak*, I am so sorry."

"I not want you to be sorry," she said, turning to face me.

"No?" I said, hoping the ice was about to thaw.

"I want you not be stupid *farang*." That word again.

"I know it was a mistake. I can get Sonthi to take it off."

"Sonthi did this?"

"Yeah, it was... kind of... his idea."

There was a little growl from her throat, it would have been quite sexy if I didn't know she wanted to kill both of us right there and then.

I picked up the phone, Sonthi was on speed dial. It would cost a few thousand baht but he was happy to help.

The *farang*

Most of the time, I think everything will be alright. Pan tells me all the time I have everything a Thai lady could want. I have a business, I have money, I can take care of my family, no problem. I also have a *farang* who loves me. My friends tell me stories of *farang* who marry a Thai lady but they still butterfly with any pretty face they see. Some even take ladies from the bar they own together. They see Thai men do the same to their women so they think it is OK. Why is that the only part of my culture *farang* can understand? They see how Thai men behave so they copy. They do not try to understand about our family, our religion or the things we have to do to make sure a family has respect in its village. I tried to explain to Paul the arrangements for our wedding but he was not interested. He seemed disappointed it would not be like in England.

"I'll never remember all that," he told me. "You'll have to prompt me as we go along."

So on my wedding day, my job would be to make sure my *farang* husband did not make a fool of himself, of me and of my family. Maybe that would be my life from now on, but I remembered Pan's words. I had money, I could take care of my family, what more should a Thai woman want. The problem was that I was soon to be married to a man who could never really understand me, or my family.

I had many things to do before we left for Buriram, I picked up my phone and called Sonthi.

CHAPTER SIXTEEN

You gave me your word

Jamie sounded apologetic on the phone but I suspected he knew it would turn out that way.

"No he's not changed his mind, I swear. He's just really excited about the project."

I was fuming, I practically ripped the phone cable out of the wall in frustration. "You said he wouldn't get involved, you said I only had to deal with you. You gave me your word. Now he wants to come and check over everything. Doesn't sound very hands off to me."

"He's in Thailand anyway, we're doing something in Bangkok, he thought it would be polite to stop by and see how things are going." Jamie was suddenly in his stride, he almost sounded convincing.

"So it's a social visit. All I have to do is give him a quick tour, lay on a few of the girls and get Sonthi to deliver another brown bag. That's it?"

"That'd be great, he might have a few questions but it will be fine."

"Questions?"

"Yeah, staff levels, stock, pay rates, marketing plans all the usual stuff. And he'll want to check out the guys who are doing the refit."

"Fuck you Jamie, you promised there'd be none of this. We don't run 555 like that, it's all seat of the pants stuff, I don't know how to deal with a guy like him."

"Well you're going to have to learn. You can't take his money and expect him to walk away."

"That's what you told me he'd do, you lying shit."

"No call for that Paul and no point in arguing, he will be there next Tuesday. I'm coming too. You'd better be ready for us."

"Tuesday, no fucking way. I'm getting married on Friday and I'm out of town from tomorrow."

"It's in the diary Paul, live with it."

The next sound I heard was dial tone.

There was nothing I could do, I didn't even know how to prepare for a meeting like that. I spoke to Daeng and told him what Jamie had said. He nodded like it was what he'd expected to be asked all along. Maybe the meeting wasn't going to be so bad after all. I wasn't happy that Doherty wanted to be so involved but it looked like we might be able to fend him off for a while anyway. I'd worry about the long term implications when I got back from Buriram.

The only other preparation I could make was to call Sonthi and tell him there was an important meeting the following week. Doherty would like some of that cake he brought over last time. Sonthi laughed.

I was wondering whether we really needed to use this schoolboy code instead of simply saying what we meant. Sonthi seemed to like it, so I played along.

The wedding planner

Clare and I had talked about weddings a few times, not our own of course, that was never on the agenda. I did have a pretty good idea of how it should all work though, the English version at least. It would all start about a week before the big day, the groom and his mates head off to Bournemouth, Amsterdam or Prague depending on how much money they could scrape together. There'd be beer, tequila, lap dancing and possibly even a brothel. The latter was generally considered to be a bad idea if the bride's brother or, God forbid; father, had tagged along. The purpose of the exercise was to humiliate the groom in such a way that he'd spend his entire wedding day in mortal fear the best man would get pissed and reveal all during his speech. The last stag weekend I attended involved stripping the man of the hour naked and tying him to a lamppost on Brighton seafront. On that occasion we couldn't even raise the funds for a trip to Bournemouth. The doctor diagnosed only a mild case of hypothermia. So Doug was passed fit for his wedding and told his beach honeymoon to Ibiza wouldn't be a problem… as long as he stayed out of direct sunlight.

Thai Kiss

On the day itself, there'd be a posh lunch for a few VIP guests followed by a disco for everyone you could think of who might buy you a decent wedding present. Costs could be kept in check by organising a booze cruise to France to stock up on cheap alcohol for the reception. That was also, of course, another excuse to get pissed. Extra points could be earned by any of the groom's friends who got to shag a bridesmaid. When I explained this part of working class culture to my bride-to-be, I was pretty sure she'd changed her mind about the whole thing. I realised my mistake and asked how a Thai ceremony might differ from what I described. The contrast was indeed stark.

I'd read a bit of history and liked the idea that, in days gone by, the bride's family had to come up with a decent financial incentive for the groom to take her off their hands. It was a sad day when dowries went out of fashion. Now, in England, the father of the bride only has to pay for the celebrations on the day. If a groom played his cards right he was looking at a huge free party, the bigger the better as everyone on the list would feel obliged to buy a present for the newlyweds.

It was clear that the Thais looked at this system and decided it would work so much better in reverse. Instead of a dowry, there's a Sin Sot, and it's the groom who writes out the cheque. There are presents, but again it's the groom who does the giving. He even pays for the party. I had to look on the bright side. Food is a big deal in Thailand and I was pretty hooked on the local cooking. Yim reluctantly allowed me to take part in choosing the food, for exactly ten minutes. My first choice was the delicious *Tom Yum* soup which I consume by the panful. Yim looked at me in despair.

"*Tom Yum* not lucky soup for wedding. It mean cheat and lie. Cannot eat or that what you do for sure when we marry."

I was instantly dropped from the organising team. Mercifully Singha beer had no negative connotations for married life, so I retired gracefully to drink a few cold ones, while trying to decipher a Thai soap opera on TV. I failed... miserably.

As we retired to bed on our second night, Yim was smiling broadly, everything was arranged. She explained that we'd be walking around quite a bit, processions were a big part of the day. There'd be no disco, but nine monks had been hired to chant for us. That, I was sure, would make the party fly. Yim finally decided there was no point in trying to explain what I'd have to do. I was to go where she told me, smile a lot, nod and even if I thought what was going on was barking mad, I'd have to go along with it.

"Same, same, after we get married," she said, "this good practice for you." I hoped she was joking.

Contractual complications

Yim appeared to have forgiven me for the screw up with the SUV. We'd been so busy at work and thinking about the wedding our sex life had taken a back seat. I'd always heard it was what happened when you were with the same person for a while. It certainly happened with Clare, big time. There were three days until our wedding and I was trying to make myself comfortable on the thin mat that served as a mattress. Yim was in the room next door, with Dao and Pim. It was, apparently, essential we maintained the myth of her virginity. I tried to explain that going to spend the night with your daughter was a very odd way of doing that. Yim's beautiful brow furrowed and she flashed me another of those despairing looks that indicated she was wondering why she bothered with a stupid *farang*. I'd finally found a tolerable sleeping position when I heard her voice from the doorway.

"Paul, you like to sleep alone?"

"No."

"I come share with you?"

Yim slipped off the old football shirt I'd given her when she once said she was cold in bed. She never really got used to hotel air conditioning. Then she lay down next to me.

"I hear you get married soon," she said smiling.

"That's right, and I'm very happy about it."

"Well, maybe you not get so much *boom-boom* when you married. Better you have now."

I was about to request further details on the availability of *boom-boom* after we were married, but Yim's mouth was tracing the line her hand had already made down my chest and stomach. I'd ask her later.

When my mobile rang in the morning, it took me a few seconds to realise where I was. Yim was gone and I'd not felt this comfortable since I woke up on Brighton seafront after Doug Taylor's stag night. I flicked the answer button, hoping it hadn't woken the girls in the next room.

"*Khun* Paul, it is very bad. There is a man here, he says he wants to see you now."

"For fuck's sake Sonthi, it's nine in the morning. I only just woke up. What's the problem?"

"He says there is a big problem with new bar. Your lawyer not do his job properly, you pay money but you not own bar. I think lawyer cheat you, but this man want to help."

"My lawyer? You introduced him for Christ's sake, this is your screw up."

"Be careful what you say Paul. I tell you man can find you bar, you use him, up to you."

Maybe that was what happened, I couldn't remember, it was late at night when I met the lawyer and now I was barely awake.

"So what do I do? What does he want?"

"Man say, you get here by five p.m. and he help you. Maybe you have to pay him little bit, but you not lose bar."

"What do I tell Yim? She'll go crazy, we get married the day after tomorrow."

"You play golf today with Phil?"

"Yes, that's the plan."

"Tell her you have to go early, then later you tell her you must go back Pattaya. Better to have fight on phone. You still be in time for wedding."

The drive was horrendous, I spent the whole time trying to work out what could have gone wrong. The lawyer seemed completely legit. How could he have duped me? If he did, surely I could prove he'd cheated me... but I'd need a good lawyer. Oh Jesus.

Thai Kiss

Sonthi told me to meet him in a layby on the main road between Chonburi and Pattaya, he said it was about a hundred yards past a Chevron garage. Sonthi's man had told him he was in fear for his life and didn't want to be seen with me in central Pattaya and definitely not near the bars. I pulled into the layby at four forty-five and settled down to wait for the men to arrive.

When the police cars pulled up, it didn't cause me the slightest concern, even when I realised I left my driving licence in Buriram in my hurry to leave for Pattaya. I knew the system by now, we'd chat, they'd look very serious as they checked my brake lights and stuff like that. Then I'd hand over a few hundred baht and they'd be on their way. The licence thing was problematic so it might cost me as much as five hundred. I'd keep it quick and simple, the important thing was that they were gone by the time Sonthi arrived with the mystery man. It was important he didn't get spooked.

I waited for the officer to approach. Sonthi told me it was better not to get out of the car if I was ever stopped. Sitting makes it look like you are being subservient. Towering over a tiny little Thai wouldn't set the right tone for our negotiation. There was a tap on the window and I tried to appear solemn and respectful as I pressed the button to lower the glass, looking up at the officer with what I hoped was the right balance of humility and steely determination. I was staring straight into a familiar face, Mongkut's.

The next few minutes flashed by as I was dragged from the car and thrown to the ground. Mongkut didn't even seem to notice I was still strapped into the car with a safety belt. I managed to press the release before my shoulder joint popped out of its socket. I could hear the click of a camera shutter from the moment the car door was pulled open and I briefly recalled the front page picture of the mangled Frenchman in Pattaya Daily News. I suspected that tomorrow I could be staring out from everyone's morning paper. I still had no idea why. Maybe the deal for the bar had gone worse than I ever imagined, maybe they thought I'd conspired with the crooked lawyer. If that was the case, I didn't understand why one of the officers was taking a crowbar to one of the side panels of the SUV. It popped off in a second and the policeman reached in and retrieved six long cardboard tubes. It looked like they'd found what they were looking for and the officer started to walk back to his patrol car. Mongkut shouted an instruction which at first the junior policeman didn't appear to understand. Then the officer walked back to the SUV and went to work detaching each of the other panels in turn. The odd thing was that he didn't bother to reach inside the bodywork, it was as though he already knew there were no more cardboard tubes to discover. Mongkut dragged me by my damaged arm and propped me up against the wheel arch of the decimated SUV. The men piled the cardboard containers onto my lap and the photographer started to check his light meter.

That was when I realised I'd seen containers like that before. They even rattled a little bit when they moved, exactly like the ones I'd collected from Mark in the pub in Borough Market. These tubes were much bigger, but there wasn't much doubt in my mind that the contents were the same. When the photographer stepped forward, there was no doubt at all; I'd be on the front page of the morning paper.

Rich... for the time being

Paul was gone, everything had changed, but I knew exactly the course my life would take from that day. I had tried for years to pretend I could have a little bit of control, but it was not to be. I thought about how it had all started, with the wave. It had taken the only man I ever loved. It picked me up and for eight long years it had thrown me around. There was the greedy businessman who killed my papa, and all the others who wanted something from me in exchange for as little as they could possibly give. I had lost count of the number of men who told me they loved me for an hour, a week or even a year. Most of them would not even be able to remember my name if they were asked. Mongkut had wanted me, only his fear of Sonthi kept him at bay. Sonthi was scared of no-one and knew he could have anything or anyone he wanted. Poor sweet stupid Paul thought he could understand me and my people, but he would pay the highest price. The newspapers were lapping up the story and pretending to be aghast at the massive haul of drugs found in his car. It was time, they said, to make an example of a foreign drug smuggler. He had refused to help the authorities find the people who supplied him with the drugs, instead he had made up a crazy story about being framed by a well known and hugely respected local policeman. They reported that Paul had picked on the officer who received the anonymous tip off, Mongkut, who made himself a hero when he intercepted the drug filled SUV. Paul had also implicated another Thai and claimed he was some sort of criminal mastermind who had set the whole thing up. Everyone knew Sonthi was only a motorbike taxi driver and occasional Muay Thai fighter. It was ridiculous to even suggest he could have the brains to organise anything as complicated as Paul described. The Press was split firmly down the middle, half wanted the death penalty for the scheming *farang*, the rest thought he was mentally ill and should be sent to a psychiatric unit for the remainder of his life.

It was the day after I was due to get married when I arrived back in Pattaya. The bar was running as normal, they never saw Paul as the boss, so why should anything change? Sonthi had phoned and told me to come to his apartment at ten p.m. I might have felt sick had I not felt so horribly numb.

"Wear something sexy, we're celebrating."

In theory I was a rich woman. I owned two bars, a huge house and I had plenty of money in the bank, but I knew why Sonthi wanted to see me. He was going to tell me how much I was going to be allowed to keep and what I was required to do to secure that small favour.

I arrived at Sonthi's apartment at exactly ten. A moment before and I would have to spend time with him unnecessarily, a moment after and there would be a price to pay for sure. He was already drunk when I stepped through the door.

"My beautiful Yim, I am so pleased to see you. Meet a very good friend of mine."

Mongkut was standing by the table looking at one of the notebooks I had seen last time I was in the apartment. The other one was nowhere in sight. The policeman looked really pleased to see me too and a terrible fear rose in my stomach. The two men were drunk, they had been celebrating and maybe I had been invited along to entertain both of them. I wanted to be sick.

"I am afraid our heroic policeman has to go now. He has more drug smugglers to catch." Both men laughed like stupid schoolboys but I was relieved to see Mongkut retreat towards the door. Sonthi looked again at the notebook as though he was checking something.

"It's all there, spend it wisely." He handed Mongkut an envelope.

It was clear the book was some sort of ledger, I guessed it recorded Sonthi's deals and gave Mongkut the chance to check he was being paid his fair share, I just couldn't work out what the other book was for and why it was absent. The second notebook did not have the monthly totals or show the fifteen per cent. As the door closed and Sonthi turned towards me, I was sure I knew the answer and I knew what I had to do next... one million per cent.

"So you got rid of him then?" I asked, trying to sound impressed.

"Who, Mongkut?"

"No, the stupid *farang*."

"I thought you'd be upset, you were pretty keen on him."

"He paid the bills, now he's gone and I'm rich. Well... we're rich. Aren't we *tirak*?"

I reached out and gently stroked Sonthi's crotch with my hand. He responded immediately.

"Well that's not what I expected. I thought you'd had a bit too much *farang* cock in your time and you couldn't recognise a real man any more."

"I did what I had to do for a while that's all. The *farang* is where he deserves to be, he was using me and I was using him. Now we have all that money. Even the new bar is in my name, Doherty has no claim on it at all. He wrote a contract with a drug smuggler. Sonthi we are rich, it makes me so horny."

I made sure I showered first in the morning, I needed to be dressed when Sonthi went to clean up. As soon as I heard the water running, I reached for his jeans, but the key wasn't there. I checked all his pockets, then the drawers and there was still no sign of it. Then I remembered, Sonthi was wearing a chain round his neck, it was starting to come back to me. There was something on that chain, maybe it was the key. I slipped out of my clothes and went back to the bathroom.

"One more time," I murmured in his ear as I started to soap his back. He'd only just started to wear the key round his neck, I had to hope he would not notice if it was gone. I waited until he was about to come before I slipped the clasp.

"Sonthi, do something for me?"

"Anything *tirak*, that was incredible, you are wasted on *farang*."

"Shave for me, your face is a little rough. It was nice last night, but I want you to look handsome when we have lunch together. I am a rich woman now and I want my lover to look his best."

"No problem, you wait for me?"

"No, I'll see you at 555 at two o'clock. I have to check on the takings for last night."

I tried to look as composed as possible as I left the bathroom and was soon pulling my clothes over wet skin as I tried to unlock the drawer. The notebooks were there and I put both in my handbag. It had occurred to me to try to get the chain back round Sonthi's neck but that sort of thing only happens in the movies, I was sure to be caught. I could not control my breathing and I was certain I was about to faint with fear but I had to do something with the key. Sonthi's bed had pure white linen and the top sheet was lying across the mattress where we left it. I pulled that back so the lower sheet was in full view, then laid the chain next to the pillow. If I was lucky Sonthi would think the chain had fallen off during the night. If he wanted to check the books, he would see they were missing. If not, I might buy myself a few hours until he noticed what I had done.

"What do you think you're doing?"

I hadn't heard the bathroom door opening and I couldn't bring myself to turn to face him. I'd been caught. I tried not to imagine what he might do to me, but the thought of Pascal and what had happened to him clawed its way into my consciousness.

"You know that Ning makes the bed when she comes in to clean up. Throw me that towel."

I thought he was sure to see that something was wrong, but he just caught the towel and the bathroom door slammed **shut.**

The showdown

Barely three hours had passed since I left Sonthi in the shower. Shortly, we would see him again. Our car turned sharply and made it through a narrow gap in the chain-link fencing with millimetres to spare. There might have been a gate there long ago but there was no sign of it now as we raced across open ground to where a motorbike was already parked. We manoeuvred alongside a wooden hut, its windows were shattered and the door hung limply from a single hinge. From the long-faded sign near the road, it appeared there had once been plans to build a huge block of luxury condominiums on this site. The plan had been abandoned. A tattered banner hung from the eaves of the hut proudly proclaiming a no-risk investment, the developers promising purchasers a guaranteed moving-in date that had passed three years before. We swerved slightly to avoid two stray dogs, apparently intent on ripping each other's throats out. A portent for what was about to unfold.

Mongkut told me to stay in the car, he would confront Sonthi alone.

"Mongkut my friend, why have you dragged me all the way out here?"

Sonthi was clearly irritated by the inconvenience. The windows of Mongkut's 4X4 were tinted black, I could see out but no-one could see in.

"Sonthi, I love the theatre and this place is so rich with symbolism. Grand plans that come to a spectacular but ignominious end, and look..." Mongkut waved his hand towards the dogs, "...there are even two old friends resolving their differences in the only way they can."

"I don't have time for riddles. You said you had something for me, what is it?"

Sonthi was standing completely still behind his motorbike. He was sure to have a concealed gun or a knife but Mongkut was totally at ease. It looked like he had a plan and everything was going exactly as he expected. When Mongkut reached inside his shirt, Sonthi's hand moved towards the bike seat, but the policeman had already retrieved the first of the notebooks.

"What is this Sonthi?"

"It's the book that lists my deals, you see it every month when I give you your cut. How the fuck did you get hold of it?"

Sonthi reached for the chain round his neck and fingered the key. He must have seen it on the bed and believed it fell off during the night, as I had hoped he would. I was pretty sure he had no idea the books were missing until that moment. When he saw the first one in Mongkut's hand the shock on his face was clear.

"This lists all your deals… as we agreed?" the policeman asked.

"Sure… yeah… of course it does. That's the deal we have. You get fifteen per cent of everything."

"Then what is this you little piece of shit?" The other notebook appeared from Mongkut's shirt and in a second was lying at the other man's feet. Sonthi had no time to think of a better lie.

"I don't know, I've never seen it before."

"Oh Sonthi, I was sure you could do better than that. You are so much more in your element when only your muscle is required. As soon a little thought is necessary, you are so… disappointing."

"I swear, it's not my book, those deals are nothing to do with me."

"How do you know what's in that book? I never said it was a list of deals. Sonthi, you need to think before you speak, you're making it so much worse for yourself."

The dogs had stopped fighting, they shook the dust from their coats and the smaller one briefly licked a gaping wound on one of its back legs. It then glanced at its opponent and they both wandered over to take a front row seat for the human drama that was unfolding.

"OK…" Sonthi admitted, looking at the ground and kicking dirt onto the damning ledger, "…I've seen the book. It belongs to my cousin, I was showing him how to do the bookkeeping, he does some business up-country and I taught him how to record the deals."

"Oh, so it's his book?" Mongkut replied, nodding his head and half laughing.

"For sure, I swear." Sonthi was looking both hopeful and apprehensive at the same time.

"But it's your handwriting and the only fingerprints on it are yours Sonthi. The police lab confirmed that this morning."

Mongkut was lying, the books had never been out of my sight from the moment I brought them to him.

"Fuck it Mongkut, it's just a little sideline. The deals there are a fraction of what I put in the other book. So I didn't pay you everything I owed, I can fix that, I can repay you… with interest."

Mongkut laughed.

"Sonthi, my brother, if only that were possible. You see, the problem now is that the sacred bond of trust we had has been broken, and I don't think it can ever be mended. Do you understand?"

"Don't be a fool Mongkut. You make a fortune out of this, do anything to me and all of that will vanish. You may have the books, but all the delivery information is coded. Only me and Sunan understand how to decipher it. I am due to see him in an hour, if I don't turn up, he will leave town today. You'll have nothing. Let me make this up to you, I'll pay you back, I promise."

This time Mongkut gazed off to the side and shook his head slowly. He genuinely looked as though he was thinking it over. I had to stifle a sob, if he let Sonthi go, I was finished. He would kill me for sure.

"So Sonthi, what should I do? What would you do if you were in my position?"

"Mongkut, you cannot kill me, that's crazy, you need me and Sunan."

"Sonthi, I have absolutely no intention of killing you, you have my solemn word on that."

Sonthi let out a sigh of triumph and I knew I had been defeated… again.

"You say I need Sunan?" Mongkut continued.

"Well as a back up I guess, but I'm the guy you really need." Sonthi's confidence was returning.

"Because you see Sonthi, I have Sunan. I have always had Sunan. He is, after all, my cousin and he and I have discussed this at length. He is just as angry about the other notebook as I am. You were cutting him out of those deals too, the same as you were cheating me."

"That's ridiculous, you're saying I hired your cousin. That would be some coincidence."

"Coincidence? Not so Sonthi, no coincidence. What I'm saying is that I sent my cousin to buy drugs from you. I arranged for two officers to intercept you and for those same officers to allow you to escape in a way that made Sunan appear to be quite the hero. He hit my sergeant a little harder than was really necessary, but these things rarely go as scripted. It was always my intention to replace you with Sunan. This conversation was going to happen sooner or later, but when Yim brought me the books today, I decided that the time had come."

"That little slut, I'll kill her," Sonthi screamed, his face twisted with rage.

"You most certainly will not Sonthi, dead men can't kill."

Sonthi laughed nervously. "What do you mean? You said you weren't going to kill me."

Mongkut spread his arms. "And I'm a man of my word."

I had been sitting in the front passenger seat of the car, there was a darkened screen which meant I could not see if anything was in the back. I had assumed it was empty. It all seemed to happen in a single movement. The rear door swung open and Sunan appeared a couple of feet from where I was sitting. I turned away as he raised the gun, so I only heard the shots. Four of them, in quick succession. When I looked back Sonthi was lying on the ground and there was a pool of what looked like black liquid spreading around his head.

As Mongkut and Sunan returned to the car, the two dogs who fled when the shots were fired cautiously wandered back to the scene of the action. As we drove out of the abandoned building site, the larger of the two was sniffing Sonthi's supine body.

We drove back to Pattaya in utter silence. I had no idea what was going to happen next, I'd asked for nothing in return for the books and I knew I was totally at Mongkut's mercy. I assumed we were going where the policeman and I could make whatever arrangements he wanted in private. I was surprised when he stopped outside the 555 bar. Sunan stepped out of the car and opened the door for me, Mongkut did not move.

"What do you want from me?" I asked.

"We will be in contact about the bars, I have an investor I want to introduce you to."

"And me, what do you want from me?"

"Ah yes, well, there was a time I would have been very happy to spend some personal time with you. You are without doubt one of the most desirable women in Pattaya, but I believe in fate, I'm a superstitious man. This morning I put my right sock on before my left and I prayed twice before I left the house. I always turn left when I leave for work, even though it is quicker if I turn right. I never choose to tempt fate."

I had no idea what he meant.

"You see, Yim, there was your young waiter who lost his life in the wave; yes Sonthi told me about your beloved Ghai. Then the Frenchman who flew from his hotel balcony, a motorbike taxi rider who's now providing lunch for the *soi* dogs of Jomtien and a stupid *farang* who will soon have a date with the executioner at Bangkwaeng. There are many dangerous things in Pattaya, but I think the most dangerous of all is to come to your bed. We will be in touch about the bars."

Thai Kiss

CHAPTER SEVENTEEN

An innocent man

"So *Khun* Paul, why did you do it?"

"Have they told you about the death penalty?"

"What do you have to say to your family?"

I couldn't see their faces, but the thin cotton hood didn't shut out the camera flashes. The Press wanted their pound of flesh too. Two Thai police guards were half carrying, half dragging me from the door of the courtroom. My knee hit what felt like a metal step and then I was pulled by another pair of strong hands into what I guessed was the back of a prison van. The door slammed shut behind me and the hood was tugged off. It took a second to get used to the light. There were two uniformed Thais, both looking straight ahead, neither making any sort of eye contact. Their body language indicated they weren't too concerned about me trying to escape. Each carried a gun at their waist and a long baton that looked a little like a baseball bat. My hands were tied in front of me with a plastic zip strap and my feet manacled and chained to a thick leather belt that circled my waist.

I waited for one of the guards to turn away and then pounced, strangling him with a chokehold, his throat in the crook of my powerful arm. As he collapsed to the ground I head-butted his advancing companion, grabbed his baton, and knocked him out with a single forceful blow. With both men unconscious, I just needed to find the key and make my escape. At least that's what I'd have done if I was James fucking Bond, secret agent and super hero, however, I wasn't. Regrettably, I was Paul fucking Murphy, serial loser, a man who obviously walked around with a huge sign on his arse that said "kick me." One of the guards looked at me but, knowing the tears were about to come, I avoided his eyes. That's when I noticed the other man on the opposite side of the truck. He was dressed in rough prison overalls, the same as me. His hair was long and unkempt, it looked like he'd not washed for days. The man had that emaciated look you see on documentaries about prison camps in the War.

"You're famous mate," he said.

"Me, famous?"

"For sure, you're the biggest dealer they've caught in a long while. All the Thais are pretty excited about it and the guys at Big Tiger can't wait to see you. They're calling you Mister Big."

I'd seen the YouTube video about Big Tiger. That was the name they gave to Bangkwaeng prison because it was supposed to devour its inmates. The BBC didn't make it look that bad to be honest, a bit overcrowded but so are the ones in Britain, so I'm told. A few of the guys I'd met in Pattaya had worse tales to tell. They reckoned the BBC was only allowed to film if they showed the place in a reasonable light. I laughed it off at the time, why would I care about what it was like inside a Thai jail?

"I'm no Mister Big. I was stitched up, someone planted those drugs on me. I'm innocent, I swear it."

"Well you'll get on great with the guys in Big Tiger," the other prisoner said.

"I will?"

"Of course, because they're all innocent too." He laughed like a madman who had seen one too many pirate movies. I waited for him to calm down.

"And you, are you innocent?" I asked.

"Well I told them I was at the beginning, but then the lawyer told me that was the best way to get the death sentence. So I confessed."

He told me about the drugs that were in his possession when he was arrested. It was considerably less than Mongkut found in the SUV.

"You didn't get the death sentence?"

"No, they said the judge was feeling merciful that day, my sentence was a mere sixty years. But they've toughened it all up a bit since then."

"Since when?"

"I went in fifteen years ago, only another forty-five to go, unless I can get a transfer back to an English jail."

"So what were you doing in court?"

"Final appeal, my lawyer found some great new evidence."

"And?"

"It wasn't so great, they turned me down."

The van jolted to a halt. There was a pause and the sound of gates opening. We set off again and I was pretty sure I'd just entered Bangkwaeng prison. I was inside the Big Tiger.

It was another twenty-four hours before the man from the Embassy came to visit. He was the first person to explain properly what had happened in the court. For all I knew, I might have already been sentenced. Christopher was what any self-respecting Brighton boy might call a posh twat. He was dressed as though he'd been summoned unexpectedly from afternoon tea on the Ambassador's lawn and his accent suggested mummy and daddy must be on speaking terms with the Queen at the very least. I hated the sight of him the second he turned up. Everything was handed to him on a silver platter whereas I had to fight for everything. The only thing was… I'd fought and lost.

I wondered whether they deliberately sent people like Christopher to deal with the likes of me. It was the establishment's way of rubbing it in a little bit more. Showing you what you could have been if you weren't born on a council estate, or your Dad didn't fuck off when you were six, or if you weren't such a complete loser.

"It was only an initial hearing. You haven't been found guilty of anything yet. They've sent you here until their investigation is complete and they're ready to bring you to trial."

"How long'll that be?"

"I'm sorry Paul… you don't mind me calling you Paul do you? I really don't know. This has become a very high profile case. It means they will want to be certain of their facts, but it's a great law enforcement story. They'll want to push on with all vigour."

"How long?" I was impatient but maybe this guy wasn't so bad after all.

"Weeks certainly. Possibly months."

"What'll I get?"

"You need to talk to your lawyer about that, the court will appoint one. But if you have money you would be far better off getting your own. The public defenders here are completely hopeless… and you didn't hear that from me."

"I need to talk to my girlfriend."

"It won't be a problem if she wants to come to visit you. You can write to her and I can arrange for you to have one phone call while I'm here. Do you have her number?"

I tapped the side of my head and smiled.

Christopher was back in no time with a mobile phone.

"You have three minutes."

I dialled four times, I was certain of the number but I even switched the last two digits on the fourth attempt out of desperation. Three times I got the message the number was unrecognised or disconnected. Only on the fourth occasion did I get to speak to anyone. They babbled at me in what sounded like Thai. I have no idea who it was, but it wasn't Yim.

"Is she Thai?"

"Yeah, she's Thai."

"Mmmmm…." Christopher said, stroking his chin.

"Mmmmm what?" I replied, stroking mine.

"Nothing, I'm sure she'll be in touch, but don't get your hopes up. Many foreigners discover that Thai families… shall we say… close ranks when this sort of thing happens. It's their culture, they avoid conflict if they possibly can."

"So what's the deal? You've been there before, what're they going to do to me?"

"You have to hope for the best… but expect the worst. The only thing you can say for sure, is that the courts are totally unpredictable… as if that's any consolation."

Christopher asked me how I was being treated. I told him it wasn't so bad. A man can get used to thin, watery soup, grey rice and the odd bit of gristle masquerading as meat for every meal, especially when his girlfriend has been telling him he could do with losing a few pounds. I was still calling her my girlfriend but I knew she was the number one suspect for setting me up. Her and the policeman Mongkut, her and Sonthi, maybe even her and rat boy, Noom, our undernourished security guard. I guess that was the test - if she got in touch and tried to help, then it was someone else; if she didn't, I'd take that as a confession.

I told Christopher about the cell, no bigger than the bedroom I shared with Yim but home to thirty-six guys from different countries and with wildly different perceptions of good personal hygiene. I spent a happy hour every day clearing my worn mattress of any bed bugs and lice. The guy next to me couldn't be bothered, so by the following day they were back. We slept head to toe in three rows and territory was jealously guarded. Concede a bit and you might have to fight to get it back, encroach on the guy next door and you've probably made an enemy for the rest of your stay. I read that book about the lady drug smuggler, Sandra Gregory. She said the best thing was to do what they said, don't pick any fights and just keep your head down. That was my plan.

Selling up

"Yim, sign here... you will be paid later, you have my word."

I could barely focus on the contract. I was dealing with Mongkut so there was probably a catch but I had no choice. Even if I had wanted to hold onto the bars, he could take them from me little by little anyway. In truth, I was desperate to get rid of them and get back to my daughter. The house would be sold and there was plenty of money in my bank account.

Mongkut raised his glass to me... the signing ceremony was over. The bars had been transferred to a Russian called Oleg Zhuzakov and I may or may not receive the money for them in the coming days. If I did, it would make me a very rich woman by the standards of the people of my village and if not, I still had enough to live comfortably with my daughter. I picked up my new phone to call her, the old one had been stolen the day Paul was arrested.

Mongkut strolled over to the bar to rejoin the Russian and I was left to reflect on what happened and how I felt about Paul.

No sooner had Mongkut sat down than the door flew open and Callum Doherty appeared, flanked by two men who were even bigger than him, and trailing in their wake, Jamie, the accountant.

"So what the fuck's going on. What's happening with my bar?"

"Mister Doherty..." I stood up to greet him with a *wai*.

"It's all over the papers about your boyfriend. Now what's happening with my bar?"

"Your bar?" Mongkut's voice was calm but demanded attention.

"Yes, my fucking bar, and who the fuck are you?"

"I am Inspector Mongkut Tharranyata of the Royal Thai Police. And if I might ask, who the fuck are you?"

Doherty looked rattled.

"Callum Doherty, I invested a lot of money with Murphy and his Thai whore."

"Mister Doherty, if that is the case then you can rely on the full protection of Thai law. Clearly we will need to examine the paperwork, you will be able to prove that you made the payments and the transfers of cash into the country will be legal and fully documented, I am sure. Obviously we will need to consult with the British authorities to confirm that the money came from legitimate sources in the United Kingdom. I think this is a simple task. If you have indeed made a bona fide investment in a business here then we will ensure you get exactly what is due you."

"Well that's alright then." Doherty sounded like he knew he ought to be pleased but wasn't quite sure.

"Of course if the bar does belong to you, Mr Zhuzakov will be very disappointed. He believes he is the new owner of both the bars."

Mongkut stepped aside and the Russian walked forward. The name clearly meant something to Doherty.

"Maybe there has been some mistake, I'll have to talk to my accountant and we can try to sort this out ourselves. Come on."

Doherty grabbed Jamie by the collar and dragged him through the door. The other men followed.

The Russian threw his head back, laughing, then drained his champagne glass and slapped Mongkut on the back.

Mongkut took a seat beside me.

"Is it over?" I asked.

"For sure, he won't be back. He is afraid we will look into his finances with the British… and my Russian friend might kill him. For Doherty, this is small money anyway, he does not care about the cash, he is upset that someone made a fool of him."

"He won't come for me?"

"He looks at you and all he sees is a beautiful face and body. You are no more than decoration, it will never occur to him you had anything to do with a deception. He will also be very wary of Mr Zhuzakov. For all he knows you may be his new business partner. He will do nothing to upset the Russian. You are in the clear and the only man he could go after is looking at a death sentence."

"Can you help him?"

"Help who?"

"Paul, of course."

"You want to save him? You want him back?" Mongkut looked incredulous.

"All I know is that he does not deserve to die."

"That could cost a lot of money." Mongkut's tongue slid across his lips like a lizard. He could already taste the cash.

"How much?"

"A lot."

Mongkut asked for a quarter of the money I was due to get for the bars.

"Will I be paid for selling the bars?"

"You have my word."

Visiting time

The previous December, Yim and I spent three days in Kanchanaburi, site of the notorious Bridge over the River Kwai. It was awe inspiring and incredibly sad. All those people died in such terrible circumstances. I was really proud of my own country for a change. About six thousand men were buried in graves immaculately maintained by a Commission set up to look after cemeteries all over the world. You couldn't help noticing there didn't appear to be a memorial for the tens of thousands of Thai and Malay workers who died, some of them because of the heroic things they did to help our soldiers.

On our last night we crossed the bridge itself (no they didn't blow it up) to get to the light and sound show they put on as part of the Kanchanaburi festival. It was great fun, even if some of the special effects fell a bit flat. It was very entertaining stuff.

"This is a disgrace, these people are savages." It was an American voice behind me. "Turning a tragedy into a piece of entertainment. Let's go."

The man's partner was in full agreement.

"It would be like staging a musical re-enactment of 9-11."

The two departed swiftly as the other spectators scoffed at their reaction.

I could see their point in a way, but I'd got used to the fact that it was the Thai way. They were a lot more relaxed about the life and death thing. Each life is, after all simply part of a journey. Death is a brief interruption until you come back for your next turn. If you've done good things in one life you come back to a better one. What football supporter couldn't identify with that? Death is just the close season and depending how well you did, you either get promoted or relegated. Whichever it is, you get over it and then you have a new season to look forward to. It made some sense to me, but then you come up with all sorts of bollocks when you think your season might be coming to an end.

The Kanchanaburi experience also set me up for my seventeenth day in Bangkwaeng. I was sitting behind a metal grille, there was then a gap to another grille beyond which I could see a bunch of westerners smiling and pointing. They had turned Bangkwaeng into a tourist attraction and foreigners were paying a few baht to come and look at the exhibits behind the bars. They even talked to us, sympathised with our predicament and shared our disbelief that these Thai barbarians would execute innocent men. Then they got their partners to line up a photo so they could show their friends when they got home that they'd got so close to a guy who was probably going to die. Some of them even told us how shocking they thought it was that the locals had turned a prison into a tourist attraction.

"Disgusting," said Don from Ontario as he showed his wife how to change the lens setting.

"Yeah, you'd have to be pretty sick to think this should be on the tourist map," I said.

Don agreed with me wholeheartedly.

I fantasised about seeing Yim, I just couldn't work out whether I wanted to kiss her or strangle the last breath from her body. In my dreams it was like that scene from Midnight Express. The bloke's in Turkey's worst prison and his girlfriend comes to visit. She takes her top off and presses her breasts against the glass partition, the prisoner then masturbates while she writhes in front of him. In my dream there was a handy button you could press to make the glass slide open.

Christopher's visits started to become the highlight of my week. That and the girl from a Bangkok charity that gave *farang* prisoners some cash to spend at the prison shop. It meant I could have some fruit, a little bit of decent meat and toothpaste and soap. And the girl was cute, not a patch on Yim of course, but cute for sure.

"Paul, there's been a development."

There was no clue from Christopher's face as to whether it was good news or bad. I clenched my fists in frustration and looked at him hopefully.

"The evidence has gone missing."

"Excuse me?"

"They've lost the containers with the drugs, or maybe someone stole them. What is important is that they no longer have that evidence to use against you."

"But they still have all the other stuff? The witness statements, the photos, everything." I was trying to stay calm and not read too much into it.

"That's true but it's going to be tough for them in court without the merchandise. They could do it legally, but it would make them look so stupid... and corrupt."

"Jesus, you mean they might drop the case?"

"They're having a hearing tomorrow, you'll be attending. They haven't even told the press. Hope for the best."

"But expect the worst, right?"

"Right."

Forgive me?

I still did not really believe the money from the sale of the bars would arrive as Mongkut promised but when I checked at the ATM, there it was. I was just about to get my card back when I noticed two other entries, one from Japan, the other from Switzerland. I texted Oshi and Ralf to say that I'd found a good man and was going to live with him in Australia. I was grateful for their help but there was no need to send me money any more.

Later that day, Mongkut explained what he had done with the evidence containers and how it should lead to Paul's case being dropped or at least changed to a lesser charge. It was time for me to hand over his fee. In typical style, Mongkut expressed his profound regret that he would not be seeing me again. He dropped me at the bus terminal and I waited for the next express coach to Buriram.

Dao burst through the door and jumped into my lap.
"I love you mama."
"I love you too, little one."
"And papa loves you too."
"I hope so, I love papa too much… but how do you know?"
"He tells me every night before I go to sleep."
Dao looked at me as though what she'd said was the most natural thing in the world. She yawned, hugged the small bear I had given her to her chest and looked up at me with those huge brown eyes that reminded me so much of Ghai.
"Do you see your papa every night?"
Dao nodded. "For sure."
I tried not to let her see the tear that was running down my face.

It was time to make dinner. Then I might let her watch some TV before bedtime. I was ashamed to be so jealous of my daughter, she really believed she saw her father before she went to sleep. That night before the wave was so clear in my mind and so was the last time he came to me in my dreams. It was the night before I went with Preben, the first *farang* to take me from the bar. Of course I had dreamt of Ghai, but we had not talked. Before that night he would come and hold me and say how proud he was of me and our daughter and how he would always be there for us. He had not come to me in my dreams since.

I opened the door to Dao's room just a little so I could be sure she was asleep. Then I took a long warm shower. I was starting to get used to sleeping alone, it was something I had rarely done since I went to work in Pattaya. It was nice to drift off to sleep and hope that good dreams might come.

I'd had one particular dream several times before. A crowded street and a young handsome man in the distance. He looked like Ghai but I could never get close enough to be sure. The crowd kept getting in the way. I knew how it ended, with me chasing through the streets but never quite catching up. Then I would be in a bar with a *farang* leering at me and asking if I wanted a drink. So, this time, I didn't expect the crowd to clear and for the man to turn towards me and smile. He carried a little girl in his arms. It was Dao.

"Ghai, my love, do you forgive me?" I asked.

"One million per cent," he replied.

Getting out

I'd become the model prisoner. Why shouldn't I? It wasn't going to be for much longer, although the guards were looking at me as though I'd lost my mind. Shark had been in Bangkwaeng as long as anyone I'd met, he was the one who said the Thais were getting nervous. Apparently a lot of prisoners got all cheerful immediately before they're found hanging by one of the Governor's bed sheets in the prison laundry. My case was a bit too high profile for them to let that happen. I just laughed.

"Trust me mate, you don't have to worry about me," I told him.

"I never said I was worried. Couldn't give a toss what you do pal, I'm only telling you what they're saying about you."

"Yeah, well thanks for that, I'm going to be just fine."

Shark had been in Bangkwaeng for ten years, I still wasn't sure if that was his surname or some bizarre nickname suggesting a lonely but lethal predator. His initial offence wasn't that serious but he didn't know how to play the game. He'd always been OK with me before, I never gave him any reason to get angry, so all I ever really saw was a grumpy bloke with no mates. I tried to get him to read the Sandra Gregory book… keep your nose clean and you'll be fine, that was the message. Shark couldn't help himself, if there was a fight to be had, he'd have it. If a warder gave him any grief, he thought the smart thing to do was to retaliate.

"So, you're one of the guys who got the Thai Kiss then." Shark said with a sly grin.

"Sorry mate you've lost me." I wanted to get away but I'd have had to push past him to get back to the prison yard, and that wouldn't have been a smart move.

"You know what a Glasgow Kiss is?"

"No but I suppose you're going to tell me."

"It's just a wee name we have for a head butt where I come from. It's what you get if you cross the wrong fella when the pubs are closing on a Saturday night. It's painful, but it's over and done with pretty quick."

"And a Thai Kiss?" I wasn't going anywhere until he finished his story so I thought I should play along.

"It takes a lot longer and it can be agonising so I'm told. Remember that first time your little lady sidled up to you and sniffed your ear?"

"Sure, everyone knows that, it's called a sniff kiss."

"Well that's where the Thai Kiss starts, and it ends up in here pal. When they've screwed you for every penny you've got and then they shaft you. Land of Smiles my hairy arse."

I wanted to tell him there and then, that it was going to turn out very different for me... luck was finally on my side, I was going to get out. Just as I opened my mouth to speak, there was the rattle of a guard's night-stick against the metal gate of the prison yard.

"Paul Murphy... visitor... now." I just shrugged and followed the man in the black uniform into the administration block.

A couple of weeks earlier Shark's words might have hurt; another reality check, another reminder that in Bangkwaeng you're on your own. Anyone who makes out they're on your side has another agenda, they either want something, or they're hoping to see you suffer so they can feel a bit better about their own lot. Still that was the story of my life, Tommy, Mongkut, Yim, Sonthi, they all stiffed me one way or the other. Well I wasn't going to let it get to me. I knew something Shark didn't, I was getting out, I was sure of that. But my mind was racing, surely it couldn't just be a cock-up by the Thai police. There had to be more to it. Maybe Yim had paid someone off, I couldn't imagine anyone else doing it. If it was her, we could pick up just where we left off, we'd still have the bar, we'd still have the house. That had to be the answer.

Christopher from the Embassy was waiting for me. It couldn't be bad news.

"There's been another development." As usual he was completely unreadable. It was impossible to say which way this was going to go.

"It's the taxi driver, the one you said masterminded it all."

"Sonthi? Just tell me for Christ's sake."

"He's dead Paul. Someone shot him in Jomtien and left his body for the dogs. He'd been missing for nearly two weeks, then they found what was left of the corpse a couple of days ago. They only identified him from dental records and a few personal effects. His bike was nearby and there was a gun and a bag of *yaba* in the seat box."

I couldn't work it out, it was too much to take in.

"That's good isn't it? Surely that's got to be good for me."

"Paul, I can tell you the facts, only a lawyer can interpret them for you. There was also a notebook, it could easily have been a list of drug deliveries, but it's hard to say."

"Stop being the civil servant, just tell me what you think… please."

"Obviously I can't say this in an official capacity Paul. It's not my area of expertise. But these developments can't do you any harm. You claimed Sonthi was behind all this, the prosecutor has already said he was an innocent man and you picked on him out of desperation. Now he's been killed in what looks like a gangland hit. All the evidence is that he was involved with drugs precisely as you suggested. Unless they can tie you to his killing its another hole in their case."

"And the drugs… the evidence?"

"No sign of them."

The hearing was a little over four hours away.

Shark was still where I left him fifteen minutes earlier.

Thai Kiss

"What are you looking so happy about?"

This was turning into my longest exchange since I arrived at the Big Tiger. I'd not seen that much of Shark since I arrived because he spent most of the time in solitary confinement. He'd only been out four days. I'd always steered clear of him before, he was a constant reminder of what you might end up like if you didn't get out. The skin around his ankles and wrists was mottled and scarred. He probably spent more time tied to the metal spike in solitary than he had in a standard cell. His teeth went long ago and there was a look in his eyes that said all hope had gone too. It was like watching a man who'd died but no one had told his body yet. The betting amongst the inmates was that he'd never leave Bangkwaeng.

"So come on Murphy, you can tell me... what you so happy about?"

"I just got some good news, that's all." I was suddenly anxious to shove his earlier jibe straight down his throat.

"Want to share it?" Shark looked like he was not that concerned either way, he was drawing a pattern in the dirt with a stick.

"I'm supposed to keep my mouth shut but I guess I could let you in on it."

"I'm honoured," Shark said, standing up and starting to walk away.

"Well based on what I've been told just now, I'd say all that crap about a Thai Kiss is wide of the mark."

"Really?" Shark turned to face me. "So what is it that you've been told?"

I sidled up close to him, looked around and then whispered. "Looks like I'm getting out soon." I couldn't keep the triumph out of my voice.

Shark looked about, leaned forward, and whispered back. "That's not what I heard."

"What?" I couldn't believe my ears. "What have you heard?"

Shark stayed close by me as he answered.

"I've been told the only way you're getting out of here is in a box, feet first."

"Who the fuck told you that?" I shouted. "Who says I'm not getting out?"

I was so angry I didn't notice the screwdriver slide down from the inside of his shirt-sleeve into his hand until it was too late.

Shark's lips parted in a toothless smile.

"Callum Doherty."

The End

Books & Short stories by Matt Carrell

Novels
I Am An Author
Vortex
Vortex… the Endgame
Blood Brothers… Thai Style
Thai Kiss
A Matter of Life and Death

Anthologies
Thai Lottery… and Other Stories from Pattaya, Thailand

Short Stories
Crazy Medicine
Something Must Be Done
A Friend in Need
Slips, Trips and Whiplash

Printed in Great Britain
by Amazon

57156810R00129